Angel Ship

Blue Phantom Book One

Vijaya Schartz

Print ISBNs
LSI Print 9780228623854
B&N Print 9780228623861
Amazon Print 9780228623878

BWL Publishing Inc.

ks we love to write ...
Authors around the world.

http://bwlpublishing.ca

Dedication

To all lovers of Science Fiction, Fantasy, and cats, enjoy the read.

TABLE OF CONTENTS

Prologue

Somewhere at the outer fringe of the galaxy...

Deep inside the rocky planetoid, a loud rhythmic chant and the pounding of drums echoed throughout the torchlit temple. Psychedelic vapors and incense twirled toward the high vaults.

Matchitehew, Sorcerer Supreme of the Stygian Order, flipped back his red mantle, exposing his immaculate white robes and the black crystal pulsing on his chest. Then he raised both arms toward the cave ceiling and focused his thoughts on the pyre.

The sacred fire flared. Good. His powers increased as the Dark Lord neared the galaxy. "Let the infernal flames burn like a beacon and summon the ardent believers to rejoin our ranks!"

Matchitehew focused his mind on activating the bellows. The strong hiss of compressed air briefly muted the ceremonial chant. Seizing the handle of the branding iron, he stabbed it deep into the fire, letting the smell of scorched metal and smoke rise toward the high vaults. His heart beat faster as the energy level in the cave increased.

The flames grew and swayed in front of the altar, reaching up toward the tall banners and their symbols of snake and dagger inside a circle. The dancing glow also enlivened the wall carvings, as if the engraved figures performing human sacrifices breathed and chanted along with the acolytes.

A hundred men and women in red hooded capes and masks formed a wide circle around the raised altar. Their pulsing chant swelled and billowed, summoning the forces of darkness.

Matchitehew rejoiced on the eve of a new dawn. His heart sang, drunk with the promise of new powers. "I had a vision confirming the ancient prophecy."

"We believe the ancient prophecy," the acolytes echoed.

"A great prince of darkness is on his way to this galaxy. The Exalted Baalmordo himself, the dark hero of many legends, has chosen to bestow his bounty and his might upon the Stygian Order." Matchitehew could already taste his revenge upon his enemies.

"Baalmordo, Baalmordo, Baalmordo..." the acolytes repeated as they swayed from side to side in a deep trance.

Beyond the fire, on the sacrificial stone, a gagged woman in white robes struggled against her bonds. Matchitehew had loved this woman once. Over two decades ago, this Anvad beauty had given him a son named Malo. Now, she would serve her higher purpose... a noble purpose.

Tonight, Matchitehew gazed with pride upon his son kneeling in front of the pyre, shirtless, ready for the trial. He had grown into a handsome man, strong muscles shining in the reddish glow of the flames.

Malo, his own flesh and blood, would receive immense power... a rare honor in the Stygian Order. The hunger in his brown eyes held great promise. Already an accomplished sorcerer, he would soon become a mighty tool of destruction to bring about a new dawn.

The black jewel on Matchitehew's chest pulsed with renewed intensity. The ritual was working. He circled the fire and climbed the three steps to take his place behind the altar. With great solemnity, he dropped his mantle, then pulled down the wide sleeve from his left shoulder, unveiling the white scar of the Stygian symbol burned into his left pectoral, the serpent dagger inside a circle.

The acolytes bowed in awe at the sight of the sacred brand. The chant subsided and the drums quieted.

Matchitehew now faced the altar upon which lay the sacrifice, and beyond it, the pyre, and his kneeling son. "Malo, tonight you take your rightful place as my First Lieutenant in the Stygian Order."

The acolytes hummed a hushed litany.

Matchitehew raised his arms, encompassing the entire cave. "Even when the serpent's head is cut off, the dagger remains. The secret circle remains. The Stygian Order remains... and eventually, another serpent rises to give it power."

"Another serpent rises," the acolytes repeated in unison.

Matchitehew turned to scan the minds of each acolyte in the circle to ascertain their trustworthiness. No traitors in his ranks this time around... only devoted believers.

"No longer shall we fear death or defeat. Under the mighty protection of the Exalted Baalmordo, we shall become invulnerable, impervious to pain, death, or failure." Matchitehew would avenge the death of his daughter and kill the traitor who caused the Stygian Order's defeat three cycles ago... whatever the cost.

The drums resumed, slow and muted at first, then louder and faster.

Matchitehew drew from his sash the golden snake dagger and held it high, poised over the blood offering. "For the Darkness to rise, the lamb must be sacrificed."

The Anvad woman on the altar struggled in her restraints and emitted muffled sounds. Matchitehew remembered how her body had felt under his. But tonight, his arousal came from a different place. He relished the blood lust thundering through his arteries.

The drums accelerated to a frenzied tempo.

A thrilling exhilaration rushed through Matchitehew. He raised his golden blade and briefly closed his eyes to savor the power, then he stabbed the woman's chest, burying the dagger to the hilt. She shook and spasmed. Red blood gushed when he pulled out the gold blade. As he dropped it, the dagger clattered to the stone floor. What a rush!

His hands shook with eagerness as he pried open the ribs and dug into the chest to grasp the beating heart. He squeezed it with strong fingers and wrenched it out, extinguishing her life. She finally stilled. How he relished the smell of the blood spattering his face and his white robes.

Then he raised the heart high, blood dripping down his forearm, to offer it to the rising Darkness. "Exalted Baalmordo, accept this offering of pure Anvad blood. May you find it sweet and worthy."

Matchitehew tossed the bleeding heart into the pyre, where it sizzled. "Soon you shall have the blood and souls of all the remaining Anvad people, the pure tribe you so yearn to consume."

As he stared at his son kneeling beyond the altar, Matchitehew saw no tears, no grief, not a thought for his mother's bloody corpse. Good. Born from a dark sorcerer and a pure soul, Malo was a true son of darkness...by birth and by choice. He would serve his father well.

Matchitehew casually pushed the woman's body off the altar's edge, and it fell into the sacred fire. The flesh sizzled and crackled. The smell of cooking meat spread through the air, mixing with the smoke, the incense, and the psychedelic vapors.

The drums slowed and their beat muffled.

"May the blood of this pure Anvad soul entice the Exalted Baalmordo to make haste. Then we shall receive him with open arms… and many more sacrifices."

"Baalmordo, Baalmordo, Baalmordo…" The acolytes whispered in a collective sigh.

"No longer subject to mortal limitations, we shall rule this galaxy. Already, the super-soldiers disbanded by our former allies are flocking back to us. They will join the ranks of our Army of Darkness. This new military force, imbued with extraordinary powers of destruction, will enforce our will upon the weak and the misguided. They will crush the opposition, snuffing any hope of rebellion."

The acolytes in red swayed from side to side, entranced by the ritual, like concentric ripples in a pool of blood. "Baalmordo, Baalmordo, Baalmordo…"

"The desperate planets at the mercy of thugs, Marauders, and slave traders, will beg for the privilege of our mighty protection. In exchange, they will pay fortunes in taxes, goods, precious metals, as well as labor. Those who refuse our help will be annihilated."

"Annihilated, annihilated…" repeated the acolytes like an echo.

Matchitehew descended the three steps to join his kneeling son on the other side of the altar. He bent to turn the sacred iron deep into the glowing ambers, making sure it also touched the burning flesh and blood of the sacrifice.

Then he rose and faced Malo. "My son, tonight, all the mistakes of your youth are forgiven. Tonight, you are reborn to become an instrument of fate, unbound by any rule, a deadly weapon imbued with powerful forces of darkness. You will lead our armies and bring the Stygian Order back from the brink of oblivion. From now on, we belong in the maelstrom of absolute power over this galaxy."

Matchitehew seized the insulated handle and pulled the branding iron out of the fire, then he raised the red-hot Stygian symbol for Malo to see. His son stared but didn't flinch.

"With this symbol I mark you as First Lieutenant of the Stygian Order." Matchitehew pressed the red-hot metal into Malo's left pectoral, above his heart, relishing the thrill of his power over his son.

As the iron sizzled and steamed, Malo remained stoic, jaw clenched, showing no other sign of pain.

Matchitehew pulled back the iron and gazed upon his handiwork. Perfect. The raw and charred circle with snake and dagger would heal into a white scar on Malo's dark skin. "The very sight of the Stygian symbol etched into your flesh will instill fear in our enemies, and awe in our supporters. Wear it proudly and use its power ruthlessly."

Malo turned his impassible face toward him. "What do you expect of me, Father?"

Matchitehew's chest filled with pride. "My vision included your first official missions as second in command of the Stygian Order."

"I yearn to serve the Order." Malo's neutral tone confirmed the sacrifice had worked. His dark eyes shone with stern resolve. His hands crackled with crimson energy, and he almost glowed with new strength and exceptional abilities.

"Through the dark power of the Exalted Baalmordo, you are now the most lethal weapon of the Stygian Order. Unless your head is severed, you cannot be killed. Your superstrength gives you the advantage in combat. No weapon can destroy your body. No blade can pierce your skin."

To demonstrate, Matchitehew pulled a knife from his sash and stabbed his son with

11

all his strength. The sharp blade did not penetrate the skin.

The acolytes murmured in awe.

No reaction from Malo. Only attentive focus. Good. Matchitehew had created his best weapon yet.

He sheathed his knife. "Your ship is equipped with Stygian shields impenetrable to conventional weapons. Your ability to read and influence people's minds is unrivaled. No ordinary being can resist your charms. The time has come to use your new skills to serve our mighty goals."

"What are my two missions, Father?" No emotion in the voice, whatsoever.

"First, you must locate the pure tribe, the Anvad people, and bring them to this temple to be sacrificed." Matchitehew thrilled at the very thought.

"Consider it done, Father." No feelings, no concerns…only the will to serve.

"And for your second mission, the most imminent threat to our resurgence is a wandering ship called *Blue Phantom*."

Malo's eyes focused faraway.

"Since the Azurans and their Avenging Angels went back into seclusion, the *Blue Phantom* and its crew constitute the only force in this galaxy powerful enough to thwart our plans. Furthermore, its captain, Blake Volkov, is the traitor who turned his cannons against us in the final battle. He caused the death of your mighty sister, and our greatest defeat. He must pay with his life."

"I heard rumors of this captain and his ghostly ship." No emotion in Malo's voice. "They say the *Blue Phantom* helps the innocent victims who summon it."

"There is no such thing as an innocent victim!" Matchitehew hated that term. "All beings are flawed, and all are guilty of one thing or another."

Malo nodded. "I understand, Father."

"Good. Repeat your orders."

Malo rose and stood at attention. "First capture the Anvad people, then Kill Blake Volkov and destroy the *Blue Phantom* and its crew."

"Perfect." Matchitehew exulted. With Malo as his weapon, he would have his revenge, and his dream of domination over the galaxy would finally come true. "Spare no expense, my son. The fate of the Stygian Order rests on your shoulders."

Malo's back remained very straight and immobile. "Praise the Exalted Baalmordo. May his will be done." The new lieutenant effected a slight bow to Matchitehew. "And your will as well, Father."

Matchitehew smiled. He hoped Baalmordo would be as easy to manipulate. The more powerful they were, the greater their weaknesses. After all, Matchitehew had once seduced the great Kalishtar Herself and fathered Her daughter. Baalmordo would provide the might needed to fill the vacuum left by the destruction of the GTA.

The time had come for the Stygian Order to bring its iron rule and superior order to the galaxy.

Chapter One

At the hiss of compressed air from the opening hatch, Kefira stopped petting Karak, her feline bodyguard. She kissed him on the nose then rose from her bunk. "Sorry, big boy. Duty calls."

The big cat slinked down from the bunk, his tan pelt rolling over powerful shoulders as he ambled back to his comfy crate-bed. Good boy.

"My apologies for the intrusion, Sardar." The old captain standing in the open hatchway bowed too low, displaying the shiny ripples of his shaved head.

Kefira rose, brushing cat hair from her silk uniform. Blue silk... because tradition forbade a Sardar to wear ordinary cloth. She straightened the blasters, swords, and Kirpan blades on her hips. "Please, Captain, call me Kefira, we are lightyears away from the palace."

"Yes, Sardar." The slightly exaggerated tone bordered on disrespect. Like the other men on this ship, the captain disapproved of her warrior garb...among other things.

She shook her short black curls in frustration at the captain's attitude toward her gender. She was the only surviving Sardar, a lofty, pure blood princess with divine powers, a direct descendent of the goddess Helsara... yet, the Anvad men didn't believe a woman should rule.

The captain kept his downcast eyes on Karak. He didn't trust the big cat's cuddly looks... for good reason. "Sardar, our scanners picked up a signal."

"Karak not like captain," her feline bodyguard hissed in her mind.

"I know." Kefira answered without speaking. Aloud, she asked, "What signal?"

The captain cleared his throat. "I didn't want to frighten the crew, so I came in person. We may have company soon. You'll want to see this."

Avoiding eye contact, the captain turned and walked away with a slight limp.

The big cat growled his satisfaction at the captain's departure and laid his head down for a nap. *"Karak protect."*

Kefira chuckled at the contradiction, but Karak's mind was linked to hers and could see everything through her eyes. She was safe on the freighter among her people, but the big cat would rush to her help if she found herself in a dangerous situation.

She stepped out of her cabin and followed the limping captain through the central corridor, toward the command bridge. What could be so frightening that the old man didn't want to alert the crew? Kefira touched the silver medallion on her chest for luck. It always reminded her of her former life... a happy life.

The corridor widened. Open hatches on both sides revealed large holds, some crowded with domestic animals and farm equipment, others occupied by elders and young families, desperate to flee the lawless cluster. Just over five thousand people... the last of the Anvad... her people.

When Kefira reached the command bridge, the few crewmen and officers stood up and bowed, acknowledging her presence, eyes downcast. She didn't need to read their minds to sense their resentment at being led by a mere woman. Then they sat again and returned their attention to their consoles.

The captain indicated the main viewer displaying a few blips. "Sardar, we have been tracking these ships through space for a while, and we confirmed that they are coming straight for us."

"Why didn't you tell me earlier?" Her voice rose louder than she intended.

"I didn't want to worry you unnecessarily, Sardar." The captain bowed. Although the words indicated respect, the patronizing tone reflected his true beliefs. A woman shouldn't get involved in fighting or politics. Too bad.

"Could they be friendly?" But there was no such thing in deep space.

"I think not, Sardar." The captain adjusted the image resolution from his console. "They look like Marauders."

"Marauder?" A cold sluice washed over Kefira. The civilian freighter had limited defenses. "How many ships?"

"Ten raptors, armed to the gills, Sardar." The captain enhanced the image further and bounced it to the main viewer.

Kefira stared at the advancing raptors, painted blood-red and black, bristling with cannons and sharp, protruding hooks. She could sense the hatred, the danger, the contempt for life, emanating from them. She could almost smell blood. May Helsara the Bountiful protect her and her people. "Broadcast a distress call, far and wide."

The captain punched several keys on his console. "Distress beacon activated, Sardar. But we are a long way from any outpost, and so far from the shipping lanes, there are no vessels close enough to help."

"Well, we planned our secret route through the emptiness to avoid any unwanted encounters. Why are the Marauders here against all odds? There is nothing here for them." Kefira's heart pounded faster. "We were so careful."

"If they attack, we will not last long against them, Sardar." The captain's voice lost its strength.

"Can we outrun them?" Kefira already guessed the answer.

"Not a chance, Sardar." The captain's voice trembled. "They have fast ships. Our freighter is an old clunker in comparison." He sounded defeated.

Kefira must protect her people. It was her divine destiny as the last Sardar alive, her main reason to exist. That, and continuing the bloodline. The Bountiful Helsara demanded it of her. "Maybe, we can bargain with them. What do we have of value?"

"Not much to spare, Sardar, but we have food, livestock, and fuel. Nowadays it's enough to attract Marauders." The captain cleared his throat. "Although, what they likely want is strong, able bodies."

"What do you mean?" Kefira shuddered, hoping she understood wrong.

"Since the fall of the GTA, the slave trade flourishes with impunity in this quadrant, Sardar."

"Slavers? Here? But we are far away from trade routes and traffic lanes. These forsaken parts are usually empty of life. So, what are they doing here?" Kefira didn't believe in coincidences. Her hot blood churned in her chest.

"I know you hated the GTA, Sardar, but it had its uses." The old captain pinched his lips together, as if realizing he'd gone too far.

"I still hate the GTA for oppressing the Anvad people and slaughtering my entire family. And their so-called peace was only a cover for exploitation. May Helsara throw their souls into the frozen hells of Laxxar!" Kefira took a slow, calming breath to clear her mind. "How did these Marauders find us? Unless… one of us tipped them off."

"That's always a possibility, Sardar." The captain looked away. "Like when your private ship was attacked, over three cycles ago… it seems you were betrayed then, too."

The memory of the attack on the *Zantar* still eluded Kefira. How she ended up with Karak in that escape pod remained a mystery. She touched her medallion as a reminder. Even the big cat didn't remember. "By the bountiful breasts of Helsara! Who would be evil enough to sell our skins to such savages?"

The captain chewed on his lower lip. "Maybe there is no traitor. Maybe whoever is coming can read minds, like you, Sardar."

"That would be unlikely." Very few had such divine abilities, and they used it for the greater good.

The captain raised his brow, wrinkling his forehead. "Unlikely, but not impossible, Sardar."

Kefira casually scanned the old man's mind, but only found fear, weakness, and misogynism. Besides, she refused to suspect any of the Anvad people, all refugees, including her. They had everything to lose. "Any idea how we might survive this encounter unscathed?"

The wrinkled face suddenly looked older. "Surrender and pray for a miracle, Sardar. That is our only hope."

"Pray to Helsara all you like, Captain, but we are not entirely defenseless." Kefira never submitted in the past, not even to the mighty GTA, when they controlled the galaxy. "I refuse to bow down to a band of Marauders."

"But we cannot win, Sardar. Our armament is limited and old, like this freighter. They'll kill us if we resist." The old captain's face slacked. "They'll kill our people."

"If we don't fight back, they will enslave the able bodies, and kill the children and the elderly. I also fear for our young women." Violent images of rape flashed upon Kefira's mind. She had witnessed long ago the ferocious nature of space scum. "We have a few cannons on the outer hull, and blasters in our armory. I say, let's use them."

The captain bowed low. "Your wish is my command, Sardar."

"Good." Was it wrong to fight back? Was the price of freedom too high? Never. "I would rather die fighting than live as a slave... or let my people be enslaved and killed."

"The Anvad are resilient, Sardar. They would survive captivity." Was the captain advocating slavery? What a coward!

"Approaching ships are coming into cannon range," the synthetic computer voice announced overhead.

Kefira walked to one of the firing consoles, sat, pushed the activation key, and grasped the control grips. "Let's give them a fight."

"Should you be doing this, Sardar?" The old man's tone oozed disapproval.

"I'm a trained warrior, Captain, and as your Sardar, I say we fight."

"As you wish, Sardar." The old captain straightened his frame, and resolve filled his tired eyes. "Man the space guns, and fire at will!"

Focused on the cannon sight, staring at the monitor, Kefira acquired a target, aimed, and fired. Her shot exploded harmlessly on a red bubble shield. The command bridge echoed and shook with the salvoes of the freighter's other cannons. But the Marauders' shields held.

Then the raiders returned rapid fire. The deck rolled as if under a powerful wave.

Kefira gripped the handle bars of the console to steady herself. "By the Land of Many Waters!"

"Shields at fifty percent," the neutral computer voice announced.

"Keep firing!" Kefira wished they had torpedoes, but no such luck on this old freighter. Besides, the enemy was upon them, now.

"Shields failing! Fifteen percent... ten percent... five percent... Red alert..." The calm computer tone didn't fit the urgency.

Red lights pulsed on the emergency strips, and alarms rang, punctuating the beat of firing cannons. Kefira couldn't focus her sights. The Marauders must have knocked down her targeting system. As she switched to a hull camera, she realized her external cannon had been ripped off the hull.

A loud bang, then the moaning of metal beams... a sinister rotary engine made the entire hull vibrate.

Kefira rose. A chill coursed down her spine. "What's that?"

"I know that sound, Sardar." The old captain shook his head. "Grappling hooks and a large drill... They're breaching the hull with a giant can opener."

Kefira tightened her jaw to stifle a scream. "Activate the emergency plan."

"Yes, Sardar." The captain nodded then pushed his com key to broadcast through the entire ship. "Prepare to be boarded! Civilians to the secret hiding compartments, fighters to your weapons and await orders. May Helsara protect us all!"

Although Kefira believed in Helsara's bounty, she preferred to control her own destiny. "Where are these Marauders drilling?"

"At the stern, Sardar." The captain pointed to the spot on the ship's diagram on his console. "Here... in the main cargo hold."

Kefira touched her collar pin, activating her personal com. "All able fighters, meet me in the main cargo hold at the stern!"

Her small contingent of warriors was loyal and well trained. They would fight to the last. Drawing her blasters, one in each hand, Kefira nodded to the old man. "Wish me luck, Captain."

The captain offered a sad smile. "Good luck, Sardar. May Helsara protect you."

Kefira turned away, stepped into the central corridor, and marched toward the stern.

"Karak fight. Karak protect." The strong mind voice never failed to reassure. The big cat remained vigilant at all times.

"You are a good boy, Karak." In her mind, she visualized her feline bodyguard. *"Bad people are coming, Kitten. The Anvad need protecting. Join me in the big cargo hold in the back."*

One by one, several fighters emerged from the many open hatches and joined and followed Kefira along the central corridor. The young men and women with a stiff jaw and a resolute stare, tightened their grips on blasters and blades. They lined up and marched behind her at a brisk pace.

Kefira had fought the generals in order to admit young women among the Anvad warriors. Now, she was glad to have them at her side. Unlike the generals whose titles were purely honorific, these young people would fight valiantly.

As she marched to do battle, she focused on the collective mood of her people throughout the ship. Her sensitive mind picked up their fear. It saddened her that she couldn't influence their minds to stop the panic. But she would do her duty.

The big cat surged from a side corridor and now loped at her side. *"Karak protect."*

She patted the furry head. "Thank you, my friend."

Today was just as good a day to die as any. Kefira's life didn't matter. Only the freedom and the survival of her people.

Chapter Two

Adjusting her oxygen mask against the thick smoke, Kefira struggled to ignore the flickering lights and the alarms sounding all over the freighter. She crouched with Karak behind a large crate and whispered in her com. "Anyone can hear me?"

No response. Was the com dead, or was she the last fighter still standing?

Several Anvad warriors lay unconscious or dead on the decking. What a waste of good lives... but they'd killed five times as many Marauders. The wounded moaned in pain somewhere in the smoke.

Still, the raiders kept trickling through the breach in the hull. How many were roaming the freighter? A hundred? How many more would pour in from the Marauders' ships?

Movement caught her eye, a flash of metal. She fired her blaster. The Marauder woman collapsed at her feet with a hole in her chest the size of her fist. Her tattooed face relaxed, eyes wide open in death.

The big cat sniffed the fallen enemy, then growled, twisted around, and leapt as another attacker emerged from the smoke.

Karak pounced and the man's skull cracked under the cat's powerful jaw. *"Karak protect."*

"Thank you, Kitten." The smoke screen worked both ways.

Screams exploded nearby. The cries of women and children being rounded up. By Helsara, the disgusting Marauders had found some civilians in their secret compartments!

Low to the deck to breathe better, hidden by the smoke above, Kefira ran in the direction of the cries. The big cat followed her in stalking mode, sneezing in protest to the fumes.

When she reached the open hatchway, Kefira flattened herself by its side and ventured a glance into the darkened hold. Way too many Marauders. One shoved an old woman who fell to the deck. A young boy crouched near the woman to help and was struck on the side of the head. Kefira's anger roiled in her chest.

She refused to accept defeat. And now, the low-lives had hostages they could use to control her. But although all seemed lost, Kefira could still fight.

Hidden, her back to the bulkhead, she closed her eyes briefly and closed her ears to her people cries to broadcast a silent plea.

"If anyone, out there, cares about what is decent and just, please don't let my people suffer this iniquity. Please... We need a miracle. Come help us..."

27

She doubted anyone would receive her mental call, or want to come if they did, but the goddess had given the Sardar special gifts to use them. Besides, she had nothing to lose.

She patted Karak's silky pelt. "Ready, boy?"

The big cat growled his agreement. *"Karak protect."*

Tightening the grip on her blasters, heart pounding like a war drum, Kefira rose and emerged from the smoke with Karak. Together, they stepped through the open hatch. Karak pounced. Kefira dodged a blade, then aimed and fired upon the Marauders. Whatever the odds, whatever happened, she would defend her people until her last breath.

* * *

Blake Volkov, captain of the *Blue Phantom*, stood under the clear dome of the observation deck. He closed his eyes to scan the black expanse with his mind.

The image of a young woman with black curly hair flashed through Blake's thoughts. She was beautiful and fierce... passionate, and in serious trouble. She also looked oddly familiar... from some faraway dream. Blake didn't believe in coincidences. She had come to him, and he must meet her.

In his mind, he studied her surroundings. Smoke, blaster fire, children's screams, a large cat. Marauders... her desperate call mentioned decency and justice. She believed her people were mostly good and asked nothing for herself.

The first worthy call in a while. Since the fall of the GTA space pirates had free rein, and many of their victims called for miracles, but few deserved to be saved.

Blake focused his mind on the young woman. She was selfless and pure of heart. He traced the call back to its origin and pinpointed her coordinates. "Got it!"

Then he broadcast a mental message for his first officer. *"Graziella? Rescue imminent, prepare to fight Marauders. Inform the crew to be ready."*

"Aye, Captain," Graziella responded in his mind. *"Order sent. Okay to proceed."*

Blake sensed Graziella's agreement and support as he applied both hands to his glowing console. He synchronized his mind with the ship's crystal engines. A rush of energy flowed through him as he became one with the ship. Then he willed himself, the ship, and its crew, to the location of the damsel in distress.

* * *

Kefira breathed hard despite her rigorous training. A blaster in one hand and a short, curved blade in the other, she found herself at the center of a fighting circle, with only the cat at her side. The Marauders seemed partial to blades and hadn't killed her, yet. Maybe, they wanted her alive... to have their fun with her... or to control her people.

She was grossly outnumbered, surrounded by dirty men and women, with snarly faces, scary tattoos, ugly scars, and rotten teeth. All of them exuded savagery through their blood-shot eyes, like the wild beasts on red-jack Kefira had fought in the bad lands. She much preferred to deal with the simple minds of monstrous beasts than with these evil ruffians.

Were the Marauders also on some kind of drug? She wouldn't be surprised.

Kefira hated them. She ducked and side-stepped, firing at threatening shadows as fast as she could. A few Marauders fell, but most still stood, thanks to their strong protective armor. The leaders among them also wore electronic shields... somewhat too sophisticated for space pirates.

Karak pounced on one big man breaking their circle. The Marauder lost his balance. His struggle created havoc as the big cat planted his long fangs into the man's throat and shook him violently. "*Good boy.*"

"*Karak protect.*"

Kefira sliced an attacker's hand at the wrist and the man whimpered clutching his stump as his blade clattered on the decking. Then she peppered the circle with short blaster shots.

Cries and laments exploded from the far end of the hold. From the corner of her eye, she saw Marauders striking and shoving helpless civilians. Some Anvad refugees huddled together for protection. Others waited stoically, placing their hopes in their Sardar, their savior, their divine leader.

If they only knew, despite her special talents, Kefira was just like them... but they would never believe it. In their mind, a Sardar was all powerful, imbued with Helsara's gifts.

As Kefira fired again, her blaster sputtered and died. "By the frozen hells of Laxxar!"

The raiders froze, all eyes on their leader. They definitely wanted her alive.

The leader snarled, baring black teeth. "So, pretty girl... you've lost!"

The hold grew quiet. As if sensing the change in the air, Karak sat down, alert, and watchful. Good cat.

"You!" Kefira marched up to the despicable leader. "Be a man and fight me in a fair fight, one on one!"

The big man scoffed and stepped forward. He probably thought he could best her easily. If he followed the Marauders' code, he must accept the challenge or lose face in front of his crew. With some reluctance, he turned off his fancy shield and holstered his blaster, next to a sword too refined to be his.

Then the leader drew and brandished a cat-o-nine-tail whip, with sharp barbs protruding from the scourges. "You, wench, need a good flogging."

The Marauders laughed and slapped each-other's shoulders, expecting an entertaining fight.

Rooting her feet to the deck, Kefira sheathed her knife and grasped the business end of her dead blaster with both hands, like a club.

The man cracked the nasty whip. She raised her improvised bludgeon then ducked low to avoid the flying barbed tails that grabbed the blaster. She pulled and the whip flew off the Marauder's hands. Then she whirled and stepped aside, ducking under the leader's arm. In one smooth motion, she rose again behind him and clobbered him on the head.

As he stumbled, she threw her improvised club at the nearest tattooed head, then grasped the big man's blaster and the hilt of his blade... a work of art he didn't deserve. Before he hit the deck, Kefira drew the fine sword and sliced off his head. Blood sprayed. The leader crumpled to the deck. His head went rolling in the middle of the circle.

The Marauders froze and stared at it in disbelief.

"Who's next?" Kefira faced the rest of the gang, her victim's blaster in one hand, his sword in the other. With decent weapons, she might be able to take them all... although there would be more reinforcements coming out of their ships.

* * *

Blake's hands tingled as he rematerialized the *Blue Phantom* in a new part of the galaxy. Through the clear dome, he now recognized different stars. A large freighter sat there, surrounded by ten raptors with bloody markings... Marauders... some anchored to the freighter's hull with chains and hooks.

Blake could sense the poisonous nature of their evil minds. Assassins, addicts, cruel perverts, greedy souls, damaged far beyond redemption. *"Graziella, do you see and feel this?"*

"Aye, Captain." Graziella's melodious voice sang in his head.

Blake had no doubt these savages deserved to die. This region of space would be a better place without such vermin. *"This evil must be eradicated."*

"I agree." Graziella usually did. They shared the same values of right and wrong.

With one sharp thought, Blake directed the *Blue Phantom*'s weapons to fire. Ten glowing torpedoes ejected from their tubes, each one hurtling toward a different raptor.

"Torpedoes on course, Captain." Graziella sang in his mind.

Blake closed his eyes as he focused on their trajectories. The Marauders had not detected the arrival of his destroyer and would never expect the attack. Not that they could avoid the deadly missiles at close range. Their shields, although fancier than most, would be no match for the *Blue Phantom*'s weapons.

* * *

A blue flash blinded Kefira. She stumbled backwards under an invisible wave and landed on the deck. The overhead illuminations flickered and died. As the emergency power switched back on, the feeble glow revealed the Marauders groveling on the deck... as if gravity was so strong, they couldn't get up. They also seemed disoriented, while she and her people slowly rose to their feet.

Her feline bodyguard joined her side, eyes round with surprise. *"Karak protect."*

The civilians in the hold stared at something behind her.

"What just happened?" Then she turned and saw him in her peripheral vision.

The tall being with majestic wings glowed as he hovered in midair, in a military style light blue uniform. His appearance brought to mind the legendary descriptions of guardian angels of the universe, rumored to help the just and destroy evil. But it couldn't be. They belonged to ancient legends.

Yet, Kefira could not deny the outlandish apparition... or his effect on the Marauders.

When he gazed at her, his turquoise eyes had a strange piercing quality... Her heart exulted, and her legs wobbled... as if she'd waited all her life to meet this particular being.

She mentally shook her head. She didn't believe in fate or destiny, or soulmates anymore... although she felt as if she'd known him her whole life.

"My name is Blake." The angel alighted on the deck, retracted his wings, then bowed to her. "Sardar, we heard your silent plea to save your people, and deemed you worthy of our help." His deep melodious voice reverberated throughout the hold.

Did he call her Sardar? Did he say worthy? But she couldn't react, tongue-tied under his spell. She could only stare at him. What was happening to her?

Then the angel snapped his fingers.

The Marauders in the hold, dead and alive, phased in and out of existence, then vanished in a blink... along with the severed head, leaving only abandoned weapons and blood on the decking.

This seemed too good to be true. Was Kefira dreaming? Was she dead? Did her confused spirit try to make sense of her demise? She cleared her throat and found her voice. "Where did they go?"

"You and your people are now safe." The angel remained stern. "As for the Marauders, they are floating in cold space, where they can't hurt anyone. None are left on your freighter. We shall heal the wounded and help with repairs, then you and your people can resume your travels in peace."

Karak strode straight to the angel and rubbed his furry head on his hip. How odd! The large feline never liked strangers, and usually prompted fear in ordinary people. But the angel bent and scratched the big head between the ears, treating Karak like a tamed house pet.

The cat emitted a loud purr then sat at the angel's feet. *"Karak like angel."*

So did Kefira. Why did he seem so familiar?

Three more glowing beings manifested inside the hold and rushed to attend the bemused civilians, many of them in need of medical attention. Angels popped in and out of existence, carrying the wounded and vanishing with them. How strange.

Kefira bowed to Angel Blake. "In the name of the Anvad people, I thank you for saving us from these savages." She exhaled her relief. "What about all the Marauder ships out there?"

"We pulverized their ships." The casual tone sounded blasé and remorseless.

Kefira shuddered. She had killed many times defending her people, but this cold and detached attitude after killing hundreds bothered her.

"Sardar... if you can hear me..." The captain's voice broadcast overhead through the ship wide system. "Your presence is desired on the command bridge."

"Sorry." Kefira offered the angel an apologetic smile. "If you follow me, I'll introduce you to the captain."

The angel nodded. "I owe you my full name and title. Blake Volkov, captain of the *Blue Phantom*."

"Blake Volkov?" It translated as black wolf. What a ridiculous name for an angel. "I am Kefira, Sardar of the Anvad people, and in my culture, my name means young lioness."

She stepped through the hatch and marched along the central corridor, the angel captain at her side, with Karak trotting behind them. No signs of Marauders onboard. Could they be all gone? It seemed Angel Blake told the truth.

Kefira stole a side glance at their savior. He was a tall, muscular man, reminiscent of genetically enhanced soldiers... like the

Space Marines of the now defunct GTA. A dimple in the chin softened his square jaw. His short dark hair and sullen brow accentuated the piercing blue eyes. His light blue garb also screamed military, although he carried no visible insignia or modern weapons… only a glowing blue sword.

"When I called for help, I didn't think anyone would be listening, especially to a mental message. Few people in the universe can detect those." Heat rose up Kefira's throat. Shame at calling for help? Or the oddly pleasurable effect of the angel's proximity?

His brow shot up. "If you don't believe in miracles, then, why did you ask for one?"

"Something to do when you are desperate, I guess. Like unbelievers sometimes pray when death is near." She gave him a once over without slowing her pace. "I certainly didn't expect heavenly angels with majestic wings and glowing swords."

He emitted a nervous chuckle. "I may sprout wings at will and fly… and I am handy with that sword, but believe me, Sardar, I am no angel."

"Then what are you?" Such powers could only have divine origins… like hers.

"I'm just a lucky man with too many flaws." He sounded detached but the great sadness she sensed in him contradicted his words.

An Anvad officer walked toward them in the wide corridor.

Kefira stopped. So did Karak and Angel Blake.

The officer saluted. "Sardar, we've lost engine power. We are stalled. We are on limited auxiliary power until we can fix the drives and restart the engines."

"Do your best." Kefira smiled. "We are safe with the Angel ship beside us."

The officer bowed then turned around and hurried into a side corridor.

Kefira resumed her walk along the central corridor and Angel Blake kept her pace. The big cat remained oddly silent.

She glanced at Angel Blake sideways. "I don't believe for a nanosecond that you are just a man. Regular men don't fly, nor do they manifest out of thin air, or make people disappear with a snap of their fingers."

"Believe what you will." He looked straight ahead, not at her.

If not from the divine, did he draw his power from the darkness, like the evil entities of legend? "Why do you think so little of yourself?"

He sighed. "As a man, I made bad choices, and enormous mistakes that cost countless lives. Now, I'm trying to redeem myself in the eyes of the universe."

"By rescuing others in need? I find that admirable." Kefira smiled and slowed her steps. She didn't want this moment to end. "I understand the need for salvation. Everybody makes mistakes. But wallowing in guilt is not healthy. It's much better to move on."

The angel emitted a nervous chuckle. "Easier said than done."

She huffed. "How long are you going to beat yourself up for what happened in the past?"

"Time is irrelevant." He sounded so serious. "Sin has no expiration date."

She lightened her tone to relieve the tension. "Did you say, in the eyes of the universe? I didn't know the universe had eyes."

"You better believe it. And these eyes have been watching and judging us since the Big Bang." His lips curled up slightly and a tiny spark reached his eyes as he gazed upon her. "I admire your positive outlook in the face of adversity."

"Thanks. It's because I don't believe in defeat… or fate… I like to decide my own." She wished she could bring him some measure of happiness and wondered why. "But you are so strong, you probably always get your wish, so why are you sad?"

He shook his head. "You have a curious mind, but I don't have to answer all your questions."

"I could read your thoughts to find the answers." She kept her tone light.

"I know." His half smile looked forced. "Only you among your people have this ability to connect mind to mind. How did you get it?"

Kefira wondered why he didn't extract the information directly from her mind, as he did when he called her Sardar. Was he testing her? "My gifts come from the goddess Helsara. Eons ago, the Bountiful One started a royal line to rule her chosen people, the pure tribe, the Anvad. Some of her divine blood runs in my veins through my family line… although it's been diluted over many generations."

"Really?" He sounded genuinely interested.

"Yes. My talents are meager compared to those of my ancestors." She sighed. "Still, to my people, I am a Sardar, a holy princess, born with special abilities, in order to lead and protect them."

"I can see that." His turquoise gaze pierced through her.

Kefira shivered with strange sensations. This man, or angel, awakened butterflies in her stomach, and turned her legs to marshmallow. Why?

As they reached the command bridge, Kefira composed herself, reminded of her responsibilities, and steeled herself to walk confidently to the center of the space. But the angel remained behind in the corridor with Karak. Strange.

Broken lights and haphazard debris on the decking attested to a struggle, but no Marauders in sight. Good.

The few crew members saluted.

Two dead crew members lay on the deck. Kefira didn't recognize them, but her heart went out to them and their families. May Helsara keep them safe against her bosom.

Another crew was bleeding profusely from a gash in the chest, a young man. The medics surrounding him attempted to staunch the blood, but as she read their minds, Kefira realized the wounded crew was as good as dead.

"Sardar!" The old captain limped toward her, pale, eyes wide with repressed fear. "What happened?"

"Apparently, we have been rescued. We are no longer in danger."

"But Sardar, there is a strange ship on the viewer that doesn't register on scanners. Yet it's here. Look!"

He indicated the main viewer where a luminous blue ship, shaped like a military destroyer with a full arsenal, hovered in space like a disembodied ghost. It wavered in and out of phase, sometimes here, sometimes not. How unusual and disturbing!

But Kefira must remain calm for her people. "I know, Captain. It belongs to our rescuers… it's all right."

"All right? It shot down and destroyed all the Marauder ships in one sweep! Then the raiders attacking the command bridge simply vanished, in some feat of sorcery." The captain froze when he spotted the tall angel in the hatchway, and stared. "By the bountiful breasts of Helsara, what is that?"

Angel Blake calmly walked toward the bleeding crewmember. "Please, allow me."

Kefira motioned for the medics to give him space. All stepped back in awe of the strange glowing man. Karak brushed her hip and settled at her side, purring, and watching with interest. The angel knelt beside the fallen crew, applied his hands to the ghastly stab wound, and closed his eyes as if in a deep trance.

The entire bridge grew quiet as officers and crew stared, waiting. Luminous energy emanated from the angel's hands. Within seconds, color returned to the crewmember's face. The bleeding stopped, and it seemed the wound closed itself under the angel's ministrations.

When the injured man opened his eyes, conscious of his surroundings, he smiled at his savior. "Thank you for saving my life."

"Glad I could help." Angel Blake rose and joined Kefira and Karak next to the baffled captain.

The medics ran back to the crewman, helped him stand up, gushing their surprise and admiration at the miracle.

"Thank you." Kefira's chest welled with gratitude and wonder. "How can we ever repay you?"

"About that… Is there a place where we can talk in private? Just you and me?" The angel touched her shoulder.

Kefira almost swooned at his touch. "Yes, of course. My private quarters." She turned to the captain. "Please, assess the losses and the damages and keep me informed."

The captain bowed too low. "As you wish, Sardar."

The big cat sneezed. *"Karak not like captain."*

"I know, Kitten." Kefira led Angel Blake toward her quarters, with Karak on their heels.

As they walked, she wondered at the strange feeling of wellbeing she experienced in the angel's presence. What kind of mental hold did he exert upon her? It was so weird. And she couldn't understand how someone who saved good people's lives could possibly be so sad and depressed.

Chapter Three

Blake followed the lovely woman and her big cat along the metallic corridors, noticing the smell of poorly recycled air. Was the cat purring? Yes. Angels had that effect on animals.

Despite the dim emergency lights, Kefira looked every bit as pretty as the first time he saw her in his faraway dreams. She had a spring in her step, and an honest, open face. Her dark eyes shone with hope. She loved her people, and she believed she could help them.

Compared to her, Blake felt old, although they probably looked the same age. But he had experienced shame and defeat. He knew the dark side of power and the many faces of greed, and ethnic hatred. As an officer in the GTA, he'd witnessed pure evil and even served it for a while… Such experiences changed a man.

Now, he protected the good and the worthy. "You seem in very good spirits, for someone whose ship has been breached, damaged, invaded, and her people violated and hurt, and some even killed…"

"I do grieve for my people who have joined Helsara in her bountiful land. But the rest of the Anvad need me." Kefira stopped in front of an unmarked hatch. "I'd rather focus on solving our current problems, than wallowing in sorrow. Lamenting over what's lost never accomplished anything."

The big cat halted and stretched. The hatch opened in a puff of compressed air.

The young woman hesitated at the threshold. "Why did you request a private meeting? Why not speak in front of the captain? The Anvad do not keep secrets from each other."

Blake hated this part of the job. "We must discuss the matter of compensation."

"Compensation?" Her voice trembled. "Of course." She stepped into what looked like very simple quarters for a princely leader. "Come in. You may sit wherever you like. Excuse the dim lights. We are low on power."

"I understand." Blake felt the large feline slinking past him and rubbing gently against his hip.

The big cat ambled straight for his food bowls, next to a comfy crate bed in a corner. *"Karak eat, Karak sleep."*

Blake smiled inwardly. Most cats could mind-speak but it took another mind-speaker to communicate with them.

"Good boy, Karak. You did well and you deserve food and rest." The lovely Kefira stood by a small couch. She attempted a smile. "May I offer you something to drink? Or eat?"

Blake sat in a comfy chair across the table from the couch and shook his head. "Nothing for me, thank you."

Better refuse the food and drink entirely, rather than have to explain why his kind didn't consume alcohol or animal protein, or anything processed... the only kinds of refreshments available on a long-haul space freighter.

"I'm a realist. I know miracles aren't free." The beautiful Kefira gave him a measuring stare. "We are very grateful for the rescue, of course, and willing to share with you whatever we have... but we don't have much. You see, we are refugees, enroute for our new home, the Land of Many Waters."

Blake lowered his gaze. "When I say compensation, I do not refer to currency or goods."

She offered a puzzled frown. "Then what do you want?"

He hesitated, wishing he didn't have to ask, but the universe had strict rules. "For payment, we require five innocent souls."

Her brown eyes rounded like saucers. "What?"

47

Blake sighed. He hated to explain. "We require five of your people to join us on our ship."

* * *

The temperature in Kefira's cabin suddenly dropped. She couldn't believe the angel had the audacity to claim such an outrageous toll. "You saved our freighter, and now you want to take five of my people with you?"

"Five innocent souls. Yes. Out of the five thousand we saved from slavery or death, it's a small price to pay." Angel Blake didn't even blink.

"But why?" Kefira stood up from the couch and paced her small quarters. "What are you going to do with them?" Could the saviors be as twisted as the Marauders?

"Not that it's any of your business, but…" Angel Blake stared at her with piercing turquoise eyes that stared straight into her soul. "The *Blue Phantom* needs a larger crew."

Kefira shuddered. She realized she couldn't refuse, but she couldn't imagine any of her people giving up their family and friends… or the dream of their promised land. "So, these five innocents will never see the Land of Many Waters?"

"Not for thirty cycles, no." The handsome angel sat very straight, immobile, steadfast, waiting…

"Three decades of servitude?" Longer than Kefira had lived. Longer than a murder sentence. She couldn't imagine serving that long. At least, the chosen five wouldn't have to die, but still, that sacrifice sounded cruel. "It might as well be a lifetime."

"It goes faster than you think." Angel Blake flashed a smug smile.

She started to like him less and less. "I need to think about this."

Kefira had already lost her elite warriors in the raid. They'd forfeited their lives to defend their people, but they'd freely chosen that path, and dedicated their lives to it. The few superior officers left were lazy nobles who inherited their title and would certainly refuse. As for the remaining civilians, they had made no commitment to serve.

"However you decide to proceed, by lottery, asking for volunteers, or by princely decree, do it quickly." Angel Blake remained unshakeable. "The price must be paid before you can resume your journey. If you fail to provide the requested compensation, we shall pick the five individuals ourselves."

"At random?" How dare he decide such things!

"Nothing is random in the universe, Sardar. Everything and everyone has a purpose." As the angel rose, his faint smile remained cold and distant. "Let me know what you decide."

Angel Blake inclined his head then vanished into thin air, leaving behind a fresh scent, like lilac in the spring.

Somehow, the temperature in the cabin dropped again. Or did her shivers mean she missed his presence? So odd.

Kefira couldn't imagine asking such a sacrifice from her people... and yet, compared to what their fate would have been without the rescue, it seemed a small price to pay indeed. Should they draw straws? Would she ask for volunteers among young single people? She refused to split up families. Should she let her people decide among themselves?

The sacrifices must be made, and the price must be paid. She faced a difficult decision, but she trusted the Anvad people. They would rise to the challenge... they always did in the past.

She wished she could volunteer herself, but her people would never agree to let her go, for fear to anger Helsara. They needed their Sardar princess to lead them. They also counted on her to insure the continuation of the Sardar line, for the future of the Anvad people.

Still... something troubled Kefira about this phantom ship, and the sad, handsome captain, who claimed he was no angel. "Computer?"

"Yes, Sardar." At least, the computer respected the etiquette due to her caste, without resentment for taking orders from a woman.

"Please run a search on the *Blue Phantom*, any ship glowing in space, and any winged beings resembling the angels of long-ago myths."

"As you wish, Sardar... but our power is currently limited." The computer emitted a few beeps.

Kefira had no doubt the angel captain would keep his word. She sensed great resolve in him. She wished she knew more about Angel Blake, before judging him too quickly.

"Karak? What do you think of Angel Blake?" Animals usually had a good instinct about people.

The large cat growled. *"Karak like Angel Blake."*

"Thanks, I thought so." Still. She needed reassurance, and she was curious. "Computer?"

"Yes, Sardar."

"Please, run a galaxy-wide search on Captain Blake Volkov." If, as he claimed, Blake wasn't a heavenly angel but a man, he would have a past, and there would be records. That would tell her whether or not he could be trusted.

"As you wish, Sardar. But in the present state of the ship, with only intermittent power, it might take a long time." The computer beeped. "Hours, days, or even longer."

"That's all right." Kefira would get to the bottom of this mystery. "Just do your best."

"Yes, Sardar." The computer beeped and went dark... probably to conserve power.

Kefira would rather conduct a discrete search than confront the powerful angel, or get caught trying to read his mind through his mental shield... he might object. Everyone had secrets... even Angel Blake. Maybe she'd learn why Blake was so somber, or why he seemed so familiar. She would find out what skeletons lay buried in his past. She would enjoy snooping and discovering more about him.

* * *

Back on the *Blue Phantom*, Blake gazed through the clear dome. A field of floating debris strewn all around Kefira's freighter attested to the attack. He shook his head in dejection. That's what his life had become... killing, destroying without mercy, and taking reluctant individuals to serve on his ship.

Graziella manifested inside the dome, tall, sculpted, tossing her short blond hair, and always cheerful. "Why the long face, Captain?"

Blake exhaled a slow breath. "I still wonder whether we really won the final battle, three cycles ago."

"Of course, we won. You brought about the fall of a great evil entity, the Stygian Order, and the formidable GTA military force that supported them." She smiled. "That was a great victory for the forces of good."

"Easy for you to say. You were already an Avenging Angel. You always fought for the light."

Graziella's pale face turned serious. "Not always…"

"Still, I'm not certain the forces of good won that day." Blake gestured toward the debris field. "I feel responsible for the ensuing chaos, for the small pockets of evil surging everywhere, unchecked…"

"You have to stop blaming yourself, Captain. This mission of yours is turning into an obsession." She bit her lips as if she'd spoken out of turn. "We patrol the galaxy to save the worthy from these pirates and Marauders. You should feel good about that."

Blake couldn't hide his guilt. Not from his First in Command. "To me, our mission resembles more and more the work of an executioner of lowly thugs."

"But you should be proud and happy about saving the galaxy from evil."

"Then why does my victory on the malevolent Kalishtar and her evil daughter

53

tastes bitter? I betrayed my superior officers and my comrades in arms. Most of my friends died on that fated day." And their death weighed heavily on Blake's conscience.

"Not all your comrades died in the final battle, Captain."

"Those who survived hate me and blame me for their defeat and their imprisonment." There was no joy in Blake's life.

But maybe, there could be. Kefira's beautiful face flashed upon his mind. Kefira… the woman from his dreams. Like a young lioness, she was fierce, full of life, and wild. The opposite of what he had become. Unlike him, Kefira was surrounded by her people. She belonged with them, and she wanted to protect them.

"Kefira is a lovely woman." Graziella smiled knowingly. Of course, she knew how he felt about the Sardar princess. There were no secrets among angels.

"Kefira must think I am a terrible person to ask for such a price in innocent lives." And Blake tended to agree. At the very least, he was a fraud. He didn't deserve the power bestowed upon angels.

"Did you mention to the beautiful Sardar princess what would happen to the five selected to join us?" Graziella smiled again.

"Of course not. I can't tell her that. It's against the rule. Their initial sacrifice must be authentic. Only the worthy..." Yet, Blake didn't feel worthy.

"I see... and your sadness has nothing to do with the fact that she is beautiful and kind and we must leave soon?"

"Of course, not." But Blake wasn't so sure. "The *Blue Phantom* has a reputation to uphold. Its tough brand of justice should incite dread among the despicable space pirates."

"I see..." Graziella nodded. "Avenging Angels must be seen as deadly weapons to be feared."

"Exactly." Blake struggled to regain his calm. "And the slightest rumor of kindness or benevolence toward the guilty could be viewed as a weakness."

Graziella pursed her lips. "And any perceived weakness could compromise our important work."

"Yes." Blake sighed, no longer certain he still believed in his self-imposed mission. "Why did you come?"

Graziella straightened and saluted. "Captain, speaking of the lovely Kefira, leader of the Anvad, she requested to see you."

A shiver scurried down Blake's spine. He found Kefira's company invigorating, and immensely enjoyable, and he dreaded facing her pain. "I shall meet her right here."

"Aye, aye, Captain." Graziella saluted and vanished.

With one thought, Blake made himself invisible.

* * *

As her feet met the deck of the angel ship, Kefira lurched forward. Graziella, the radiant woman angel, helped her regain her balance then let her go. Strange mode of transportation, dematerializing from one place to rematerialize in another. Advanced technology? Or just weird abilities?

Although, from the outside the angel ship had the shape of a military destroyer, the inside looked like a cathedral with high vaults, buttresses, and glass-like pillars. Strange material for a spaceship. It radiated a blue glow, providing soft illumination throughout.

No wonder the angel ship looked like a ghostly apparition in dark space. It actually glowed.

"Thank you, Graziella." Kefira couldn't help but smile at the beautiful angel.

"You are most welcome." Graziella smiled back. She looked like an Amazon, tall and sculpted, with flawless skin, short blond hair, and striking turquoise eyes. Although strong, she exuded compassion.

The battery light on both of Kefira's blasters extinguished at the same time. She drew one out and shook it, then she tapped it, but the power cell read empty. "What happened? Both my weapons are dead. I had fresh power cells."

"Sorry. The special kind of energy running the *Blue Phantom* automatically disables all electronics. Don't worry, after you recharge your blasters, back on your ship, they will work again." Graziella's melodious voice reminded Kefira of her mother's. Her very presence was soothing. What a strange power to exert on another being.

The beautiful Graziella pointed to an arched portal in the blue crystal bulkhead. "Through this opening is where our captain will meet you."

Angel Graziella turned around and vanished into thin air, leaving behind her the faint fragrance of a rosebush, like the ones blooming in the gardens of the Sardar palace on Kefira's former home planet.

Was everyone on the *Blue Phantom* a work of art? So far, the angels Kefira had glimpsed, human-looking or otherwise, seemed perfect in every way. All of them had striking blue eyes. They all looked young but seemed to think and act with great consideration and wisdom, a quality most often found in older people.

Kefira walked toward the tall arch in the translucent bulkhead. She found herself in a vast space, mostly empty, under a clear dome. Through it, she could see the stars, and her freighter, surrounded by a debris field, and the floating corpses of many Marauders.

She shivered at the fragility of life. Closing her eyes, she inhaled the sweet vapors and listened to the soft musical harmonies whirling around the dome. The mix of fragrances transported her mind to an idyllic early childhood… before the love of her life disappeared, before the invasion of her planet… before her family was accused of treason and slaughtered by the GTA.

Now, she was the last of her kind, the last Sardar of the Anvad to guide her people to a promised faraway land, away from civilization. In that distant part of the galaxy, where pirates and Marauders would never venture, Helsara would protect her people, like she had protected their ancestors.

Angel Blake manifested in front of her… or had he been there, invisible, watching her all along? She guessed the latter. She sensed his energy and could almost read him, but not quite.

"I'm glad you came." He looked straight through her, cold and detached, but was it a pretense? She sensed so many protective barriers around him. This man, or angel, didn't want to be read.

"Doesn't all that carnage and debris floating outside in space bother you?" Kefira felt entitled to ask. After all, she was paying his price in Anvad lives.

"It reminds me evil exists and must be eradicated." He sighed and gazed faraway through the clear dome. "Would you have preferred we didn't save your people?"

"Of course, not." Now, she felt guilty for asking.

"After justice is done, there is no room for regrets. Only the mission at hand counts." Such determination… but his jaw clenched. He was hiding deeper feelings.

Kefira gently focused on his thoughts and hit a mental wall. Why was he so guarded? She wanted to know more about him and his kind. "How do you do that, making yourself invisible, materializing from nowhere?"

He smiled. "Oh, you picked up on the invisibility thing?"

"Yes. The blood of the goddess Helsara still flows in my veins." Had he forgotten she had powers? "Are you using some kind of technology?"

"Not really. Our ship's special energy source neutralizes conventional technology. I dematerialize or manifest the same way I sprout wings and fly… just by thinking about it." He offered a sad smile. "Did you come to a decision about our compensation arrangement?"

"Yes." She paused, taking a breath. She refused to show weakness. "It was a difficult choice, but my people are very grateful for their lives, and they decided in the end. I have five volunteers ready to join your crew."

"Are they pure of heart?" His blue eyes seemed to scan deep into her very soul.

"Yes. We are called the Anvad for a reason. Anvad means pure. The three young men and two young women chosen are exemplary, and willing to sacrifice their freedom, so the rest of their people may reach the Land of Many Waters… our promised planet."

"Their sacrifice is admirable. I thank you, personally, and in the name of my crew." He clasped his hands behind his back and gazed at the black expanse beyond the dome. "The *Blue Phantom* is a very large ship, and although most functions are automated, we need more hands on our many decks."

"When should they transfer to your ship?" Kefira closed the few steps between them. "Right now, everyone is working on repairs."

"They can come aboard as soon as you are ready to resume your voyage." Why was he staring at her with such sadness in his eyes?

"We assessed the damages, and it will take a few days to get the freighter in full working order." Kefira sensed an opportunity. "Would it be too much to ask for some help from you and your crew?"

"Help with what?" His face opened and relaxed and the light in his eyes brightened. "We are always happy to help the worthy."

She took heart from his enthusiasm. "I'm afraid our cannons were destroyed, and we have no spares."

He straightened as if digesting the request. "Our weapons are not compatible with your technology."

"That's unfortunate." Kefira suspected the freighter would be safe for a while, but she was reluctant to leave the company of the angel ship... and that of its handsome captain. "How shall we protect ourselves from other space pirates along the way?"

His brow shot up in mild surprise. "Are you asking for protection for the remainder of your voyage?"

"Yes... if it's not too much to ask." She smiled in apology, hoping he would accept. "I don't want to impose... you must be busy."

"Not as busy as you would think." His melodious voice hung in the air. "Not all who call for help deserve to be rescued."

"Wow! You decide who is worthy and who is not?" It sounded like a heavy responsibility.

His face relaxed into a rare smile. "How far is that promised planet? Are you even certain it exists?"

"Of course, it exists!" How could he doubt her word? "It's the planet of our faraway ancestors, damaged by solar flares over ten millennia ago. Now, it has recovered and become livable again... like a virgin paradise."

He seemed amused by her reaction. "How do you know it hasn't been settled by another tribe, or been claimed by pirates?"

"It's too isolated, far away from other planets, far off the trade routes... of no value and no interest for the greedy."

"How can you be sure?" His inquisitive gaze warmed her. "And what if there are more solar flares?"

Finally, a sensible question. "Our scientists determined that our original star has now entered a stable phase that will last roughly a million cycles."

Angel Blake nodded gravely. "An eternity for us, a mere blink in the life of a galaxy."

"So, will you accompany us the rest of the way?" Her heart galloped in her chest as she waited for his answer.

Angel Blake considered her for a moment then sighed. "All right. You win. We shall accompany you for the rest of your voyage."

"Thank you, in the name of my people." Kefira felt giddy. She couldn't help but smile like a dimwit. "If you don't mind, we are planning a gathering to celebrate the miraculous rescue. The Anvad would love to have you and your crew attend, so they can thank you properly."

"We would be honored." Angel Blake flashed a brief smile. "We'll also bring some supplies, since yours must be limited."

"Wonderful." Kefira's chest overflowed with gratitude, so happy her people would be safe for the rest of the voyage... and she looked forward to spending all that time with the gorgeous captain of the *Blue Phantom*. For some reason, his very presence made her feel safe.

Chapter Four

Through the clear observation dome of the *Blue Phantom*, Blake watched Kefira's freighter, floating among the debris field. He didn't know what to expect from an Anvad celebration, but he relished the idea of spending time with the beautiful princess. He couldn't stop thinking about her... and smile. She made his heart sing like never before... but this kind of happiness wasn't for him.

Since the historic final battle, three cycles ago, he and his crew never relaxed. He still ran the *Blue Phantom* in the military style he'd learned in the GTA. Discipline, cleanliness, dedication to the mission, all were paramount. But times had changed. There was no galactic war, only pirates and Marauders. Perhaps, he should allow his crew to have some fun once in a while.

"Graziella?"

His first officer manifested inside the dome and stood at attention, in her light blue uniform, hand on her sword hilt. "Aye, Captain."

"Extend the Anvad's invitation to the entire crew." Some R&R might be good for them. After all, they hadn't attended a single party since they set out on this mission.

"Wonderful idea, Captain." Graziella relaxed her stance and flipped her short blond hair in a familiar gesture. "I will invite them. But most of them might decline, you know, on account of the food." She made a sour face.

"I know." And Blake agreed. "But they did invite us, and we do not wish to be rude."

"Since when do we care?" Graziella chuckled then winked at him. "You mean, you do not want to upset the lovely Kefira."

Blake sighed. Angels couldn't hide their thoughts from each other. "I'm still the captain, and I wish for the crew to attend."

"But these mortals still drink fermented beverages and eat processed foods... even meat." She almost gagged.

"True." Blake sighed.

Not so long ago, he and his crew also ate animal protein... but as the Azuran crystal at the core of the *Blue Phantom* bonded with the ship and made it glow, it also transformed the crew. As they grew wings and acquired new abilities, they lost the capacity to process impure foods.

He cleared his throat. "Arrange for fresh produce from our hydroponic hangars to be delivered to their freighter for the occasion."

"Aye Captain." Graziella flashed a one-sided smile. "And desserts from our galley?"

Blake chuckled. His first officer loved sweets. "Yes, Graziella, and desserts."

* * *

Dressed in dark red, with black veils covering their faces, the families of the dead Anvad recited the litanies and lit traditional glowing lights in commemoration of the young lives cut short.

Kefira presided, also wearing dark red, black, and gold, the traditional colors of the Anvad. "These thirty-three young men and women dedicated their lives to the protection of the Anvad. As we fought alongside, I witnessed their sacrifice. They died with honor and deserve your praises. They will forever be recognized in Anvad History as examples of courage and dedication. May Helsara keep them near and bless their souls."

"May Helsara bless their souls!" the mourners repeated.

Soft music seeped from the bulkhead as the mourners circled the sarcophagi painted with the red, black, and gold stripes of the Anvad flag.

Everyone stood very straight and silent as the music stopped, and the thirty-three pods slid silently into the void of space.

"May we all be reunited some day in the arms of Helsara the Bountiful, after a life well lived." Kefira's voice trembled a little, but she straightened her frame. A Sardar must never show weakness.

"May we all be reunited in Helsara!" repeated the mourners.

Then came the condolences and hugs. Although Kefira couldn't hug anyone. Hugging a Sardar would be an inconceivable lack of respect for any Anvad.

Kefira left discreetly to join Karak in the corridor. She removed her veil and her mourning cape, handed them to a lady's extended hands, then made her way to the main hold. Although deeply saddened by the loss of precious Anvad lives, she must make sure the rest of the tribe remained in high spirits.

She straightened her dress as she walked. She hated fancy clothes, but Anvad protocol only allowed her to wear rich gowns or military garb… always of the finest silk.

She petted Karak. "At least, you don't have to worry about clothes."

The big cat hissed. *"Karak protect."*

From the corridor, Kefira smelled the aroma of roasting meat and fresh baked goods. Soft music and laughter wafted in the air. As she stepped into the main hold, the celebration was already underway. The space, decorated for the occasion, dripped with shiny garlands and blinking lights. Along the bulkhead, long tables displayed exotic fruit and fresh food, drinks, and even sweets... a rare treat.

Several angels mingled with the Anvad, who bowed to them in gratitude. Despite the brutal experience with the Marauders, her people seemed to enjoy the festivities, happy to be alive.

Kefira had a slight frisson as she spotted Angel Blake in a dark corner of the hold. Tall and imposing in his light blue uniform, glowing sword at his side, he observed the crowd and seemed in deep reflection.

The first computer reports from her search, mentioned winged angels on the planet Azura and on the Byzantium Space Station. Emboldened by these positive results, Kefira walked toward Blake. She had new questions for him.

On her way, she waved, nodded, and smiled at the many deep curtsies from her people. Unfortunately, the miraculous rescue had reinforced their belief in her divinity. They thought their Sardar alone had saved them by summoning the angels.

Butterflies fluttered in her stomach as she crossed the hold toward Blake, intensely aware of his blue gaze upon her. As she approached him, he straightened and offered a strained smile. Did he ever relax?

She couldn't help feeling light and invigorated by his presence and smiled. "Thank you for the food, Captain. Fresh fruit and vegetables are a rare commodity on a lengthy space voyage. And the desserts are a big success."

"My pleasure." Angel Blake offered a half smile. "The desserts were Graziella's idea."

Kefira would have to thank the gorgeous female angel. "How do you happen to have so much to share?"

"Hydroponics." Angel Blake locked his hands behind his back, as if he didn't trust himself with them. "We have a large ship with a small crew, so there is plenty of available space to grow food, and an abundance of crops."

"I see…" Kefira found him fascinating and wanted to know more. Now that she had him cornered, she would make the most of it. "How often to you stop for supplies on populated planets?"

"Never." He closed his mouth in a tight line.

She kept staring and waited.

He sighed. "We are self-sufficient, like an independent state, like a floating island."

"Like a space station?" So many things still baffled Kefira about the *Blue Phantom* and its crew.

"Most space stations rely on supply ships. The *Blue Phantom* does not." Was it a hint of pride in his voice?

"I hear the Byzantium Space Station is also self-reliant." The computer report

69

mentioned the Azurans as angel-like beings with wings and blue eyes, and amazing abilities... who also owned and ran the Byzantium Space Station.

"Byzantium is an Azuran enclave. The *Blue Phantom* does not recognize Azuran rule. We are not Azurans." The statement sounded final.

"Then what are you?" She wanted to add *Who do you serve?* but she feared he would clam up if she asked.

"We are independent from any planet or government, and completely self-sufficient. We live in the vastness of space." His face closed again.

The music played louder. A few Anvad couples now danced in the clear central space. Kefira noticed the beautiful Graziella dancing with another female angel, smiling and giggling. The few other angels stood around in small clusters remaining among themselves. Not a very social bunch.

She laid a hand on Blake's arm, enjoying the intoxicating contact. "Would you like to dance?"

Angel Blake cleared his throat. "Sorry, Sardar. Dancing is not among my list of skills."

Kefira smiled. "Could I get a copy of that list for future reference?"

Blake chuckled. "It's highly classified, Sardar."

She pouted. "Too bad."

Angel Graziella left the dance floor and walked toward them with the other beautiful female angel. Both smiled at Blake, who saluted them with a nod.

Graziella grabbed two steaming cups from a passing tray and offered one to Kefira, and the other to Blake. She smiled to Kefira. "Have you tried our crimson tea?"

"Thank you." Kefira took the warm cup. She tasted the tea and found it sweet, aromatic, and extremely pleasant. "This is a rare treat."

Blake sipped then nodded. "It is made from the petals of a tropical flower found on Azura. But, of course, we grow it aboard the *Blue Phantom*."

Blake seemed to exchange thoughts with Graziella, but Kefira couldn't read them. How odd. She watched the two gorgeous women walk away toward another group of angels. These beings had very strong abilities that made Kefira feel inadequate, less than a Sardar. She felt a tinge of envy but quickly dismissed it.

Soft music, conversations, and laughter hung in the air. Her people seemed happy. Kefira raised her cup to Blake and took another sip of tea.

She wondered if the crew of the *Blue Phantom* indulged in romantic relationships, since they never stopped in ports of call. But she would be too embarrassed to ask directly.

Still… She found her courage and smiled at Blake. "There are many women among your crew… and in position of responsibility, no less."

"Yes, of course. Why is that surprising?" He frowned at her. "You rule the Anvad, and you are a woman."

She looked down. "The Anvad are still a male-dominated society. I made a few changes, but I rule only because I am the very last Sardar carrying Helsara's divine blood. When I take a mate, he will become Padshad and have power over me. I will lose my authority. My only responsibility then will be to bear children to continue the Sardar line."

Angel Blake frowned. "That hardly seems fair."

Kefira took a deep breath and observed Graziella and her friend talking and socializing nearby. "They are very beautiful, aren't they?"

Blake sipped his crimson tea. "I guess they are… I never noticed."

"How can you not?" Even Kefira had noticed. Was Blake hiding his true feelings? Why? "You seem to be very close with Graziella."

"Yes, Sardar. She is my first officer, second in command on the *Blue Phantom*." His back straightened and he looked rigid.

"I see…" It meant they were together a lot. "Is that all Graziella is to you?"

"Sardar!" Blake gave her a once over and a disapproving stare. "Respectfully, I believe my relationship with my crew is none of your business."

His repeated use of her title, and his refusal to answer slapped Kefira in the face. As a Sardar, she wasn't used to being denied anything. She wished she weren't so jealous. It was beneath her. But how could she compete with the gorgeous Graziella? Such perfection and beauty of body and spirit would render any woman insecure.

Blake's gaze softened. "I would think a beautiful princess like you must have many noble suitors. Anyone special in your life?"

"There used to be." Kefira flinched at the painful memory and caressed her silver medallion.

"Who was he?" Blake's sudden interest and gentle voice made her feel special.

Kefira struggled against bitter tears. "He was a bright young man from a good Anvad family. We studied and traveled together on my ship, the *Zantar*. We were very much in love... that was before everything changed in the galaxy."

"What happened to him?" Blake's blue gaze sharpened.

"My ship was attacked... I wish the *Blue Phantom* had been there to rescue us that day." A rush of emotions knotted Kefira's throat.

"If it happened before the final battle, there was no *Blue Phantom* then. It couldn't have answered your call," Blake declared, matter-of-factly.

"There was no distress call for help. It happened too fast." Kefira repressed the sobs threatening to overcome her. "I didn't even realize we were being attacked. I was hit over the head and fell unconscious."

"I'm so sorry." His hand on her arm felt wonderfully comforting.

"I lost my crew and my ship, and the man I loved at the same time. All gone, without a trace, lost to the black expanse... and the wound is still raw despite the passage of time."

"By what miracle did you survive the attack?" Blake's interest in her made her feel better.

"I have no idea." Kefira swallowed the knot in her throat. "I woke up in an escape pod with Karak purring beside me. I don't remember anything about the battle, or if there was one... or how I escaped. All I have to go on is a recorded warning in the escape pod's memory, saying the ship was under attack."

"What about your big cat?" Blake set his empty cup on a passing tray. "What does he remember?"

Karak rubbed against the angel's hip. *"Karak protect."*

Blake indulged the big cat with a scratch on the head. Kefira did the same. Their hands almost touched.

Kefira's heart skipped a beat. "Karak's memory is blank as well... although I suspect he dragged me to the pod when I was unconscious and saved my life."

Blake narrowed his piercing blue eyes at her. "Isn't that lack of memory in both of you rather strange?"

Kefira shivered under his scrutiny, holding back tears. The wound was still fresh. "I thought so, too. But I didn't have much time to think about it. When my pod was rescued and I returned home, the GTA had slaughtered my entire family. I was the only Sardar left to lead the Anvad people... and they counted on me. So, I set aside my strange and devastating experience and focused on helping them."

Blake laid a light hand on her shoulder, and it seemed all the hurt from the tragedy was lifted from her soul. In that moment, Kefira wanted to remain at his side for the rest of her life. But she mentally shook herself and regained her senses. It wasn't real. She couldn't trust her feelings around him. These angels had to exude some kind of pheromones. It was all very confusing.

"What about you? Anyone special?" If he said Graziella, she would die of humiliation.

He smiled, as if he sensed her attraction to him, and maybe he did. "There is no room for relationships aboard the *Blue Phantom*. Besides, the radiation that makes the ship glow in the dark keeps us sterile."

"Really?" Kefira's hope sank. How could such a gorgeous man be sterile? As a Sardar princess, having children was her sacred duty, to continue Helsara's direct line into the future.

"Being an angel requires sacrifices."

She raised her teacup and eyed it suspiciously. "Should I worry about that tea? Could it make me sterile?"

"No worries." He chuckled. "It's the crystal in the ship having that transformative effect on our bodies. As we gain our abilities, we also lose our capacity to procreate."

Kefira realized she was still very attracted to him, but she should fight his influence. It wasn't real. Besides, he couldn't have children. She couldn't think like a little girl with selfish dreams of happiness in the arms of a kind, handsome man... even if he were an angel. Her life belonged to her people.

In the Land of Many Waters, reduced to a virgin planet, there would be no fancy labs to continue the Sardar line through scientific means... at least, not for a few decades. So, she would have to find a consort who could produce an heir the way Helsara intended.

* * *

The next morning, as she sipped the crimson tea Angel Blake had kindly provided, Kefira felt renewed. She walked to the private console in her quarters. "Computer, how are the repairs going?"

The computer beeped. "The repairs are going smoothly, Sardar. We now have full power. Normal life is returning onboard, and we should be able to resume our voyage in a day or two."

"Great." Last night's enlightening conversation with Blake... and the lovely dreams that ensued, had restored Kefira's peace. She would focus on her duty.

In a few days they would be on their way. After they reached the Land of Many Waters, Angel Blake would be gone forever. Kefira belonged to the Anvad and could never take him as her mate, but she would always have the dreams to comfort her.

Now, she was ready to tackle the task at hand. She sat at her private console and set down her warm mug. "Computer? What else should I know?"

"Sardar? I have the results of the search you requested on Captain Blake Volkov." The electronic voice sounded upbeat, as always.

Blake's face filled the monitor screen. He wore a black cap and uniform jacket, and his dark eyes and harsh expression made her cringe inside. He looked so different, and so angry. The uniform was reminiscent of the

GTA, but other institutions used black as well. Kefira shivered.

She no longer considered Blake a threat... only a wonderful possibility that could never happen. An impossible dream. Still, this disturbing picture of him demanded an explanation. "What did you find?"

The computer chimed. "Blake Volkov disappeared from the records three cycles ago, Sardar. But prior to that, he has a complete history preserved in the archives of the now defunct GTA."

"The GTA archives?" Kefira had assumed they'd been destroyed.

"Yes, Sardar. Most of the GTA records survived the purge and were made public by the victors."

Might Blake have been a Resistance fighter or a prisoner? "Was he arrested for opposing them?"

The computer beeped a few times. "No, Sardar... quite the contrary."

"What do you mean?" Confusion clouded Kefira's mind.

"Blake Volkov was a highly decorated Fleet Captain in the former GTA." A symbol of a snake and dagger inside a circle popped on the console screen. "He was also an official member of the Stygian Order."

"What? It can't be!" Kefira's small hairs stood up on her arms. Even though that evil had been eradicated in the final battle, the

Stygian Order had left a black mark on the entire galaxy. "It has to be a mistake."

"No mistake, Sardar." The computer beeped. "Tasked to annex many planets unfavorable to his powerful overlords, Fleet Captain Blake Volkov ruthlessly oppressed those who resisted, always getting lucrative results. Which awarded him many accolades from the GTA High Council."

Stunned, Kefira could barely articulate. She swallowed hard, reminding herself facts did not lie, but records weren't always accurate. How could this evil GTA captain become an example of vertu? "What else do the records say?"

"In his defense, Fleet Captain Blake Volkov turned his destroyers against the Stygian Order in the final battle, and his betrayal was instrumental in the ultimate victory."

Unable to remain seated, Kefira rose from her private console. "Are you telling me that before the final battle, Angel Blake was a ruthless GTA oppressor, a worshipper of evil, who then turned against his masters, became a traitor, and saved the day?"

"Exactly, Sardar. In precisely that order." The disembodied voice sounded proud.

Kefira still couldn't believe it. "And now, he's some kind of Avenging Angel?"

"The GTA records stop after the final battle, Sardar. As for the mentions of the *Blue Phantom*, its crew, or its mission, they started afterwards. But it's only rumors and hearsay. Nothing official."

Kefira's throat constricted. She couldn't process the information. "It doesn't make any sense!"

The computer beeped. "I also found interesting bits of material about Captain Volkov's family."

"Tell me everything." Kefira hoped it would help her understand.

"Blake's father, a prominent GTA general, led the mission to punish the Anvad people and end the reign of the Sardars."

Heat rose up Kefira's throat. "You mean, Blake's father ordered my entire family slaughtered?"

"Yes, Sardar. And old General Volkov also participated in the slaughtering." The lack of emotion in the computer voice sounded wrong.

Kefira's throat clenched. How could this be? "Where is the father now?"

"He was killed in the final battle, Sardar."

"Good riddance." Kefira wished she'd slain the bastard herself... although in those days, she had no warrior skills.

"In the Volkov's family files, a side note indicates that Blake's grandfather publicly opposed the GTA. For his rebellious audacity, he was condemned to forced labor in a mining colony in the frozen hells of Laxxar... where he likely died from exposure and exhaustion many cycles ago. No one

80

survives more than a cycle in these frozen mines."

"At least one person in his family had enough courage to stand up for justice." But what did that make Blake? How did a tyrant turned traitor become a savior? Or was there such a thing? Kefira didn't know what to believe.

"On a different note, Sardar, an Anvad ship was spotted on long-range scanners a few hours ago, heading straight for us. It is still too far away to recognize, but the faint radio-wave emissions are definitely Anvad."

"Strange. The entire Anvad fleet was destroyed." And Kefira's plan didn't include other ships joining them part way. "Could it be that an exiled Anvad group from a distant colony, also located the Land of Many Waters, and decided to head there?"

The computer beeped. "It would be unlikely, but not impossible, Sardar."

"The timing is too much of a coincidence." And Kefira didn't believe in coincidences. "Why didn't our captain let me know about this approaching ship when it was spotted?"

"An Anvad vessel is not considered a threat, Sardar. The captain didn't want to intrude on your sleep, or alarm you for no reason."

"Right." Kefira was tired of being treated like a fragile princess. "Tell the captain I'm coming to have a word with him."

Kefira didn't appreciate surprise visits on this voyage. Not even from an Anvad ship. Too many weird coincidences. At least, the new information about Blake had effectively stopped her infatuation with the handsome angel. He was nothing more than a cold-blooded GTA turncoat who didn't deserve her attention.

She should just forget about him... but could she?

* * *

Under the clear observation dome of his destroyer, Blake focused his mind and scanned the advancing ship. He shuddered as his enhanced abilities sensed evil onboard. Not just evil... the kind of evil that can swallow an entire quadrant. Although that evil was skillfully camouflaged... as if by dark sorcery.

From his short stint in the Stygian Order, Blake remembered the feel and the taste of ritual blood sacrifice. Blood and fire, to be exact. The knife poised over the innocent victim... evil incantations summoning entities from other worlds... He shuddered and shook the gory images from his mind.

How could he have attended such rituals without doing something about it? But he was only one man at the time, powerless against so many. And he did take action when the opportunity arose… during the final battle.

Still, he blamed himself for not reacting sooner… although it would only have gotten him killed. His calculated military move in the final battle had saved the galaxy from a ghastly fate… for now.

But this incoming ship carried a dangerous entity, a powerful sorcerer with blood lust on his mind. It must be destroyed as soon as it came into torpedo range.

As he refocused his mind on the advancing ship, Blake could see the red glowing shields and shuddered. They seemed a hundred times more powerful than the Marauders' shields. They also reeked of Stygian sorcery. Even the *Blue Phantom's* special weapons would be inadequate against such shields.

In the final battle, when he'd turned his destroyers against the Stygian Order, his torpedoes weren't enough to penetrate the Stygian shields either… until his clever strategy and the moral strength of the Azuran angels outsmarted and defeated the might of the sorcerers. Only then could Blake destroy their ships.

Such evil was too strong to fight face to face. Blake must go at it sideways. Undermine and destroy the sorcerer first, then the ship.

In any case, he must warn Kefira and the Anvad captain. Together, they might be able to formulate a plan.

Chapter Five

Malo paced his luxurious quarters aboard the Anvad raptor. Why did the Marauders ignore his call? He rubbed his left upper chest through the padded silk vest. Although the branding burn had healed, the scar still itched and pulled at the skin.

His hired goons should have found the freighter and reported to him by now. He'd given them clear directions about the Anvad's route and current location, and promised each their weight in gold for capturing the entire tribe... and delivering Kefira... alive.

What good was his power if he couldn't even get Marauders to do his bidding? A First Lieutenant and skilled sorcerer shouldn't have to do anything himself. And yet, here he was, chasing his prey, instead of waiting for its delivery.

Malo closed his eyes and focused his sharp mind on a particular signal. Like he had done many times before, he synched his mind with the special medallion he'd given Kefira before leaving her. Drawing power from the collective consciousness of the Stygian Order, he scanned the dark expanse in front of him.

There! He couldn't see Kefira but he sensed her presence. She was surrounded by the Anvad tribe, inside their freighter.

But where were the Marauders? Had they been delayed? Had they reneged on the deal? There would be severe reprisals if they did. Could they have jumped on the freighter and parked their ships inside it? Not likely. In any case, they should have reported to him by now. Something smelled fishy, and Malo would find the culprits. They would pay with their lives for not delivering on time.

He relaxed against the back of the silk couch and sighed.

Kefira was there, but he couldn't see her, or read her thoughts. Her Sardar powers protected her mind. So, he focused on her location and made contact with the weak-minded captain of the freighter. The old man had no idea his thoughts could be read so easily from afar. The Anvad were innocent but gullible and easily manipulated.

Malo picked up on the captain's thoughts and closed his eyes to explore the old man's recent memories. The answers he received chilled his blood.

What? The Marauders had failed? How could this be? Malo couldn't stand failure, but he controlled his rage. If the despicable pirates were still alive, he would make them pay... but their death would explain their silence.

Malo focused on the weak captain's mind and explored his memories. Someone with superior armament had intervened... a strange ship that phased in and out of existence... and glowed blue in dark space.

Could it be the *Blue Phantom*? The old captain believed the phantom ship was still there, but Malo couldn't detect any ship in the vicinity, not even the freighter itself. Still, it could be his chance to kill two birds, fulfill both missions in one sweep.

His mind vision failed him, as if the ships were cloaked or shielded. No matter. Soon, Malo would be there in person. If he wanted things done right, he would have to do the job himself.

Brute force may have failed, but it wasn't the only way to accomplish his goal. Since the Marauders had botched the mission, he'd use his powers of seduction and misdirection. He was a master at playing the role of the innocent... after all, his late mother had been Anvad. It was in his blood.

He couldn't wait to see Kefira in the flesh again... He could still smell her sweet perfume. They were quite a pair, once, and he hoped she still loved him. The last time he was with her, he'd sent her away in an escape pod. It wasn't her time to serve her purpose.

That day, Malo had stolen Kefira's ship and abducted his mother to bring her to his father. Then he'd completed his training as a sorcerer, culminating in his recent initiation... and his mother's sacrifice by blood and fire. He hated her for hiding his father's identity all this time. Now, she had served her purpose.

Above all, Malo hated the Anvad. He should have been raised and educated as a Sardar. His powers were obvious, even as a child. But the Anvad had refused to recognize his abilities. If he didn't get his abilities from Helsara, they must have come from evil sources. Well, they weren't wrong. Still, they would pay for the insult.

Today, as First Lieutenant in the Stygian Order, in possession of all these new abilities, Malo was ready for the next phase. He was coming for Kefira... and the rest of the Anvad people would pay for rejecting his gifts. Now, he was powerful beyond their imagining. And they would be sacrificed, all of them... by blood and fire.

The Anvad were pure and innocent. The perfect sacrifices to entice the new Prince of Darkness, the Exalted Baalmordo. With the dark prince's help, Malo would dethrone his father and rule the galaxy. He hoped Kefira would join him on his throne.

* * *

"Captain!" Kefira marched into the command bridge, her hand on Karak's collar, finding strength in his presence. "What is it I hear about an incoming ship?"

"Sardar." The old man eyed the big cat fearfully as he bowed. "We decoded the ship's signals. It seems the Anvad vessel coming toward us is the *Zantar!*"

"My *Zantar*? The ship I lost over three cycles ago?" Kefira dared to hope. The return of her ship reminded her of Malo. Could he have survived?

The big cat picked up on her thoughts and growled. *"Karak not like Malo."*

"I know, Kitten." She petted the cat, who was probably jealous of Malo's affections.

Kefira caressed her silver medallion, Malo's last gift. Her pulse raced at the memory of their love. She'd missed him so much, as a friend, and as a lover.

Angel Blake manifested in midair then alighted on the command bridge. "There is something you should know about that ship, Sardar."

"Oh, really?" Kefira could barely keep her anger under control as she glared at him. As a prominent GTA officer, he'd oppressed peaceful tribes… his father had slaughtered her family. "And what is it I should know, exactly?"

"I sense a dark presence lurking aboard that ship, Sardar. Its shields are imbued with dangerous sorcery." Angel Blake shook his head. "I sense imminent danger. Something is very wrong."

Karak sat up at the angel's feet, as if taking his side and blinked at Kefira. Traitor.

"I don't sense any evil aboard the Zantar." And Kefira had clearly felt it in the Marauders' ships.

The big cat shuddered, shaking his pelt from his ears to the tip of his tail. *"Karak not like evil."*

"I know, Kitten." Kefira closed her eyes briefly and scanned the vicinity. "Why don't I sense that evil you speak of?"

"Because that ship is cloaked in a false aura of tribal togetherness, and friendship." Angel Blake's tone indicated disdain. Did he consider these values as weaknesses?

"Togetherness and friendship are the core values of the Anvad people. We are one people, and we trust each other implicitly." Kefira said it proudly. "Someone like you wouldn't understand."

Blake glanced up and frowned. "What do you mean, someone like me?"

"Karak like Angel Blake." The big cat growled and plopped down, resting his head on Blake's boot, making his preference clear.

"Fleet Captain Blake Volkov used to oppress peaceful planets for the GTA, he used to worship evil, and he betrayed his own people... his own family." Kefira

90

stopped before blurting that his father had slaughtered her family.

"Oh!" Blake flinched and his gaze fell to the decking. "I see, you checked on my past."

The old captain gasped then he turned around, avoiding eye contact.

"Yes. I'm aware of your sordid past... and that of your family." Kefira didn't find the satisfaction she expected from confronting him.

Karak rolled on his back, four paws in the air, as if to distract Kefira. The big cat hated when she was upset. Sweet boy... and yet, he sided with Blake.

Blake straightened and faced her squarely. "We all have a past, Sardar. It doesn't mean we can't change. I am no longer the person you describe. I never really was. I just didn't know how to get out of a vicious situation, but I finally did... and now, I'm doing my best to redeem myself and make amends."

"Well..." Kefira didn't have a good repartee. Blaming him for his past after he saved the entire galaxy, and after he rescued her people, seemed petty. She didn't want to be that kind of person. But she couldn't trust him either. "Only time will tell which way the scales tip."

"Exactly." Angel Blake sighed. "So, please, do not dismiss my warning.

Something is very wrong aboard that Anvad ship."

"I'll take your concerns under consideration." Kefira wouldn't trust him blindly, especially since she couldn't think clearly in his presence.

He had a strange influence on her feelings and her thoughts. She needed to get away from his angelic charm and think for herself. She wasn't a child anymore. She had responsibilities.

"Sardar?" The captain sounded excited. "We are receiving a transmission from the *Zantar.*"

Kefira's heart raced. "Send it to the main viewer."

Blake stepped to the side, away from the recorders, almost as if he didn't want to be seen.

The main viewer flashed the face Kefira had missed for over three cycles, the face of her first and only love, Malo's beloved face. Her heart missed a beat. He was alive!

How she'd missed his kind brown eyes, his smile, his ability to make her feel special. Her hand went to her medallion. He looked even more handsome than she remembered. There was a new aura of strength and confidence about him, a new radiance.

The big cat stood up and hissed as he stared at the screen. Karak never liked Malo.

"Hello, Kef, my young lioness. How I missed you." Even his voice sounded more caressing than before.

"Malo?" Kefira's voice squeaked. She could barely speak. "I thought I'd lost you forever."

"As long as I lived, nothing could keep me away from you. The hope of seeing you again is what kept me alive all these cycles away from you."

Kefira's head reeled with the shock of his presence. "What happened after the attack on the *Zantar*? Where have you been all this time? And how did you find me now? And you have my ship…"

Karak emitted a low growl from deep in his throat, like a warning.

From the viewer, Malo smiled. "I can't wait to see you in the flesh and hold you in my arms, Kef. I'll be there shortly and I'll explain everything."

The screen went blank, ending the communication.

Kefira stared at the dark viewer. Did she just daydream? No. This was real.

Blake stepped toward her, biting his lips. "I wouldn't trust a single word this man says."

"He's not just any man. He was my childhood friend. We were in love. He was chosen to be my mate and continue the line of the Sardars." As she said it, Kefira realized she was no longer certain this would happen.

93

"People change..."

Things had changed. But Kefira still belonged to Malo. "We were destined for each other since birth and mated in the eyes of Helsara."

Angel Blake scoffed. "I thought you were the kind of woman who made her own destiny."

"I am." Kefira straightened her back. "But I also have to consider my sacred duty. I must do what's best for my people... produce an heir." Yet, Kefira wasn't certain she wanted to return to Malo's arms. Much had happened. Would they still be compatible?

Blake gave a brisk salute, clicking his heels. "Since the freighter's repairs are complete, and you have an armed Anvad raptor to accompany you the rest of the way, it seems you are now in good hands. You no longer need our services."

Kefira felt as if she'd been punched in the stomach. "You are leaving?"

"Yes. I just ordered the five Anvad volunteers to be brought to the *Blue Phantom*." He gazed into her eyes with infinite kindness. "Farewell, Sardar. If you ever need our help again, you only have to call me in your mind."

"Fine." Kefira steeled herself against the tears threatening to flow. She would miss the way Blake made her feel. "Bon voyage,

Captain Volkov." She turned to the big cat. "Come, Karak."

Then she marched out of the command bridge with Karak at her heels. She didn't want anyone to see her cry.

She heard and sensed the vibrations in the air when Blake vanished... and detected a faint lilac fragrance.

She never should have let herself care about him. Despite all the things he'd done, he made her feel good about herself. But they were from completely different worlds. He belonged to his ship and his crew, galivanting about the universe, and he couldn't have children. A relationship between them could never work.

Kefira belonged to her people, and Malo was always meant to be her life mate and the father of her future children... so why did Blake's departure make her cry?

* * *

Blake watched Kefira's freighter from the clear dome of the *Blue Phantom*. "Invisibility mode!"

"Aye, Captain." Graziella, standing next to him, blinked as she made contact with the ship's systems.

The luminosity dimmed then flashed. Blake's vision blurred slightly as the *Blue Phantom* switched modes. Then everything returned to normal. Except that they couldn't be seen or detected by even the most advanced scanners.

"Are we leaving, Captain?" Graziella asked instead of reading his thoughts... out of consideration?

"No." Blake never intended to leave. "Something about the approaching Anvad ship bothers me to no end."

"Other than the handsome Malo?" Graziella's tone almost teased.

Blake would never admit jealousy. He just wanted to make sure Kefira and her people would remain safe. "I can't tell what it is, but I smell sorcery. This ship brings trouble."

"So... you let her believe we were leaving? It almost sounds like lying."

"You know angels do not lie," Blake huffed. "But yes, we are keeping watch, ready to intervene. Just in case..."

They observed together as the Anvad ship slowly approached the freighter. It was a raptor, small but heavily armed, clean and shiny, and in tip top shape. Kefira's private ship, the perfect vessel for a Sardar princess and her entourage.

Focusing on the shiny hull, Blake could discern the shimmer of a reddish shield, much stronger than any shield he'd seen before. Just as he suspected. "Can you feel the vibrations of that shield? It wears the same signature as those of the Stygian Order."

Graziella's eyes widened. "Could the evil sect be active again? So soon after their debacle?"

As the raptor drew closer, Blake flinched. "I sense the presence of a dark sorcerer aboard Kefira's personal ship."

"Could it be her former lover, Malo himself?" Graziella's tone turned serious.

The *Zantar* anchored itself to the freighter.

Blake focused his mind on Malo. "Odd. Something is preventing me from reading the young man's thoughts."

"Sorcery?" Graziella stared at the ominous raptor. "This Malo character seems to exert a strong emotional pull on the Sardar princess. Maybe he put a spell on her... or he is no longer who she remembers."

"Or maybe, she never knew him at all." The way Kefira had ridiculed his warning still stung. She no longer trusted Blake. She might revise her judgement when she sensed Malo's evil for herself. But she would have to discover it on her own. Blake hoped she would find out quickly.

"What do we do?" Graziella's optimism knew no bounds.

"Nothing right now. Since Kefira poked into my unsavory past, she hates me." As much as he wanted to protect her, Blake couldn't interfere. "I must respect her wishes and stay away."

Besides, this attraction between him and Kefira would never work. He was damaged goods, and she had a people to lead. And now, she hated him as much as he hated himself.

"Don't worry, Captain." Graziella offered a strained smile. "Kefira is sharp and capable. She will come to her senses about this Malo."

"I hope she does before it's too late." Blake couldn't stand to see her hurt. "She is smart, but also trusting… and duty-bound."

Graziella's clear blue eyes blinked, an indication she received a mind message. "Captain? The new recruits are ready for their briefing."

"Good. Let's do this." Blake smiled at the prospect and dematerialized.

* * *

Blake rematerialized in a mostly empty cargo hold. The five Anvad youth who volunteered to serve, three young men and two young women, stood there, fidgeting. Two stared at him with widened eyes, while the others raised their gaze to the glowing bulkhead and cathedral ceilings with barely veiled fear.

Graziella materialized next to Blake.

He didn't need to read the new recruits' minds. Their anxiety froze their faces. "Welcome aboard the *Blue Phantom*."

The new recruits straightened their backs, military style. Good.

Blake smiled inwardly. "You are on a former GTA destroyer. As you can see, it has undergone many transformations. Our Blue Crystal drive infuses the bulkhead with its energy and changes the substance of its bulkhead into a sheer material that glows blue. That's why the inside looks like a cathedral, and why the ship emits light in black space."

Graziella smiled. "Hence, the name, *Blue Phantom*."

"It can also become invisible at will." Blake enjoyed their look of surprise. "No ordinary engines or weapons onboard, just blue crystal technology powered by the commanding crew's mind. Only worthy angels can command the *Blue Phantom*." Although Blake often questioned his worthiness.

One recruit gaped while others looked around in pure awe.

"You will notice that sophisticated weapons and electronic devices do not function aboard this ship. Our energy core drains their batteries. But we have special weapons engineered to work with Blue Crystal. This ship also has cloaking abilities that allow it to escape long and short-range scanners… and we can travel at the speed of mind. You are very safe onboard."

The Anvad youths seemed to relax a little. Blake smiled inwardly. They were in for a treat.

"I regret the circumstances are not ideal for your first experience aboard the *Blue Phantom*, but we are on an ongoing mission. For three cycles now, we have been helping the innocent persecuted by evildoers."

"That's why you saved our freighter from the Marauders?" The tall young man in the middle seemed eager to learn.

"Yes." Blake liked the boy. "And we are currently shadowing the Anvad freighter, because we suspect your Sardar and the rest of the Anvad are still in danger."

"Danger from what?" The same young man spoke clearly.

The other recruits looked at each other with worry in their eyes, probably thinking about their friends and families still onboard.

"Deep space is never safe, and evil can take many forms. But don't worry. We are powerful, and invisible to eyes and scanners. We shall intervene if, or when, the need arises." Blake smiled. "In the meantime, you will report to Graziella."

"A woman in charge?" The tall young man frowned. "The Anvad culture considers women less capable, and better suited for breeding than command."

"Well…" Blake enjoyed that part. "On this vessel, you'll discover that men and women are equal in every way."

The two female recruits giggled, while the three young men struggled not to show their disapproval. They would learn… in time.

Graziella smiled. "You must have questions. This is your chance to ask."

"What are we expected to do?" The tall young man asked. "We are not angels like you."

"Not yet." Blake pursed his lips to stop talking.

The recruits frowned and glanced at each other.

Blake nodded to Graziella to take over.

Graziella took a deep breath. "You will be given jobs. You will tend the growing of the food, cook, clean, meditate in your spare time, and strengthen your link to the Formless One."

"The Formless One?" The short young woman narrowed her eyes. "Is this a cult?"

Blake took a deep breath. "The Formless One speaks through the crystal that permeates this ship and makes it glow. The Formless One's only concern is to keep the balance of good and evil in the universe. We serve to keep that balance."

"But we believe in Helsara the Bountiful." The other girl seemed upset. "Praying to another deity goes against our religion. It would be an insult to Helsara."

The other recruits fidgeted from foot to foot, twitched, or twisted their hands. They valued their beliefs.

Blake raised appeasing hands. "You can keep your faith in Helsara as long as you wish. We do not pray to or worship The Formless One. We meditate in harmony with the universe. We learn to recognize the presence of evil, and we practice humility and compassion. As you do this, you will notice changes in your body and your mind."

"What changes?" The tall young man again.

Blake nodded. "Our most guarded secret is that none of us were born as angels, but as regular sentient beings. There is a force at the heart of the *Blue Phantom*, that transforms us gradually into what you see in us now. We grow wings, we gain abilities, like reading minds, dematerializing in one place to rematerialize in another. We can become invisible, and we can sense the truth through layers of deceit."

"You mean… we will become angels like you?" The short girl's eyes widened.

"That's exactly what I mean." Blake couldn't help but smile. "For some the transformation happens in a few days, for others it takes weeks or months. But it happens eventually. Also, we cannot lie. So, we trust one another and rely on each other."

The new recruits exchanged appreciative glances and nods.

The tall young man straightened. "The Anvad also do not lie and rely on each other."

"Good." Blake was well inspired to call on the Anvad. They would make a worthy addition to his crew. "Another detail... as long as we remain in the proximity of the blue crystal, we are under its protection and quasi-immortal."

"We cannot die?" The girl's eyes rounded in surprise.

"I wish." Blake chuckled. "We can be killed through violent means. But when wounded, we heal quickly, and we never age. We remain young and strong forever."

The eyes of the recruits widened in awe.

A young woman raised her hand. "What's the catch?"

"Two things." Blake watched as their expression sobered. "One, we can only use our abilities to serve the forces of good. And two, as a result of the proximity to the crystal, as long as we are exposed to it, we are sterile."

The recruits remained quiet, glancing at each other, trying to digest this information.

Graziella smiled. "Any other question?"

Not a peep from the recruits.

"I wish you luck." Blake remembered his first weeks on the *Blue Phantom* after the crystal took it over. It was a magical time of discovery and wonder, a short time of innocence, before the burden of his commitment hit home. "Enjoy your stay and your transformation. After you get your wings, you will have a better understanding of how the universe works."

"Can we ever leave?" A young man asked. "Our Sardar said three decades of service."

"Three decades during which you will not age." Blake smiled. "But after you become an angel, time is irrelevant. In truth, once you get your wings, if you really want to leave, I can't stop you. But it would mean losing your immortality along with all these wonderful new abilities. No one has ever left the *Blue Phantom*."

After nodding to Graziella, confident the recruits would be safe in her capable hands, Blake saluted the five young people then dematerialized. He had to research Malo and the resurgence of the Stygian Order.

* * *

Kefira paced her quarters, waiting for Malo to arrive. So many thoughts roiled inside her mind, she couldn't make sense of them. Malo was alive! How could it be? She should be jumping for joy and planning her wedding. So why wasn't she? Did she still love him?

She checked her reflection in the large mirror and removed her weapons belt, blasters, and blades. She felt light and naked without them. She smoothed her hair away from her face and straightened her medallion. She managed to smile in the mirror. It made her dark eyes shine.

Then she rummaged into a drawer. Where was her perfume? Found it. She spritzed a bit on her hair.

Had she changed much in over three cycles? She wore a silk uniform now instead of precious robes. She'd become a warrior, but her advisers wouldn't let her wear drab military garb. She had to project the image of a Sardar. And she'd trimmed her hair. What if he didn't like it?

She no longer was the innocent little princess swept away by a handsome young man. The Anvad liked their women sweet and docile. Would Malo still love her as a strong, independent woman?

She had grown so much since he'd disappeared. Grief, loss, and responsibilities had reshaped her. She'd found purpose. She'd learned to rule, and she became good at helping her people. She had earned their love and their respect.

What happened to Malo all this time? She imagined him sold into labor, escaping… such experiences could change a man. They would have to be reacquainted.

The hatchway chimed.

Karak glanced up from his nap, bared his fangs and hissed.

"Be nice, big boy. Malo is an old friend." Her heart beat a savage tempo. "Open."

The sliding panel revealed the tall young man she remembered, wearing flashy yellow and red silk. He hadn't changed a bit. No apparent scar or sign of torture from his captivity. His dark gaze and roguish smile still made her heart sing.

"Malo!" She ran toward him and threw herself into his arms. She inhaled his familiar scent of spices.

He chuckled and held her close. "I dreamed of this moment for so long. How I missed you and your sweet scent, my little lioness."

Karak growled and turned in his bed, showing them his back in disapproval. Silly cat.

Malo chuckled. "Your pussycat will get used to me again."

"I thought you were dead, and I would never see you again." She expected a kiss, but it didn't come, so she hid her disappointment and reveled in his familiar embrace, congratulating herself for wearing perfume. She enjoyed the contact with his strong body. He always made her feel so safe.

She reluctantly separated herself from him. "Sit down. Have some tea. I want to know everything."

Malo sat in the big chair, and she served crimson tea from the angel ship. Brushing aside Blake's image, she sat on the couch across the low table. "Start from the attack on the *Zantar* last time we were together. What happened? I woke up in an escape pod with Karak."

The big cat growled menacingly. He really didn't like Malo. Grouchy cat.

"I found you and Karak unconscious on the bridge, and I placed you both in the pod and launched it. I knew we were doomed, and I hoped you would escape and survive." It sounded perfectly logical, yet...

Warm tears welled in Kefira's eyes, but she refused to cry. "Thank you for saving my life. Why didn't you escape with us?"

Malo hesitated. "My mother was also on the *Zantar*. I was hoping to save her, too... but I was too late... she was killed, and I was taken... then sold into slavery."

"I am so sorry about your mother." Exactly what Kefira had guessed... as if he'd read her mind. But Malo didn't have Sardar blood and had no such abilities. Besides, she'd learned to shield her private thoughts.

She searched his face, wrists, hands, and his silk-clad body for signs of duress, like starvation, torture, or other telltales of being enslaved, but saw none. "How did you escape?"

"Let's say, I bid my time and planned my escape, waiting for the perfect opportunity. When it presented itself, I reclaimed my freedom, then I found your ship and stole it back." His eyes were dark pools of deep waters.

"Just like that?" Again… he told her exactly what she expected to hear, remaining vague, giving no details. "Sounds so simple, yet it must have been difficult."

He smiled and reached for her hand across the low table. "I will spare you the gory details. Let's not spoil this happy moment. I dreamed of it every day while in captivity."

She enjoyed his reassuring contact and extended her mind to read his but couldn't. As if he shielded his thoughts… but that was impossible. Could she be losing her abilities?

She'd always read Malo's thoughts before. He gave her permission long ago, and he could never tell when she invaded his mind. That's how she knew he'd never lied to her, and his love was true.

But she didn't feel so certain of it, now. "This connection we used to have between us… it feels different."

"It's to be expected." He caressed the palm of her hand with his thumb. "We have both grown in a different environment all this time apart."

"It makes sense." Still, she missed their former closeness. Kefira hid her unease behind a smile and shielded her thoughts… just in case. What if this man wasn't really Malo but an impersonator? She'd also heard of skilled shapeshifters. It sounded farfetched but not impossible… although she couldn't imagine why anyone would bother to mount such an elaborate scheme.

Yet, something didn't add up, and her gut twisted in warning. She couldn't afford to trust the wrong man. The fate of her people was at stake. "I missed you."

"So did I." His loving smile was heavy with promise. "In my darkest hour, the memory of our love always gave me hope and courage."

"I am so glad you survived." But Kefira wondered... would his return prove positive for the Anvad people?

"What caused the debris field around your ship?" Malo's brisk tone demanded answers.

Kefira hesitated. She felt interrogated. "We were attacked by a flock of Marauders."

"Really?" He didn't sound surprised at all. "How many?"

Despite his warm smile Kefira felt compelled to answer and she didn't like the feeling. "Ten raptors."

"How did you survive the Marauders?" That hard-to-resist inquisitive tone again.

Kefira realized he was manipulating her, but she couldn't resist answering. "We fought back... and then we had help."

Malo nodded gravely. "From the *Blue Phantom*?"

"Yes." Kefira realized her former lover was reading her thoughts... or he knew a lot more than he told her. "How did you know?"

"Just an educated guess." Malo leaned back in his chair. "Where is the *Blue Phantom* now?"

"Gone, vanished." Somehow, Kefira was glad she couldn't tell him more. That's all he would get. "You never told me how you found us."

"Well…" He flashed an apologetic smile. "I have my ways."

"What ways?" No one should have known their route, yet the Marauders found them, and Malo found them… coincidence? Kefira didn't believe in coincidences.

"How I found you no longer matters. We are back together now. Things will be easy for us from now on." His smile remained unreadable. "You should join me aboard the *Zantar*, where our princely quarters are much more comfortable than this dreary cabin."

The very idea of bunking with Malo on her old ship revulsed her. "Sorry, Malo. But my people need me here. I feel my duty is to remain as close as possible. They need to think of me as one of them… not the lofty princess in her ivory tower."

"Suit yourself." Malo rose and his dark gaze blazed. "But think about it. We are fated mates. Sooner or later, you'll realize we still belong together."

The big cat rose and sat up next to Kefira, lending her his strength. She thanked him by scratching his head.

"Sorry, Malo. Today is not that day." Despite the traditions and Helsara's blessing, Kefira couldn't picture herself returning to his bed as if nothing had happened.

Malo walked briskly out of her cabin and the hatch closed with a hiss of compressed air.

Karak purred and rubbed his head against her shoulder. Good cat.

Kefira shuddered with dread. Angel Blake may have been right about something amiss aboard her old ship. She could feel a web of lies and deceit around it. But Blake was gone, and she would have to deal with the problem herself. Although, she had no idea what the problem was.

Chapter Six

Once aboard the *Zantar,* Malo threw his black jacket on the crushed velvet couch of his royal accommodations. At least it was warm here. That freighter was cold in comparison. He dropped to the couch, then leaned back into the silky pillows.

Kefira proved more difficult to influence than he'd anticipated. Despite their former trusting relationship, she remained guarded. And why couldn't he read her mind? But her Sardar powers were no match for his. Soon, she would beg him to share his bed again.

How could she choose to live in the dark and sinister cabin of a lowly freighter, rather than on this luxury vessel? He smiled, realizing the Anvad royal colors happened to be the same as the colors of the Stygian Order, black, gold, and crimson. How appropriate.

Closing his eyes, Malo visualized the captain of Kefira's freighter and tangled the man's weak mind in a sorcerer's web. The old captain proved easy to manipulate.

Malo used his most convincing voice. "Captain, you must change course and keep it a secret from everyone else. Here are the new coordinates. All will be well. It's for the good of the Anvad. Trust me. I am your new leader. Our Sardar princess will be grateful and reward you richly when we reach our new destination."

Malo felt his words registering into the captain's mind. Then he imprinted the new coordinates into the old man's brain and visualized him implementing them into the navigation computer. The freighter's turn would be wide, and unfelt by the crew or the passengers. "Perfect."

Then Malo focused on the minds of all the Anvad people on the freighter and imprinted a special message upon them. "Remember the old Anvad laws. Your Sardar is no longer your leader. Your future ruler has returned to lead the Anvad according to your most sacred traditions. I will be your Padshad, and all will be well."

His takeover would be smooth and orderly… even steeped in traditions.

The engines of the old freighter kept purring, and none would be the wiser about the change of course. If anyone noticed, Malo would invoke some unexpected danger necessitating a detour.

* * *

From the observation deck of the *Blue Phantom*, invisible in space under its undetectable cloak, Blake watched Kefira's freighter veer off course. Why did it change destination? He closed his eyes to see Kefira in his mind but hit a mental wall. Malo's raptor, clamped to the freighter's hull, had extended its red shield to wrap around both ships, making communications impossible.

Blake's blood roared in his ears. Was Kefira in danger? Did the charming Malo intend to harm her? No. Blake would have sensed it, and he detected no immediate danger to her life. Still, something was very wrong. He sensed a strong evil presence and suspected foul play.

In his mind, Blake traced the freighter's new trajectory to its probable destination, but it didn't lead to any habitable planet on any space map. It did, however, cross a vast asteroid field. One of these space rocks seemed large enough to be a planetoid with sufficient gravity and an atmosphere capable of sustaining basic life.

Whatever the case, Blake switched direction as well, and followed the freighter toward its new destination.

He hoped Kefira was all right. He would never forgive himself if she suffered under his watch. His feelings for her escaped his comprehension. They went far beyond kindness or compassion. The very thought of losing her made him sick. If the scumbag ex-boyfriend touched one hair on Kefira's head, he would pay with his life.

Could Blake be in love? Impossible. He never fell in love and had been an emotional mess since the final battle. He lived for his all-important job. Love was never part of the equation.

Besides, he must not get involved with mortals, especially not a royal princess with strong ties to her people. Kefira had her duties to serve the Anvad, to see them settled, rule them... and continue the Sardar line... while he must roam the far corners of the galaxy, protecting the innocent for millennia to come... unloved and without progeny.

Also, Blake was a wanted man. If the Stygian Order had resurged, the price on his head would be high. Evil wallowed in revenge and retaliation, and he refused to endanger Kefira's life by his mere proximity.

* * *

Kefira stopped mid-movement, the blaster she was cleaning all but forgotten. "Karak, can you feel the change?"

The big cat pivoted his tufted ears and froze, listening. *"Karak hear wrong purr."*

"There is a strain in the drone of the freighter's drives." As if the route had grown rocky, as if the Bountiful Helsara no longer smoothed their way, or no longer blessed the Anvad refugees... as if they'd veered off the divine path to the promised Land of Many Waters.

Had the freighter changed course? Impossible. Only she could give such an order. Not even the captain had that authority. Had there been a mutiny on the bridge? No. Kefira would have sensed it.

"Computer, did we change course?"

The computer beeped. "Aye, Sardar."

"Who ordered it?" That should be interesting.

"No one, Sardar. The new coordinates carry the captain's code."

How dare he? "What's our new destination?"

"Unknown, Sardar. I detect no known star system on our new trajectory."

An ominous foreboding drenched Kefira like a cold sluice, chilling her from head to toe. What had that mean old captain done now, and why? She needed answers.

She would give the old man a piece of her mind, but not on the com system. Important communications should happen face to face if one wanted to discover the truth.

Kefira struggled to keep calm as she donned her weapons belt, adjusting her blasters and her blades. "Come, Karak. I feel something is very wrong on the command bridge, and I may need your protection."

The large feline sprang up, at the ready and shook his pelt. *"Karak protect."*

"Good boy." No doubt the big cat had noticed her unrest and caught the urgency in her voice.

Karak followed her through the open hatch then loped at her side along the straight corridor leading to the command bridge. They didn't meet anyone. All the hatches to the many holds remained closed. How unusual.

Kefira quickened her pace. Her entire body shook like a badly calibrated frigate caught in a blizzard on the frozen hells of Laxxar.

She stepped onto the command bridge and marched to the main console. "Captain!"

At her side, Karak growled, baring his fangs.

The captain glanced fearfully at the cat then rose from his seat and bowed. "Yes, Sardar."

The other officers on deck remained seated, attentive to their stations, eyes glued to their consoles. Not saluting their Sardar constituted a flagrant lack of respect. What was happening?

Kefira glanced at the navigation screen, confirming a new, unknown trajectory. "Why did we change course? I didn't order it. This is an outrage. Helsara is not pleased. Resume course to the Land of Many Waters immediately."

The captain bowed respectfully. "So sorry, Sardar... but my orders come from a higher authority."

"What authority? I am your Sardar, the highest authority here." Kefira couldn't believe the captain's insolence.

"You no longer are in charge, Sardar. I now answer to the most powerful leader of the Anvad."

"Helsara Herself?" How could he invoke the Goddess to disobey a direct order?

"No, Sardar. The order and the new coordinates came from our new ruler, Padshad Malo."

"Padshad Malo?" An arrow through the heart couldn't have hurt more. How dare he act as supreme ruler? Kefira steeled herself and her hand went to her blaster.

The captain stepped back and bowed. "Sardar, your chosen mate is the only noble male qualified to rule over the Anvad people. You are but a princess, Sardar. Padshad Malo's authority overrules yours... I suggest you bow to his authority and give him a male heir to succeed him."

"Never!" Kefira's chest roiled with hot raging currents. "Malo and I are no longer a mated pair. He is noble by alliance only and has no Sardar blood whatsoever. Therefore, I am your only ruling Sardar."

The captain straightened and averted his gaze. "The Anvad people do not see it that way, Sardar. Padshad Malo is demonstrating divine powers, like mind-speak. It is obvious Helsara Herself favors him with Her gifts."

"What?" When did Malo get such abilities? No wonder Kefira couldn't read his mind. But she was willing to bet his powers didn't come from Helsara.

"You and Padshad Malo were a mated pair before he vanished, Sardar." The captain's voice took a soft tone, as if to soothe a child. "Since his return, as your fated consort, he is now the only legitimate claimant to the Anvad throne."

"This is a nightmare!" Kefira's head reeled. She grabbed a safety bar on the side of the console, to steady herself.

But the old captain was right. In the eyes of the Anvad people, she and Malo were once officially promised to each other, and bonded as lovers before Helsara. Since the massacre of the royal family left no male heir, Malo's claim to the throne was legitimate... even if he had no Sardar blood, even if she no longer shared his bed.

But Kefira would have something to say about this ridiculous technicality. "Where is Malo now?"

"Our beloved Padshad is resting in his royal quarters aboard the *Zantar*, Sardar." The captain bowed low.

"His royal quarters?" How dare he claim the *Zantar* as his own? "Come, Karak. Let's go see this self-proclaimed Padshad."

She marched out of the command bridge with Karak in tow.

* * *

Malo levitated above the couch; legs crossed in midair. Closing his eyes, he focused his mind on Matchitehew. "Father, can you hear me?"

"The Great Matchitehew always hears his son." The booming voice resonated all around. An inky black cloud manifested above the deck. The Sorcerer Supreme of the Stygian Order walked out of it. He always liked theatrical entrances. "Have you succeeded yet?"

Malo would show him he was worthy of command. "You know I have, Father. I am in full control of the Anvad people as their new Padshad, and their freighter is headed for the temple."

"Perfect." Matchitehew smoothed his silky white robes. "Soon, when the Exalted Baalmordo arrives with his armies, we shall need many innocent blood sacrifices."

"You will have all the pure blood you need, Father." Malo congratulated himself for his smashing success, proving once again that only he could get the job done right… although his father would never admit it.

Matchitehew narrowed his black eyes. "Any news of the *Blue Phantom*'s whereabouts?"

"The phantom ship intervened to protect the Anvad freighter from my hired Marauders, but it vanished before I arrived. Obviously, Captain Blake Volkov is not only a traitor, but also a coward. He's probably halfway across the galaxy by now." Malo shrugged. "Once the Exalted Baalmordo is here, the *Blue Phantom* won't be a threat anymore."

"Right." Matchitehew took a deep breath and his jaw clenched. "But I want Captain Blake Volkov to pay for his betrayal of the Stygian Order... and for the death of my beloved daughter, your half-sister, Ciara."

Having never known his infamous sister, Malo didn't care about her death. Actually, he resented his prodigal sister. She had been trained from birth while he was abandoned among the Anvad and kept ignorant of his magical lineage. Now, his father never missed an opportunity to humiliate him by flaunting his sister's superior abilities.

But she had been killed in the final battle. Good riddance. It was Malo's turn to become heir to the Sorcerer Supreme.

"We'll get Captain Volkov later, Father." Malo easily masked his anger and uncertainty under a confident smile. "Don't worry. He will pay in the end... with more than his life."

"I hope so, Son." Matchitehew's eyes narrowed. "What about the Sardar princess? Is she carrying your child yet?"

"Not yet." Damn the man to always point out Malo's failures. "She still hasn't warmed up to my miraculous return, but do not fear. She will soon bear my heir." One way or another, and that might be fun.

"We may need her as a divine blood sacrifice when the Dark Prince arrives. If she isn't pregnant by then, we'll harvest her DNA. Your heir needs her divine bloodline, but the child can be born from a surrogate, or matured in a lab."

Malo resented being bullied by his father, but he showed none of his anger. He wanted to keep Kefira as long as possible... as his lover. "I believe a child born from his biological mother would be preferable, Father. For health and longevity purposes, of course. The mother can be sacrificed after she gives birth."

"I see..." Matchitehew gazed into Malo's eyes and sighed. "But time is of the essence, my son. Harvesting the girl's DNA is faster and easier."

"Don't worry, Father. I'll have her pregnant before we reach the temple." Even if Malo had to force himself on her... repeatedly... the very thought brought an exciting shiver coursing through his entire body.

"I'm waiting for you, Son. We'll talk again when you get home." Matchitehew vanished in an inky black cloud.

Malo wouldn't let his father intimidate him. With his new powers, he could get anything he wanted, and he wanted Kefira all to himself, for as long as he wished it. Now that he was in a position of great power in the Stygian Order, Malo couldn't trust anyone. But Kefira had loved him and pledged her loyalty when he was nobody. Her heart was true. Although, if she ceased to entertain him, or became a nuisance, he'd discard her to the sacrificial dagger himself.

* * *

Kefira, with her feline bodyguard loping at her side, reached the hatch connecting the freighter to the *Zantar.*

An armed guard in crimson uniform stood in their way. Strange garb, too. Definitely not Anvad, and kind of freaky with red armor, blind helmet, and a hooded red cape. He carried unfamiliar weapons as well… a glowing spear… possibly ancient… or just alien.

She marched toward the hatch and stopped in front of the guard. "Move aside, I want to speak to Malo!"

Karak growled and bared his fangs for good measure. Good cat.

The guard didn't move a muscle. She heard the subtle click of a communicator coming from inside the helmet, then the guard moved aside, and the hatch opened.

As she stepped inside her old ship, Kefira could barely breathe in the oppressing and suffocating atmosphere, hot and hostile. What happened to her raptor? It looked gaudy. Had it been so long since she called it home? Such luxury, too. How many had toiled or suffered to pay for it? She'd never thought in these terms before, but she had changed in the past few cycles. She knew what things cost in labor and lives.

She walked past open hatches where she glanced a few crewmen, all wearing crimson uniforms like the guard at the entrance. A quick mind probe told her none of them were Anvad, yet they were disciplined and dedicated to their tasks... and each would gladly die to protect their leader, Malo... and they thought of him as the First Lieutenant of their Sorcerer Supreme. Strange title.

The big cat sniffed and snorted his disapproval. He didn't recognize his old digs either.

When she approached the hatch of her old quarters, Kefira noticed the new seal on the door... a circle, and inside it, a serpent dagger. Definitely not an Anvad symbol. But she'd seen it before, on the computer files of Blake's shady past. It was the seal of the Stygian Order!

A chill coursed through her at the toxic energy generated by the seal. It reeked of evil. Was Malo a prominent member of that disgusting sect? Helsara help her!

The hatch slid open in a puff of compressed air, and Kefira stepped inside. "Malo, we have to talk."

"Indeed, we do." He remained seated on the luxurious red couch, barely looking at her, focusing on his drink.

She ignored his lack of respect. As she gazed around the bold, aggressive decor, she didn't recognize anything. "What have you done to my ship?"

"I'm doing well, thank you." Malo flashed a charming smile and leaned back into the plush cushions. "I upgraded your little raptor with the latest weaponry. You should be grateful. It even has a special shield that can stop any known missile, as well as any unwanted thought from getting in or out."

"Is that a threat?" Was he telling her she couldn't use her Sardar gifts to call for help? Rage simmered low in her stomach and started to rise. "We are no longer mated. You have no right to claim the Padshad throne!"

He chuckled. "The Anvad law disagrees with you, my little lioness."

Kefira took a deep calming breath. A confrontation wouldn't work to her advantage. And killing Malo would only get her executed, since the Anvad considered him their legitimate Padshad. "Why did we change course? Where are we going?"

"That's for me to know and for you to ignore. See, you do not have to carry the burden of the Anvad anymore. You can relax and forget about ruling. I'm here to lead our people and to protect you." The patronizing tone grated on her ears.

Kefira struggled not to raise her voice. "I do not need your protection, and I can rule by myself."

The big cat brushed her arm with his head. "*Karak protect.*"

She calmed the cat with a soothing thought.

"Look at what you have become." Malo rose and walked around her, glass in hand. "Why did you chop your beautiful hair? Where are your jewels? Your eyes and lips are bare. And this manly garb and swagger make you look ordinary at best, and almost vulgar. I'm disappointed in your less than appealing appearance. I was expecting more from you."

Despite her resolve, the pointed barbs clawed at Kefira's confidence, but she could fight for herself. "Appealing appearance? That's your first concern when our people are facing extinction? They are the last of the Anvad. Their only hope is Helsara's promised Land of Many Waters. You are playing fast and loose with their destiny."

"A noblewoman should always look pretty and attractive... and always obey her mate." That patronizing tone again.

Kefira huffed. Did he really think she wanted to please him? Although, she did, once...

"I expected a better welcome upon my return." He walked around her, glancing at her from time to time. "We were a happy couple once. If not for yourself, you should still care about your looks... for our people... and for me."

The deceit and manipulation she saw in him repulsed her. "For you?"

"Of course." He looked her up and down with a disapproving look.

"In case you didn't notice, things have changed for the Anvad." Kefira struggled to keep her voice even. "Your disappearance and the slaughter of the royal family left me in charge. I had to grow up fast, and I faced the challenges alone. Successfully, I might add."

"How unseemly for a woman to brag." He tsked as if reprimanding a child. "If you are smart, you'll correct your attitude, young lady. I advise you to resume our relationship in the eyes of our people and in the eyes of Helsara. It's your only hope to survive the coming changes."

"What changes?" It sounded ominous. Did he say survive? "Are you threatening me?"

"Call it what you will, my little lioness, but as your new Padshad, I must deal with any opposition ruthlessly and mercilessly." He smiled. "I only have your wellbeing in mind."

"What happened to you, Malo? We were happy, in love, planning a future." She also remembered he already had a taste for power, always hoping to rule, even when several pure blood Sardar males stood before him in the line of succession. But he never reeked of evil before.

"We can be happy again." The fake smile didn't warm up his dark eyes.

A sudden thought shook Kefira's core. Was Malo's young love motivated by the promise to rule, even in the early days? Did he always have his eyes on the throne? "You only want me at your side because it solidifies your claim to the Padshad throne."

"It is unseemly for a woman to dabble in politics!" His voice took a sharper edge. "And it is forbidden for a woman to accuse her mate of wrong doing."

Still, Kefira must know the truth. "What really happened three cycles ago? Was my ship attacked by Marauders? Or did you stage the attack to steal my ship? I bet you never were enslaved."

"Small, unimportant details." He shook his head at her. "You are too smart for your own good, my little lioness. Let's say, I had important things to do, and I needed to borrow your fast little ship, and I needed you out of the way. A woman could never understand."

Kefira realized she'd been duped by Malo all along. "Were you also in league with the murdering soldiers who slaughtered my family? To insure no one would contest your future claim to the throne?"

"The GTA ordered your family killed. Not me." His smug smile indicated he wasn't innocent either. "But you shouldn't concern yourself with such ugly details."

"And how did you find me in the black expanse after all this time?" She realized he must have been tracking her all along, but how?

"I have my ways." His gaze fell to the medallion on her chest.

She followed his gaze and stared at it. His last gift. So that was the tracking device. Kefira grabbed and pulled on the medallion, breaking the chain, then threw it on the deck and trampled it. "What other shameful deeds did you perform, in your quest for power?"

He chuckled. "I thought the Marauders could bring you and the Anvad to me, but since they failed, I had to cut short my vacation and come in person."

Kefira had been too trusting. Now, he had veered the freighter from its original path, and wherever they were headed, she knew it was wrong for her people.

"Cat got your tongue?" Malo's confidence remained unshakeable. He sat back on the couch with his drink and gazed at her, analyzing her.

Karak growled, low in his throat, and bared his fangs.

Good cat. Kefira patted Karak's head. She realized Malo was capable of great evil, and she didn't want him to harm the big cat. "Easy, boy."

A strong, willful wave emanated from Malo. Kefira realized he was trying to subdue her mind. She shielded herself from it, but it gave her an idea. She turned to Malo and decided to play his game, letting him think his shameful trick was working.

She smiled. "Well, now that all the cards are on the table, we know each other better. If you had shared this with me way back when, we could have been ruling together a long time ago… and we would already have a child to continue the Sardar line. It's what you want, isn't it? To cement your position as ruling Padshad?"

Malo narrowed his dark eyes. "So, you don't hate me?"

She forced a chuckle. "I am disappointed that you lied to me and went behind my back to get what I realize now is legally yours."

Did he suspect a lie, or did he believe his controlling ruse was working? Kefira rejoiced that she could shield her thoughts from him, but a Sardar never lied... Could she be damning her soul?

He relaxed on the couch and patted the spot next to him. "Then come and prove your love to me right now."

"Padshad, I must ready myself for you. As you said, I look a fright, and I'm not worthy of you if I look like a vulgar soldier." Kefira took a step back and bowed demurely. "I need to retire."

"I will allow it." Malo grinned. "We'll meet tomorrow at the celebration of my return. We shall be crowned together, in front of the Anvad people, as the royal couple we were always meant to be."

"As you wish, Padshad." Kefira bowed deeply, pivoted, then walked with small demure steps through the exit hatch, with Karak in tow.

Once out of sight, she pounded each step and vented her anger. Why couldn't she rule as a woman without him? Such antiquated notions didn't belong in this time. Besides, the goddess Helsara was a feminine deity. Kefira should have changed the law when she was in power... but at the time, no one challenged her rule.

She also realized something evil had happened to Malo. She sensed the darkness in him. Would she have to kill him on the nuptial bed, and risk being executed, in order to save her people? Could she make it look like an accident? She didn't want to shed Malo's blood, but she would, in order to save her people... whatever the consequences for her.

For now, she'd purchased some time, and she had important preparations to make.

Chapter Seven

Kefira tossed and turned, struggling with nightmares. She smelled blood, lots of blood. Threatening figures in dark military armor, half human, half machines, sprung from a faraway galaxy, like a raging horde of bloodthirsty hounds.

This unholy legion of tall Cyborg soldiers with superhuman strength slammed, crushed, and slaughtered entire populations. They uttered evil litanies and the wicked blades surging out of their artificial limbs elicited screams of indescribable pain, as if the evil creatures found pleasure in the suffering of their victims.

Kefira watched in horror, paralyzed, helpless, as they sliced throats then drank the warm, viscous liquid straight from the severed carotid arteries. The Cyborg army craved blood to survive and to give them strength. They looked at the Anvad with hunger and thirst in their cruel eyes. They especially relished the blood of the pure, the worthy, and the innocent. Above all, they coveted the life force of her people.

She screamed as she recognized Malo commanding these unholy legions. Through mind control, he forced the leaders of Helsara's chosen tribe to deliver their flock to the bloodthirsty Cyborg! He'd promised to deliver the Anvad to these unholy monsters… Malo was leading her people straight to the slaughter!

"No!" Kefira awoke in a cold sweat and sat up on her bunk, panting. "Bountiful Helsara, what kind of vision did you send me?" Her entire body shook with dread. Helsara never lied.

Was this the shape of things to come? Was Malo conspiring with these evil forces? Since he'd plastered the symbol of the Stygian Order on the bulkhead of her old ship, anything was possible. Kefira shuddered. She must heed the warning.

Karak came up to her bunk and bumped her shoulder. She scratched then kissed the furry head and felt calmer. "Thanks for your love, Kitten."

"Karak protect." The big cat brushed his head against her shoulder.

Kefira stepped out of bed and grabbed her uniform. Malo had tried to influence her mind, and without her gifts, he would have succeeded. Now, according to her vision, he was leading the freighter straight to these bloodthirsty hordes.

She needed a plan to stop Malo. Kefira's people were in grave danger, all because of her lack of judgement. Now, she alone must protect the Anvad from this terrible fate.

She needed help… but she suspected the Anvad were already under Malo's influence and would be reluctant to revolt against him. Still, she had to try and convince a few of them… but it might prove difficult. Would it be in vain?

She distractedly petted the big cat. "Any idea, Karak?"

"Karak like Angel Blake." The big cat purred. *"Angel protect. Karak protect."*

"You might be right, Kitten." Why did she have to disrespect Blake? Despite his sordid past, he'd saved her and her people from the Marauders. But she had insulted him about his previous life choices, and now he was gone. She missed him. She wished she could share her vision with him. He would know what to do.

But it was too late. The new shield Malo had placed around the freighter didn't allow communications of any kind. Still, she must try.

She closed her eyes and focused on the handsome angel. *"Blake, I'm sorry I judged you harshly. Wherever you are, if you can hear me, please listen to my plea. I beg you, don't let my people die at the hands of such unholy creatures."*

No response, although he'd promised he'd be listening. But her call may never be heard. Malo said his special shield prevented any signal from getting in or out. Besides, after her scathing insults, Blake probably didn't want anything to do with her. By now, the angel ship must be helping more deserving souls, halfway across the galaxy.

She regretted her strong reaction to Blake's past. No one was perfect, and Blake had behaved admirably since she'd met him. He'd showed only kindness. People could change, even the most dedicated GTA Fleet Captain. She wasn't the same as three cycles ago, and Malo sure had changed... for the worse.

Abandoned and alone, Kefira must do whatever was in her power to prevent her people's genocide. Her powers couldn't match Malo's sorcery. She couldn't influence her people's minds. But Malo couldn't read her thoughts if she kept her mind closed to him. Her only advantage. If she failed to raise her people against him, as much as she hated the idea, cold-blooded murder might be her only recourse... even at the risk of damning her soul.

* * *

Blake smiled as he walked on a mossy ground, among tall trees, on an unknown planet, holding Kefira's hand. Their steps were light and so was his heart. Birds trilled in the high branches, the air smelled like spring blossoms after the rain, and small animals scurried into the bushes at their approach.

They laughed and talked about small nothings. Her lovely face turned up to him and he drank in her dark gaze. They were happy in love. They lay down in a meadow and he kissed her soft lips. His head whirled at the possibilities.

He shook himself and opened his eyes. He stood on the observation deck of his cloaked ship. He couldn't afford the distraction of daydreaming.

Blake stared at the slow-going freighter, far ahead, small and alone in the darkness of space. He'd figured out its destination, a far-flung planetoid. At this snail pace, it would take the Anvad several days to get there.

"Captain!" Graziella materialized inside the observation dome. "We are intercepting multiple distress calls. It seems a Cyborg army is cutting a swath of destruction through the galaxy, devastating peaceful planets, slaughtering every living being in their path."

The statement sounded widely exaggerated, but angels couldn't lie, and Blake had seen evil in action before. He closed his eyes and visualized the advance of the Cyborg army, devastating planet after planet.

A cold shiver rippled through him as he remembered the horde of demons he'd fought in the final battle. As if the past repeated itself or came back to haunt him. He had been a simple man then, fighting on the wrong side. Now he could see the assaults through the victims' eyes… and he felt shame.

A clear 3D chart appeared in front of them.

Graziella focused on it. "They seem to be heading for the same destination as the freighter."

Blake shuddered at the thought of losing Kefira to these monsters. "I don't believe it's a coincidence."

"We have to stop them!" Graziella's strong voice rang through the clear dome.

"We are only one ship with a small crew. We are not equipped to stop an entire army." If history repeated itself, Blake also suspected the enemy ships would have Stygian shields imbued with spells and alien sorcery, like the shields on Malo's raptor. They might be impervious to his special torpedoes.

"We can't let this happen. We must do something." Graziella bit her lips. "Fighting evil is what we do."

"Yes, it is." Blake must honor his vows, no matter the cost. "But we can't go into battle against such a malevolent army alone. We'll need reinforcements."

"Who's left to help us?" Graziella frowned. "Since the dismantlement of the

GTA, there is no organized military force left in the galaxy... and the Azurans are out of reach."

"I still have a few contacts in high places." Blake wondered whether any of his Azuran friends would answer.

"We could use their legions of AIs and Avenging Angels right now." Graziella's wistful tone and sigh indicated fear.

"I'll see what I can do." Blake hoped he could rally some old allies. "Meanwhile, set a new course to intercept this Cyborg army."

"Aye, Captain." Graziella drew an intercept line on the 3D map.

"And make sure we remain in stealth mode." That was their best chance against the darkest evil. "They are not expecting us. Maybe they won't see us."

"Aye, Captain." Graziella waved at the 3D map. It melted away, then she vanished.

As the *Blue Phantom* veered off, Blake watched Kefira's freighter disappear, alone, in the blackness. It tore at his heart to abandon her, even for a short time, but he had his own obligations... and stopping the invading Cyborg army might be the best way to protect her. He would catch up with her later.

He hoped Kefira would be safe enough until he returned. He couldn't stand it if she became a casualty of evil. The very thought pierced his heart like a poisoned dagger. He should never have allowed himself to care for her. He was an angel on a mission, not someone's snug-bunny.

He took a deep breath, to clear his mind from Kefira's beautiful face and soulful eyes.

Blake didn't believe in coincidences. The arrival of the Cyborg army and the abduction of the Anvad freighter must be connected. Maybe their common destination indicated the seat of some new evil power in the quadrant. If so, it must be destroyed at the source… before it became unstoppable.

But the distressing news of this Cyborg army reminded Blake of the events preceding the great battle, three cycles ago. He would need to convince and rally all the armed vessels he could find. He shuddered at the immensity of the task.

Since the final battle, most warships had been disarmed and repurposed. The Azuran angels had closed their home world, their space station, and their outpost temples, from the rest of the galaxy. They remained out of reach.

Furthermore, Blake realized, he had never faced a Cyborg army in his entire military career. He didn't know what to expect, or how to fight them and win. He would need a crash course in Cyborg warfare.

* * *

Kefira felt like a traitor as she spoke in hushed tones to her former military advisor in a deserted corridor. "Malo is leading us to be slaughtered by a horde of bloodthirsty monsters. We must get rid of him and save our people."

The man listened respectfully, then shook his head. "Sorry, Sardar, but what you are proposing is treason of the highest order."

"Would you rather see our people devoured by demonic machines?" She struggled to keep her voice down.

The man offered a condescending smile. "Sardar, if such a threat exists outside of your so-called visions, Padshad Malo is perfectly capable of protecting us. You shouldn't worry about such things. You have a coronation today. You should rejoice at finally realizing your life's purpose."

"How can I rejoice?" Kefira pushed down her frustration. How she wished she could influence her people's minds, but she couldn't. "I have devolved from sole ruler to brood mare, while a bloodthirsty army is threatening our very existence."

"The first duty of a Sardar princess is to ensure the continuity of the royal bloodline, to honor Helsara." The man straightened his frame and locked his hands behind his back. He wouldn't help her.

Kefira couldn't control her frustration anymore and raised her voice. "And who will protect the Anvad, when their Padshad is a wolf in disguise who sold them to their enemy?"

The man raised his brow in indignation. "Sardar, you should refrain from such sacrilegious accusations."

Kefira realized she must leave before the man had her arrested. She pivoted on her heel and left in a huff. This was the third person she thought she could trust, and the third refusal to help. Malo's influence controlled everyone on board. They all behaved like sheep... except her... because her Sardar gifts protected her from his mind control. But what could she do, alone?

Back in her quarters, a sumptuous dress of gold and silver threads was spread on her bunk. Where did it come from? Malo's ship? She flinched. The coronation was only an hour away.

Could she delay this coronation event? Any excuse she could make wouldn't deter Malo from being crowned without her, and she would lose all power. At least, as the crowned queen, she would have some authority... and if anything happened to Malo, she would be in charge with the full power of the crown.

Could she kill Malo and make it look like a natural death? She would have to try. Sardar women had been controlled by men for generations, but in that time, they'd learned and passed down their secret knowledge from mother to daughter. Kefira never thought she'd need their help, but she was glad she'd kept their clandestine traditions.

From a hidden drawer in the chest containing her clothes, she retrieved a small vial, leaving the larger bottle safely tucked there. The deadly poison from Helsara's flower, to which Kefira had built up immunity over many cycles, might save the Anvad people from being led to the slaughter.

Kefira slowed her breathing to calm her mind. Used to living like a warrior since she'd lost everyone dear, Kefira had long renounced ladies in waiting. She slipped into the voluminous gold and silver dress, thanking Helsara for the skinny corset and fluffy skirt. Not fluffy enough to hide a blaster, but she was able to strap her father's dagger to her thigh. Then she hid the small vial between her breasts.

She hoped the secret weapon of the ancient Sardar women would give her the advantage.

Kefira checked herself in the full-size mirror. The gold and silver enhanced her dark skin. She smoothed her hair back and held it with a golden pin. Then she applied a little gold on her eyelids, some gloss on her lips, and a dash of her favorite perfume. She must look the part of a proper Sardar princess, pretty and submissive.

A knock on the metal hatch interrupted her thoughts.

She took a calming breath stared at her face in the mirror and composed herself. She had the truth of Helsara on her side. She would succeed. "Open."

The old captain in full dress uniform, including white hat and gloves, stepped inside and bowed low. "Sardar, all is ready in the main hold for the coronation ceremony. I was sent to accompany you there."

Kefira forced a smile. She effected a small curtsy and took the captain's offered arm.

The big cat rose from his bed. *"Karak protect."*

The captain frowned. "That animal isn't coming to the ceremony, is he?"

Kefira chuckled. Malo also hated the cat. "Sorry, Captain. But since Karak is my only remaining bodyguard, he must follow me everywhere. A Sardar princess should never be without a skilled protector. Helsara's rules."

The captain shook his head and grumbled under his breath.

Kefira steeled herself and matched his limping steps along the central corridor, while the big cat followed silently on velvet paws.

At least, Kefira would be crowned queen. After Malo died, if she could make it look like a natural death, she would regain control of her people, with the absolute authority of her new title, and no more competition.

Then she would abolish that stupid rule that prevented Sardar women from being crowned queens, without a husband to rule over them.

* * *

Malo knelt in front of the Shamaness. As she set the crown on his head, he glanced sideways toward Kefira. She was breathtakingly beautiful. He'd chosen the dress well. He imagined the holographic records of the event would rival in grandeur the best ceremonies in Anvad history. Not a small feat on a grungy freighter.

She also seemed subdued and docile, but he didn't trust that side of her. Did she learn to lie and hide her feelings in his absence? Could he trust her to support him in his ascent to rule the galaxy? He hoped so. But if she betrayed him, he would sacrifice her.

Finally, the Shamaness crowned Kefira with the traditional jeweled circlet worn by all the Anvad queens before her. Amazing that the crown jewels had survived the sacking of the palace. Although the Sardar didn't foresee their massacre, they had hidden their treasures where only a Sardar could find them. And Kefira had retrieved them to finance the exodus of her people. Good thing she kept the crown and circlet.

The Shamaness bowed and stepped to the side of the stage, to stand beside Karak, the repugnant feline. That farce of a bodyguard would have to go. Maybe Malo could arrange an unfortunate accident... like a glitchy hatch mistakenly jettisoning the cat into cold space.

As if guessing his thoughts, Karak wrinkled its nose at Malo. Good thing the disgusting creature couldn't read his mind. But Malo wouldn't have to suffer its presence for long.

He took Kefira's hand, and both rose and bowed to the cheering crowd. Kefira smiled to her subjects, but Malo found her smile strained, empty of true feelings. What had become of their love? She wasn't the trusting young girl he'd fallen in love with, who adored him unconditionally. When had she learned to hide her feelings? He didn't trust this new side of Kefira.

But it didn't matter. Willing or not, she was his now, and soon, she would carry his heir, a legitimate Sardar prince, to succeed him after Malo became Sorcerer supreme of the Stygian Order.

* * *

During the traditional banquet, food, drink, music, and dance filled the main hold.

The circlet on Kefira's head made her feel more confident. At least, she was queen. Karak never left her side, and she was grateful for the cat's loyalty.

She scratched the big furry head. "You are a good boy, Karak."

The big cat purred under her ministrations. *"Karak protect."*

Kefira kept smiling to everyone, accepting congratulations and good wishes with Sardar grace. Inside, however, she could barely contain her anger. The extravagant feast had depleted the freighter's food supplies... including the fresh fruit and vegetables provided by the *Blue Phantom*. If her plan worked, and she could resume course to the Land of Many Waters, it would have to be on tasteless and meager rations.

She suspected Malo splurged because he planned to deliver the Anvad to the bloodthirsty Cyborg army sooner than later. But he wouldn't win. The small vial tucked between Kefira's breasts would insure his quick demise.

From across the hold, Malo stared at her with the hungry eyes of his earlier passion. He walked toward her, elegant in black silk, a curved Kirpan blade at his hip. She remembered happy days with him, and felt guilty about her plan, but things had changed.

As he reached her side, he took and kissed her hand. "Should we dance to show our people how happy their new Padshad and his queen are?"

Kefira hated leaving Karak on the sidelines, but she must play the game. She cringed inside as she followed Malo to the center of the hold. They danced to the rhythm of the sitars and flutes and tambourines.

She realized the movements of the dance were submissive for the woman, bowing, kneeling, as if adoring the male, while the man strutted and towered over her. The signs of inequality of the sexes were often as subtle as the graceful movements of a dance. Something she'd never noticed before, but she might change it in the future, given a chance.

When the music stopped, Malo smiled. "My young lioness, it is time to let the people rejoice on their own, while we retire to fulfill our conjugal duties."

Kefira smiled as sweetly as she could, but she felt like retching. The very idea of copulating with him, as well as committing cold-blooded murder, made her sick to her stomach. But she only had dangerous choices.

They crossed the hold, hand in hand, smiling and waving to their loyal subjects. Well... loyal to Malo, thanks to his sorcerous hold on their minds.

Kefira was wailing inside, but she found comfort in the fact that Karak was still following her faithfully. Good boy. He might have to protect her tonight.

* * *

"Captain?" Graziella manifested in the observation dome. "We are approaching the battlefield. Lots of debris in orbit. Many ships were destroyed. This planet fiercely defended itself... yet they fell and now the Cyborg army has landed its shuttles and is exterminating the civilian population."

Blake sighed at the sight of the enormous ships of unknown origin floating in orbit like black leviathans. He'd never seen this design before, slick, with black scales. They had Stygian shields, and the intensity of their evil vibrations made him cringe. They had destroyed everything in their path, including the planet's orbital defenses. How could the *Blue Phantom* possibly help anyone against such a formidable force?

"Captain, we are receiving more distress calls from ships in jeopardy in the vicinity."

Blake closed his eyes to visualize the vessels in distress. "There is only one ship worth saving among those. It's on the other side of the battlefield. Let's concentrate on that one. Snail speed and complete stealth mode. We do not want to attract attention. We are outnumbered a thousand to one."

"Any news from the Azurans?" Graziella's musical voice seemed full of hope.

"None. Either they can't hear us, or they are ignoring our calls." Blake hoped it was the former. He couldn't imagine the Guardian Angels of the universe ignoring his call to rally against such evil... or turning a blind eye on the resurgence of the Stygian Order.

Chapter Eight

"Welcome to your new residence, my little lioness." Malo kissed Kefira's hand and let her in first.

As she stepped into the luxurious royal cabin of the *Zantar*, Kefira could barely breathe. She felt oppressed, as if the bulkhead would close and suffocate her. The entire ship reeked of sorcery, but she couldn't let fear influence her mind. She must get the Sardar poison into the drink. She might get sick from it, despite her built immunity, but she'd survive, while Malo would not.

He led her to the couch.

Karak sneezed in protest to all the changes in the royal cabin, then leapt to his former favorite spot, draping himself over the back of the couch.

Kefira sat, finding the cat's proximity reassuring. "Do you have anything to drink?"

"Of course." Malo pressed a small panel on the bulkhead.

A valet in a red coat entered the salon and bowed. His pale skin, long white hair, and faded gaze contrasted with the swarthy skin tone of the Anvad.

"Bring celebration wine for the Padshad and his queen." Malo turned to Kefira. "I shall return promptly." Then he stepped into the adjacent bedchamber.

Without a word, the attendant went to a corner bar and returned holding a tray, with a bottle and two glasses. Keeping a wary eye on Karak the valet set the tray on the low table then unsealed the bottle with a flourish and set it on the table as well.

The big cat hissed at the valet. Fear flashed in the man's pale eyes. He bowed and left quickly.

Kefira saw her opportunity. She pulled the vial from between her breasts, opened it and poured the contents into the open bottle. Then she stashed the empty vial in the hidden pockets of her bulky petticoat, making sure her father's dagger was still strapped to her thigh. That would be plan B... just in case.

Her heart jumped when Malo stepped into the salon, clearing his throat. He had shed the coronation cape and stood in black silk splendor, svelte and dashing, still wearing the Kirpan blade at his left side. He was so handsome... but evil often had powers of seduction.

A rush of memories flooded Kefira's mind. Malo smiling, laughing, attentive. He was once kind, good and loving... or so she thought. But she couldn't let the past stop her. By Helsara, she hoped he didn't suspect anything of her plan.

He smiled and sat beside her on the crimson couch. Then he seized and raised the bottle, examining it intently. "What should we drink to, my little lioness?"

"Whatever makes you happy, Padshad." Kefira smiled sweetly, wondering if deceit and murder would make her a sinner or a saint in Helsara's eyes.

Malo poured the wine for both of them. He raised his glass. "You go first."

Kefira took her glass and raised it, looking into his dark, evil eyes. "To the Anvad people. May they thrive under our rule, with Helsara's blessings."

"Now, you drink." He stared at her, as if daring her.

Kefira drank a sip under his stare, glad that the poison was odorless and left no aftertaste. She smiled. "What will you drink to, Padshad?"

Malo chuckled. "I drink to your foolhardy bravery, my little lioness."

Kefira wondered what he meant. May Helsara protect her.

Malo emptied his glass in a few gulps and set it on the low table with a flourish and a sigh. "Excellent harvest."

Kefira's heart beat like a runaway drum. The effects of the poison were swift, especially when gulped quickly. She only had a sip, and because of her immunity, she couldn't feel anything, but Malo would soon drop dead.

The big cat watched Malo intently. Did Karak understand what Kefira had done? Most animals understood more than people realized.

Malo scooted closer to her on the couch. "Do you remember how happy we were when we studied and traveled together? We were golden, the perfect couple, chosen by Helsara."

"I remember. We were following Helsara's will at the time, and there were no obstacles to our love." Was he trying to seduce her with memories of their past relationship? It wouldn't work. Besides, it was too late.

"Well, you do not have to follow Helsara anymore." He gently pushed back a short curl behind her ear. "Now, you can follow me and support me in all my endeavors. Together, we shall rule the entire galaxy."

"The galaxy?" Kefira realized Malo's ambition had no bounds. "Isn't ruling the Anvad people enough?"

"Nothing is ever enough." Malo flashed a diabolical smile. "And anything is possible with the right military might."

The Cyborg army from her vision flashed on Kefira's mind. Was he going to sacrifice the Anvad people to these unholy creatures, for a chance to rule the galaxy?

"Now, to the business of producing an heir." Malo rose from the couch and took her hand, showing no signs of weakness or dizziness. "After all, according to Anvad law, it's our first and most sacred duty, isn't it?"

"Yes, of course, it is." Kefira couldn't believe Malo could still stand. She rose as he pulled her up. What now?

Karak growled and stepped down from the back of the couch and onto the pillows to follow Kefira.

Malo gave the cat a malevolent stare and pointed an accusing finger. "No beasts allowed in the bedroom."

Karak seemed to shrink into himself, emitted a tiny kitten's meow then collapsed on the couch, passed out, sound asleep, snoring softly.

Kefira's heart sank at this demonstration of Malo's superior powers. Her worst fears had realized. The dagger strapped to her thigh seemed to throb. But without Karak, her plan B would certainly fail. "What did you do to him?"

"Don't worry. Your infernal cat is just asleep." The sarcastic tone didn't bode well.

"How did you do that?" Kefira shuddered at the extent of his abilities. Where did they come from? The Stygian symbols on the bulkhead came to mind, but she wasn't familiar with the sect's particular skills. Did his magic also make Malo immune to the poison?

"Making animals sleep is just a parlor trick." Malo smiled as he invited her into the bedroom. "About our happy childhood, there is a detail you missed."

"What detail?" Kefira had read Malo's mind many times when they were children. She thought she knew everything about him. But obviously she missed the warning signs of his predisposition to evil.

"My mother was a noble Anvad woman, but not a Sardar. As a girl, she resided in the palace as one of your mother queen's ladies." He closed the hatch behind them.

"Yes, I knew that." Sadness struck Kefira as her dead mother's face flashed in her mind. She felt trapped. "Where are you going with this?"

"Women, even noblewomen, are curious by nature." Malo sat on the bed and removed his soft leather shoes. "The secrets they uncover give them the illusion of importance and power."

"I never thought of it that way." Kefira kept him talking, expecting him to drop dead any moment. She hoped she wouldn't have to use plan B, especially without Karak.

Malo slowly removed his sword belt with its curvy blade and set it on the side table, keeping his back to her. "As it happens, my mother discovered many secrets at the palace, but she was wise enough to keep them to herself. And after I came along, she was also bent on protecting me."

"It's natural for mothers to protect their children." Kefira kept the bed between them, in no hurry to remove her clothes.

He turned to her quickly. "You wouldn't try to poison me with Helsara's sacred plant, would you?"

Kefira gasped at the unexpected question and struggled to lie to his face. "Of course, not."

"Good." He chuckled. "Because you would be wasting your time. The favorite poison of the Sardar women was one of the secrets my mother uncovered. She fed me small doses throughout childhood and taught me how to make it to maintain immunity."

Kefira fumed. The lump in her throat grew heavy as a stone. She gasped. She still had the dagger, but without Karak as backup, was she strong enough to overcome Malo?

And even if she succeeded, a stabbing death could never be ruled as natural heart failure. Her people would punish her severely for murdering their Padshad. Then who would protect the Anvad?

* * *

Malo observed the little liar, enjoying the strong emotions flashing across her face at the news he was immune to her poison. Disappointment or anger? "I knew all along

157

you planned to betray me. Your attempts at plotting against me with the Anvad generals didn't go unnoticed. You were promptly reported."

"You knew?" She stared at him, immobile as a statue in her gold and silver dress, but he still couldn't read her thoughts.

"I guessed, as a Sardar princess, you would try to kill me with Helsara's sacred plant. So, I excused myself, giving you a chance to poison the wine." How he enjoyed watching her horrified face as he told her. "No point denying it. I saw you do it. You really have changed, Kef. The little lioness I knew would never murder anyone in cold blood."

Her eyes could have thrown daggers. "You tend to change when you are betrayed by your lover, when he steals your ship, leaves you marooned in space, and has your family slaughtered, then plots the genocide of your entire people, just to satisfy his greed for power."

"Not bad." He chuckled to hide his surprise at her keen insight. "How did you figure it out?"

"I am Sardar. I can sense evil, and this ship reeks of it." She straightened with that entitled arrogance of the Sardar. "Helsara sends me visions to help me protect her people."

"Helsara is long dead." How he resented her Sardar pride. "There are greater powers in this galaxy, believe me."

"What powers?" She seemed so angry... how adorable.

Malo untied the collar of his black silk shirt. "My father happens to be one of the most powerful sorcerers in this quadrant."

"Your father?" She frowned. "I thought you never knew who he was."

"I didn't at the time, but a few cycles ago, my mother told me all about him. That's when I decided to jettison you and your cat in an escape pod, steal your ship, and join him." He opened his shirt, revealing the branding scar on his left pectoral.

Kefira gasped. "You wear the brand of the Stygian Order?"

"Oh! So, you know what this is?" The little minx was full of surprises.

"I did my research." That Sardar arrogance, again.

"Good." That simplified Malo's task. "My father is Matchitehew, Sorcerer Supreme of the Stygian Order. I am his First Lieutenant, and one day soon, I shall succeed him." He inclined his head and winked at her. "You could rule at my side."

Like a lioness, Kefira growled and jumped on the bed, brandishing a dagger. A dagger? How quaint.

Malo blocked her arm, seized her wrist, and rolled her over on the bed. But she was stronger than he anticipated. She locked his head between her knees and threw him off the bed. When had she learned to fight like a warrior? He didn't like this new side of her.

Still holding the dagger, she faced him, panting, her face distorted by hatred.

Taken aback by her loathing, Malo had to gather his thoughts. He couldn't let her win. He must overcome her by other means. He focused to paralyze her with his mind, but it didn't work. The little Sardar was immune to his magic. Fark.

So, he willed the bolts of the side table to unscrew and sent it flying to hit her head.

She ducked and avoided the flying table. His sword and belt fell off it and clattered to the decking. Then she launched herself at him with surprising strength. Her dagger stabbed his bare chest... in vain. The point couldn't penetrate his skin. She stabbed and stabbed and stabbed again. Not even a drop of blood.

She froze, eyes wide. "What's happening? What kind of sorcery is that?"

Malo simply smiled. Ever so slowly, he removed the dagger from her frozen hands. "Sorry to disappoint, Kef, but I'm not that easy to kill."

Kefira paled.

Malo pushed her back with his mind and threw her across the room.

She flew off, hit the bulkhead, then wavered and collapsed on the deck. Then she struggled back to her feet and faced him again. Stubborn little hellcat.

This time, Malo had no patience left. With his mind, he drew his Kirpan blade from the scabbard. Ignoring her widened eyes full of fear, he stepped to trap her against the bulkhead and held the sharp point to her throat.

How he enjoyed her fright. "So, you are not so proud now, Sardar."

She struggled as he pinned her against the bulkhead, and her face distorted with rage. "You are evil. I hate you. I will find a way to kill you."

"Promises, promises. Only one problem… I cannot be killed." Malo threw her on the bed and lay on top of her. "Just as I thought, Kef. I like your bravery, but you are no match for me. And you will pay dearly for your treason."

Her dark eyes reflected the angry storm inside her. "Are you going to kill me?"

"Oh, I won't kill you." Malo chuckled. He would enjoy taming the little shrew. "I have other plans for you."

"What plans?" Her eyes grew wider.

"We are going to make beautiful children together." Their children would inherit her spunk and be more powerful for it.

She spat in his face. "I will never submit."

"Yes, you will." Malo wiped the spit from his cheek. "And if you don't, I will enjoy inflicting pain upon your young body, and I shall leave deep, ugly scars on your perfect skin… and in the depths of your soul."

Maybe he would act on his threat… and maybe he wouldn't. But he thoroughly enjoyed the fear in her widened brown eyes.

* * *

"Captain?" Graziella appeared inside the observation dome of the *Blue Phantom*. "We are approaching the source of the distress signal."

"Reduce speed." Blake scanned the only ship worth saving in that entire battlefield. The civilian passenger vessel was attempting to flee. "Slow down the approach. We don't want the Cyborg to detect us."

"Aye, Captain." Graziella closed her eyes as she synched with the ship

In full stealth mode, the *Blue Phantom* prowled along the hull of an enormous black leviathan, smooth-scaled and mysterious. No protuberances to indicate external cannons, yet it seemed ominous. Many smaller ships darted in and out of its open maw.

Closing his eyes, Blake focused on the smaller vessels. They also carried Cyborg soldiers. He sensed no notion of rank, and no leaders among them. As if they acted as a hive, a collective entity. Their only thought was to destroy, inflict pain, and drink fresh blood. They needed it to survive.

Was it a flaw in their design, or was the bloodlust introduced on purpose, to motivate and control them?

Blake opened his eyes as a fast projectile from a small surviving raptor in the decimated flotilla splashed on the bright red deflector shield of a large Cyborg ship. The missile burst harmlessly in a shower of sparks. The black leviathan then blasted a thin red beam of energy that pulverized the small raptor into a shower of tiny chards. Very efficient weapons. Blake was glad the *Blue Phantom* was cloaked. Otherwise, it would make a large target.

Aboard the angel ship, rising heat, and an overwhelming sense of doom, made it difficult to breathe. It seemed the Cyborg leviathan exuded dark vibrations, evil magic that might impede angelic abilities.

With his mind, Blake guided the *Blue Phantom* away from the leviathan and toward the civilian passenger vessel in distress. Several small Cyborg craft were attached to its hull like barnacles. It had been boarded.

Blake let his mind wander along the corridors of the passenger ship. It crawled with bloodthirsty Cyborg behaving like beasts. The passengers hid in small clumps from the predators, their fear palpable. These half machine monsters had no conscience, no compassion, no reasoning capabilities. They only craved blood. Their superior strength made them unstoppable.

Blake shuddered. Unlike the Marauders, they would be difficult to overcome.

His heart went out to Kefira. He hoped she was safe. He kept imagining her in the hands of these monstrosities, and it made his blood boil… a very unseemly emotion for an angel. He must stop these monsters before they reached Kefira. These Cyborg would pay dearly for the lives they took.

"Let's remain invisible as we materialize aboard that passenger ship. We must kill the Cyborg fast, before they sound the alarm and bring reinforcement. Then we carry the civilians still alive to the *Blue Phantom*, and leave as soon as all the survivors are onboard.

"What will you do, Captain?" Graziella cared about her captain.

"I'll capture and bring back a few Cyborg soldiers directly into our brig. I want to interrogate and study them. We need more information about this new enemy."

"That sounds dangerous. If they communicate with the rest of the hive, they could give them our location." Graziella's blue eye softened. "Be careful, Captain. These treacherous Cyborg may have unknown capabilities."

"No worries. I'll insulate the brig. They won't be able to communicate with the outside." At least, Blake hoped so.

Chapter Nine

Still reeling from Malo's incredible claim, Kefira berated herself. How could she have been stupid enough to think she could handle Malo on her own? Was he really unkillable? She'd seen the dagger's point refusing to penetrate his skin. No reaction on his part, and not even a drop of blood.

Now he'd pinned her on the bed, holding her wrists over her head. She must free herself to save her people. As she struggled in his grip, the exquisite dress of gold and silver ripped.

Looking for a weapon, any weapon, Kefira spotted Malo's Kirpan blade precariously balanced at the edge of the mattress. Maybe his own weapons were imbued with magic that could kill him. In a desperate effort, she twisted and lunged for it.

Almost! But not quite.

"That blade can't hurt me either." Malo snarled and pulled her back to the middle of the bed. "And don't think you can escape me, little lioness. No one escapes me."

Kefira's hope dwindled. "I will escape, and you will pay."

"You can't escape, and I can't be killed." He caressed her cheek, like he used to do when they were in love. "And soon, you'll be begging for my loving attentions... we shall be lovers again."

Kefira shuddered at his intimate touch. By the frozen hells of Laxxar, she wouldn't let Malo make a puppet of her to control her people. "Then you better arrest me, because I'll never stop trying to kill you. You are evil. I know that, now. And you betrayed the Anvad people. You are leading them to the slaughter, and you do not deserve to live!"

"Wow!" Malo chuckled. "You are in no position to threaten me, my little lioness. I could take what I want right now, but I want you broken, willing, and begging for my love."

"I will never beg." Her hatred escaped through the words.

Malo tsked. "If you refuse my love, I shall have you caged... until you change your mind."

Kefira felt the blood leave her face when a pair of shackles snapped on her wrists above her head. Where did they come from? Did he keep shackles by the bed? Of course, he would.

Malo flashed a diabolical smile. "Guards!"

Four tall men in red uniforms, armed with blasters and wearing helmets, stepped into the cabin's bedchamber.

When Malo pulled her off the bed, Kefira resisted and struggled with the shackles. Still, he forced her to her feet.

"Take her to the brig. And return that expensive coronation dress and jewels to my coffers. She is unworthy of them."

"Aye, Padshad." Two of the guards flanked Kefira, each grasping an arm, holding her upright.

Despite her shackles, Kefira fought against their grip. "The crown jewels belong to the Anvad people!"

"Exactly." Malo faced her and sneered. "And I am their Padshad, so they are mine."

Malo addressed the two other guards. "Get that big sleeping beast in the main cabin off the couch and jettison it out of an airlock. Only primitive cultures enjoy living with filthy animals."

"No!" Kefira raged and struggled but the guards held her firmly. How could Malo be so callous as to execute an innocent animal? She made contact with Karak's mind. *"Wake up, Kitten. Wake up and flee. Now. Hide. Quickly."*

She sensed the big cat stirring in the other room. *"Karak protect."*

"No, Kitten. Hide now. Protect later." She feared Malo might just snuff out the cat's life with a simple thought.

"Karak hide."

"Good boy. Stay safe and hide, Kitten. I'll call you when I need you." Kefira felt relief as she sensed Karak slinking away through the main cabin hatch into the corridor.

"What are you waiting for?" Malo shouted at the guards. "Take her away. And jettison the cat!"

The guards tightened their grip on Kefira's arms and shoved her forward.

Malo flashed her a condescending smile as she walked past him. "Good riddance, my little lioness. Soon, you'll beg for my love… you'll see."

Kefira couldn't resist. She turned around and spit at Malo's face.

A guard hit her temple with the butt of his blaster, and all went black.

* * *

Blake couldn't wait to return to Kefira's freighter. Some deep feeling told him she was in danger.

Graziella manifested before him in the observation dome. "All the rescued civilians are safe, and the three Cyborg prisoners are contained in total isolation. What are your orders, Captain?"

"We shall provide the civilians a ride to their chosen planet, but make sure one remains with us. Three decades of service on the *Blue Phantom*. You will brief the new recruit."

"Aye, aye, Captain." Graziella saluted and vanished.

Blake dematerialized and willed himself in the brig, outside the cell holding the three Cyborg prisoners. He remained invisible as he observed them through the clear crystal barrier. One Cyborg removed his helmet and Blake shuddered at the unholy sight.

Nothing human about these creatures. They had animal faces with sharp metal fangs, retractable blades, and rotary weapons as part of their artificial arms.

Black armor covered the bodies, but the faces showed furry skin between the multiple metal plates and devices. Each had one electronic eye implant. Since those no longer worked aboard the angel ship, they must be blind in that eye. Something to remember. They had weaknesses.

Severed from the rest of the hive, the three prisoners seemed lost and confused. One banged his head on the bulkhead, another walked in circles, and the third just lay there. Since the crystal disabled all electronics, they were unable to use their weapons or contact their ship to get new orders.

They didn't talk among themselves but grunted. Could they speak at all? Or did they only communicate with digital implants? Despite their humanoid shape, they seemed incapable of coherent thinking. They were blunt tools, engineered to be controlled.

Tempted to explore their minds to find out, Blake hesitated. It was never a good idea to get inside the mind of evil creatures. From his past experience in the Stygian Order, he knew sorcerers to be crafty. The Cyborg mind could be boobytrapped. He could lose his sanity, or even his life.

But the Cyborg might be less dangerous to explore while disconnected from their master, and unable to report their location. Besides, Blake had little choice. If he wanted to defeat these creatures, he must learn more about them. Knowledge of how their minds worked could give him an advantage.

Taking a deep breath to calm his fears, Blake closed his eyes. He ventured his consciousness inside the head of the prisoner reclined on the bunk, as he seemed the least aggressive. Blake struggled through oppressing channels to get access to the Cyborg's thoughts... if he had any. The Cyborg mind resisted his intrusion but was no match for Blake's abilities.

Simple mind indeed. Blake sensed no individual soul, no principles, no conscience, no sense of right or wrong inside the Cyborg mind... only hunger for blood and awe for their divinity, an exalted Prince of Darkness named Baalmordo, who always led them to feed on fresh blood.

These Cyborg had been artificially engineered from bio-material and machine parts, to inflict chaos and destruction. They had no will of their own and blindly followed orders from their dark prince, who remained in constant contact with their minds.

Except for now, while isolated from their master's signal. That's why they usually acted like a hive and now seemed lost. Without standing orders, these three didn't know how to behave.

Blake had never heard of Baalmordo, but he'd dealt with evil entities in the past. From what he understood, this unholy prince must be very powerful. The formidable Cyborg army he controlled with his mind attested to his might.

An angel guard walked by the cell, and the three Cyborg stepped up to the clear wall and sniffed the air, showing signs of agitation.

Still inside the Cyborg mind, Blake experienced the blood lust first hand. The Cyborg bared their fangs and pointy metal teeth and roared, then they pounded the clear crystal with metal fists, to no avail. The clear bulkhead was alive and could hold extraordinary pressures.

Then they wanted to pierce it, but the crystal had disabled their rotating blades, which refused to come out of their forearms. So, they banged the clear wall harder. Still, they yearned to get to their prey.

Blake's consciousness slammed back into his body, as if he'd been kicked out of the Cyborg mind. What in the frozen hells of Laxxar?

He shivered. These Cyborg had the ability to sense intrusion from the forces of good and they had the power to react against them. Like an automatic reflex to kick out any foreign thought. A clever precaution in the design.

As a result, Blake realized they couldn't be reprogrammed and controlled by their enemies. Only Baalmordo could give them orders. Clever. But that would complicate things.

Even more concerning was the fact that the Cyborg bloodlust had returned of its own at the sight of a potential prey. Since they were disconnected from their evil prince, it came naturally. It wasn't controlled or learned behavior, but an essential part of their programming... something impossible to remove on a large scale.

These ultimate killers could never be turned. They would have to be exterminated. Every single one of them. And there might be tens of thousands on each of these Leviathans.

The task seemed impossible. Blake needed some advice and help from a higher source.

Closing his eyes, Blake released a calming breath. Then he focused his mind on the Azurans scattered throughout the galaxy, whether roaming in space, on the Byzantium Space Station, or on Azura itself.

"O Azuran angels, in the name of the Formless One, forgive my intrusion and listen to my plea. A powerful evil is wreaking death and destruction among peaceful planets, killing the innocent, feeding on their lifeblood. The dark entity leading them is named Baalmordo. He commands armies of bloodthirsty Cyborg and works in league with the Stygian Order, which has resurged."

No answer came.

"Without your help, nothing stands in the way of their conquest. Please help the unfortunate who stand in the path of these unholy hordes. Lock on to the Blue Phantom's beacon and join us in our desperate attempt to stop this great evil. Any help you can give would be appreciated."

Blake waited, hoping for a response… Only silence echoed in his mind. The Azurans had truly gone dark and silent throughout the galaxy. Maybe they didn't consider Baalmordo a threat to them, or maybe they didn't think these populations deserved to be saved. Still, he mentally activated the *Blue Phantom*'s silent beacon, the kind of signal only angels and Azurans could detect.

In any case, Blake couldn't face the armies of evil alone, even less defeat them. Yet, he must rescue Kefira and her people.

He couldn't stand it if Kefira died, and the Anvad were innocent, truthful, and deserving. He must find a way to save them.

Having made his decision, Blake marched under the vaulted crystal arches toward the control room. He could have dematerialized, but he needed to burn that aggressive energy he'd gathered from his mind-trip into the Cyborg mind.

As he entered, three angels stood in a circle, minds linked, piloting the *Blue Phantom*.

"Graziella? Set course for the planetoid where the Anvad freighter is headed."

"Aye, aye, Captain. Setting new course, now." Graziella's blue eyes clouded as she linked her mind to the ship. Then her eyes cleared again. "What are we going to do about the Cyborg prisoners? Jettison them into space?"

"No. Keep them in the brig. They can't hurt anyone there. And they might prove useful when we hatch our plan." Blake might have an idea on how to use them.

"You are the boss." Graziella's pout of disapproval wouldn't change his mind.

"Don't worry. We fought worse evil once, in the final battle." Blake didn't relish having to do it again.

"But we had legions of Azuran angels to help us." Was it fear on Graziella's beautiful face?

"I doubt the Azurans will come this time." Blake would probably be killed in the rescue attempt... along with his crew... but he couldn't let Kefira die. He must do something. Besides, saving her wasn't selfish or personal. He'd vowed to fight evil for the rest of his extended life. Although self-imposed, it was his most sacred mission.

Graziella sighed. "Still feeling guilty about your past, Captain? You have redeemed yourself a hundred times over."

"Perhaps in your eyes... but the guilt is still there." Blake feared the guilt would never leave him.

* * *

Aboard the *Zantar*, still attached to the hull of the Anvad freighter, Malo savored his victory over Kefira. She was still proud, but he would whip that Sardar arrogance out of her.

Looking at her now, on the brig monitor, half-naked, unconscious, and shackled with a chain to the bulkhead of her cell, it was difficult to imagine she could be dangerous at all. A few bloody cuts on her skin attested to her struggle, as well as the welt on her temple, from the guard's blow.

That guard would have to die, too, for acting without orders and striking the queen. He could have damaged her, or worse. She was Malo's property, and only his to discipline.

Too bad the big cat had escaped, but the beast would be found eventually, and thrown out of an airlock.

Malo had enjoyed unraveling Kefira's predictable plot, although he'd not expected her to pounce on him with a blade. That was rather disconcerting. When had she become such a hellcat? Before he rewarded her with his seed, she would have to become loving and submissive, the only way he liked his women.

Given the right incentive, she could be turned around, and he had five thousand incentives on the Anvad freighter. He would relish her emotional pain as he forced her to watch when he tortured children to break her rebellious streak.

A familiar tingle announced a powerful visitor. An inky cloud manifested on the deck of his royal cabin on the *Zantar*, then the cloud dissipated, and his father, Matchitehew, walked out of it onto the deck.

Malo turned off the brig monitor, erasing Kefira's image.

"Son, I hope you have good news." The sorcerer's long robes, the theatrical voice and the gesturing of the wide sleeves evoked ancient opera spectacles.

"Yes, Father." Malo nodded slightly. He refused to bow to anyone. "I was crowned Padshad of the Anvad, and Kefira is confined to the brig, for treason, and for trying to murder me on our coronation and official mating night."

Matchitehew perused the cabin with a critical eye. "I told you she is not worthy of your attentions. You are more powerful than any Sardar. She doesn't deserve you. Let's collect her DNA, that's all we need from her. Then we'll sacrifice her."

Malo wanted to contradict his father, tell him Kefira was precious to him... yet, he couldn't. Some strong spell barred him from expressing his true opinion or his discontent... but he could use his magic to navigate around the interdiction. "We still have time, Father. She won't be any trouble anymore."

"Good. I'm expecting you soon. I'm counting on you." His father took an emphatic pause. "The Exalted Prince of Darkness, Lord Baalmordo, is on his way."

"Understood, Father." Malo kept his head high, refusing to demean himself with a bow.

Matchitehew narrowed his eyes at Malo then vanished in his inky cloud.

Left alone, Malo freed his rage. He didn't agree with his father about sacrificing Kefira, but he couldn't oppose him. No matter. He would pretend to agree with the old man... until he killed him to take his place as the most powerful sorcerer in the galaxy.

* * *

Alone in her transparent jail, Kefira rose from the bunk to explore. Her chains rattled as she walked to the clear flexglaz wall. Her head still pounded from the nasty blow to her temple. She felt strange then realized she only wore underwear.

The guards had taken away the precious coronation dress but didn't provide clothes, not even overalls. She felt self-conscious in her corset and garter, and she was willing to bet Malo enjoyed every second of her humiliation. But she wouldn't give him the satisfaction of shrinking in shame.

She saw no guards around, but she noticed the many recording devices, all of them out of reach, outside the security flexglaz. She shuddered as she realized Malo was probably watching her from his cabin. How creepy.

Although she knew the *Zantar* had a brig, she'd never visited it before. She never realized what it would be like to be locked up in one of its cells.

She was a Sardar, and she had done everything in her power to stop Malo. Unfortunately, that wasn't enough. May Helsara help her people. They would pay the price of Kefira's failure. She would be responsible for their massacre. She wanted to cry but held back her tears. As long as she lived, she must keep fighting.

At least, Karak had escaped, and she was glad for it. She sat on the bunk, closed her eyes, and focused on the big cat. *"Where are you, Kitten? Are you okay?"*

"Karak okay. Karak look down, watch bad men."

Kefira guessed what he meant. He must be perched in the rafters of the cargo hold, precariously walking on the metallic crossbeams buttressing the frame of the *Zantar. "What are the bad men doing?"*

"Mean warrior. Many gun. Ready for battle."

Malo had a small army on the *Zantar*? Why should that surprise her? The raptor could certainly carry armed men in its hold. She should have known that even with his newly found powers, Malo would never venture into a challenging situation alone.

She realized that if he hadn't seized the crown by legal means, he would simply have taken the freighter by force. He was no better than the Marauders he'd hired to do his dirty work.

To think that she once found him charming and attractive... How could she have loved such a disgusting cur?

A slight noise in the vicinity of her cell caught Kefira's attention. Someone was coming. *"Stay hidden, Kitten. I'll talk to you soon."*

Malo walked into the brig, leering at her through the clear flexglaz with open interest.

"So, did you have time to think about your situation?"

Kefira stared back without flinching. She wouldn't give an inch.

"Stubborn, as usual." He blinked and broke the stare. "Well, let me rephrase that. You will submit to my will, or your captivity is about to become extremely uncomfortable. I would even say, unbearable."

Kefira shuddered. Did he mean to use torture? "What do you want from me?"

"I want you to reassure our people that they are in good hands with their new Padshad, that no harm will come to them, that I will protect them as you have." He frowned. "It seems they still trust you, despite my influence."

"I will do no such thing." Kefira scoffed. "A Sardar princess never lies."

"But a Sardar princess poisons her mate and rushes him with a blade in the bedroom?" Malo's sneer radiated anger. "Drop the pretense, Kef. You are in no position to bargain. And if you do not conform, we'll play a little game. A game where you'll scream and beg for mercy."

"I will never submit." She hoped she could live up to the brave words.

"Not even to save a young child from torture?" Malo's smile chilled her spine. "And if you still refuse to do what I ask, that game might end with your untimely demise."

Kefira shuddered. She was ready to die, but could she stand the torture of a child? "I will not submit. No matter what torment your twisted mind plans for me."

"Wrong answer, little lioness. We shall meet again, soon, and you will not enjoy our next meeting. In the meantime, you are confined to your bunk." Malo waved his hand in the air.

Kefira's cuffs beeped, and the chain dragged her back toward her bunk. There, the magnetized cuffs stuck to the bulkhead with a thump, forcing her to lie or sit on the thin mattress, with her hands attached to the metallic headboard. "This is cruel and useless. You know I will not submit, so why are you doing this?"

Malo chuckled. "If you don't know why, think about it. Now, you will rot on your bunk, with no bathroom access, no food, no water... until you cooperate. And if you don't, you'll die of thirst and starvation. It's a very painful way to die."

"You are a monster!" The words came unbidden, but Kefira didn't regret them.

Malo shrugged. "It's not smart to insult your Padshad, little lioness. I hold your life in my hands. You should treat me with more respect."

Respect? Kefira wanted to scream but kept her mouth shut. No need to make things worse.

"I see we understand each other." Malo smiled, then turned on his heel and walked away.

Kefira watched through the flexglaz as his stiff back retreated and disappeared through the open hatch.

If only she had trusted Blake... But he had vanished, and with him her only hope was gone... or maybe not.

She may have other resources. She had Karak. And the *Zantar* used to be her personal ship. A Sardar ship. Had Malo taken control of all the original software? Or, in his lazy overconfidence, had he neglected a few non-essential or hidden subroutines?

If she could speak to her ship through a roundabout way, perhaps Kefira could escape her cell and regain some control... maybe.

If caught, however, the punishment would be quick and final... but since she already faced a most painful death, she had nothing to lose.

She closed her eyes and prayed. *Helsara the Bountiful, please protect your daughter.*

Chapter Ten

Sitting on her cell bunk, leaning on the bulkhead to which her magnetic shackles remained stuck, Kefira shivered, partly from the cold, but also with fear. Would it work?

She huddled in a ball and hid her mouth behind her cuffs. Then she hummed a short nursery rhyme her mother taught her as a toddler, *Help me, or the wolf will eat me.* She didn't see a voice monitor in her cell, but it should have one. She hoped the computer could hear her.

And in case the guards were listening, she hoped her humming would seem harmless, and no one would suspect anything amiss. They'd probably think she'd lost her grasp on reality... unless Malo knew about the secret code. After all, he'd known about the poison. But Kefira must keep hope alive.

A short musical phrase answered her little song through the bulkhead. The faint melody of a flute repeated itself, barely distinguishable from the purring of the air scrubbers.

Kefira recognized the melody of *I can hear you wherever you are* and rejoiced. Yes. The hidden emergency subroutine still worked. She managed to keep a sad face for the recorders. If Malo knew about the secret subroutine, he would have disabled it. Or maybe not.

Could Kefira recall all the subtleties of the secret musical code? That was a long time ago, and she never had to use it, until now. Still, she remembered the nursery rhyme for hostile takeover and hummed *Billy, Billy, the mean bully*.

The musical response of *Mommy, what should I do?* requested further instructions.

Why didn't she pay more attention to her mother's teachings about her ship's security features? A teenager at the time, she considered them ridiculous, and the eventuality she would need them unlikely, or even farfetched.

Her mother knew the life of a Sardar princess could turn lethal at any moment. She'd tried to prepare Kefira for the worst, but the young often ignored the warnings of their elders.

Kefira realized her mother was wise, and wished she'd listened more closely to her instructions. Now the woman was gone, slaughtered by the GTA on the suggestion of the Stygian Order, and probably on Malo's direct orders.

Swallowing the lump in her throat, Kefira wiped a tear. She must clear her thoughts and focus on saving her people.

She replayed in her mind her mother's directions to use the code, trying to remember the rhyme best fitted to her situation. *Open the flood gates* would flush poisonous gas in the corridors, holds, brig, and common areas, but not in the royal quarters. Not an option. It would kill the red soldiers, but Karak would die, and so would she, while Malo would be protected.

Let the kitten run free might unlock her cell and her cuffs, but how would she get past the guard station? She didn't see any guards, yet, knowing Malo, there would be several on duty. Could she stage a distraction to lure them away?

Don't be afraid of the dark would cause a general black out, but during a blackout, the detention cells would remain locked and require manual operation from the outside. *Fire, fire, the house is on fire* would ignite an inferno in the main cargo hold. Security features would instantly seal the cargo hold then expose it to space to extinguish the fire. It would also flush all untethered cargo into the black, including the soldiers camping there… and Karak.

Wracking her brain, Kefira recalled the code phrase that would give her back control of her ship. For that, she must have access to a console. Then she remembered there was a command console near the galley.

It could work, but she must save Karak. She closed her eyes. *"Kitten, can you hear me? Where are you?"*

"Karak watch bad men. Karak protect."

"Get out of the cargo hold, Kitten. Use the air shafts and go hide in the galley's pantry behind the food crates, where you used to play. I'll meet you there shortly."

"Karak go. Karak hide. Karak love crate."

"Good boy." Kefira smiled, sensing the big cat's excitement. Karak especially enjoyed playing in the pantry, jumping in and out of empty crates, and climbing the stacks, like half-buried pyramids in a jungle.

For her plan to work, she must use the proper sequence. First, open the cell, get out, then start the fire. Then order the blackout to blind the cameras and get past the guards, so Malo couldn't see or stop her. Then meet Karak in the pantry, regain control of the Zantar through the galley console. Then what?

What about Malo? He was too strong for her, especially with his new powers that made him impossible to kill. How could she confine him to the brig? And his loyal subjects were still under his influence. He could command them to arrest her with his mind, and they would obey.

She would have to keep him unconscious. Any attack against a Padshad, even an evil one, might get her executed by her own people. Not an easy task. Maybe she could seal his royal cabin and flood it with gas. There was no lethal gas in the royal quarters, but there was sleeping gas. What was the song for that? *Sleeping beauty in her castle*?

Free of Malo's influence and faced with the facts, the Anvad people would see him for what he was and decide his fate with a clear mind. Then she would turn the freighter around toward the safety of the Land of Many Waters. Helsara be praised. Her plan might work.

She didn't know how much time she had before the freighter reached its dreaded destination. Hours? Days? More? She must act quickly.

* * *

Blake jumped up from his bunk and shook his head to return to the reality of his spartan cabin on the *Blue Phantom*. He'd had a vision of Kefira again, and she was in even more danger than before. He shouldn't have left her alone to deal with Malo.

He couldn't be sure of anything, since he couldn't communicate with her, but he kept having flashes of her, bound and suffering, and calling for help. And he couldn't stand the thought.

He rubbed his pounding forehead and focused on his first officer. "Graziella?"

"Aye, Captain." The melodious voice bounced off the crystal bulkhead. "Can't sleep?"

"Dreams again. Let's hurry to that planetoid, or we might be too late." He hoped he could save Kefira. "If we want to rescue the Anvad, we must get there before the Cyborg army does." Even though their bloodthirst slowed them down as they stopped to feed, they wouldn't be far behind him.

"Should we manifest instantly in their vicinity?"

"No. The Stygian sorcerers may have some weird barrier protection around the planetoid. Let's manifest far enough so they don't detect us, then approach slowly in stealth mode."

"Aye, aye, Captain." Graziella's voice sang. "The freighter is getting closer to the planetoid, but we'll still get there before they do."

"Good. Let me know when we arrive." Blake cleared his voice. "Thank you Graziella."

"Understood. Graziella out."

Blake needed to clear his mind to consider his options. Meditation always gave him the clarity he needed. And sometimes he gleaned new ideas from the universe itself.

Like all Azurans and other angels did for hours each day, Blake sat in midair and crossed his legs, harmonizing his mind with that of the universe. "May the Formless One empower me to do the work of the angels of light."

As he closed his eyes, soft music streamed in his head, and many defensive options against the Cyborg army scrolled on his close eyelids.

He could send a prisoner back with a virus that would communicate to the entire hive, disabling the Cyborg army. Or, he could intercept the signal commanding the enemy and send a different order instead. Ordering them to kill the flesh and blood members of the Stygian Order might be helpful... but not enough.

Of course, he might find a way to kill the Prince of Darkness himself, Baalmordo. Neutralizing the source of the signal would render his Cyborg army catatonic. Or, Blake could order the Cyborg to fight and destroy each-other. But Baalmordo would certainly interfere, and he seemed very powerful.

Blake's first priority was to save Kefira and her people. For that, he would mount a stealth rescue. But could the Stygian sorcerers detect an angelic presence in their midst? Since the Cyborg mind did reject him, it seemed plausible, but the Cyborg weren't engineered by the Stygian Order. Their master was Baalmordo.

"O Formless One, please give me the means to help the forces of good against this horrible threat. Please share your immense knowledge." The Formless One never took sides but valued the balance between good and evil, darkness and light. In this case, the harmony was broken by a formidable evil force.

Blake's cabin resonated with faraway voices, all trying to help him. He focused on these voices. Other angels throughout the universe were sharing their knowledge with him.

Then Blake saw it. The weakness he could exploit. The means to disable the Cyborg army. It was all there, evident for him to see… yet, how could this weakness be exploited to his advantage?

"Thank you, O Formless One, for allowing me to see the ultimate truth through the layers of deceit."

* * *

"Karak hide, play with crate."

"Good boy. I'll be with you soon." Kefira sang the rhyme to free the kitten and waited.

A definite click, a beep, and a green LED light indicated her shackles had been released. Then the cell door opened. She exhaled a slow breath, in an attempt to keep her heartbeat down. Warriors didn't let emotions overwhelm them. She needed a cool mind.

She remained seated on her bunk, pretending to be shackled still, aware of the cameras focused on her. Next, the fire song. The computer answered and executed her order. The main hold was probably burning now, but as per hostile takeover protocol, no alarms sounded. Not yet. Then, she sang *Sleeping beauty in her palace.* That would neutralize Malo in his royal cabin.

By now, the red soldiers in the hold should have been vented into space with the burning cargo. Kefira startled as a few secondary alarms sounded, creating chaos. Yes. She hoped Malo was asleep by now, not watching the monitors.

She rose from her bunk and tiptoed through the open door. Once in the corridor, she hummed the blackout song, and all went dark and silent. The emergency lights came on, but they wouldn't last long. The corridor was empty. Good.

She noticed a door marked *Supplies* and quickly entered the closet. Looking for something to wear, she pulled a maintenance jumpsuit from a neatly folded pile, and a pair of boots from the shelf. Perfect. And the hat would hide her black curls.

She should find night goggles. According to hostile takeover protocol, after twenty seconds, the emergency lights would fail as well, and it would be total darkness. She ruffled through the drawers and found a pair. Then she waited.

When the dim emergency lights in the closet went off, she donned the goggles. That was her clue. She opened the closet door and stepped into the corridor.

Through her night vision goggles, she could see perfectly, while the guards, arms extended in front of them, followed the bulkhead and attempted to get their bearings.

As she reached the guards' station, they all stumbled upon each other in the dark, yelling and swearing. No one watched the door as she walked through the dead curtain of the security gate, without as much as a beep.

She knew the layout of her old ship and took the shortcut to the narrow stairs leading to the second deck, where the galley was located.

She crossed the galley with its familiar aroma of cooking oil and spice. Then she entered the pantry. "Where are you, Kitten?"

"Karak hide." The cat emerged from behind a stack of crates

Kefira smiled when she saw him. "Can you see in the dark, Kitten?"

"Karak see." The big cat rubbed his shoulders against her hip.

Kefira scratched him behind the ears, enjoying the vibrations of his loud purring. "Good boy. This way. Let's go."

She found the command console near the galley and rejoiced. Soon, she would retake control and make an official broadcast.

Time to be a queen.

She applied her hand on the console. It came to life as it recognized her Sardar DNA. The monitor wavered then stabilized. "Restore power and lights."

The lights flickered then came back on line. She must speak to her people. "Connect me with the freighter."

"Aye, Sardar." Several sections of the monitor lit up in green. "Connection open."

Kefira should also contact Blake. "Computer, lower the red shield."

"Unable to comply," the computer answered evenly.

"Why not? I am Sardar, this is my ship, and I gave you a direct order."

"Shield command is encrypted and can only be controlled by Padshad Malo himself, Sardar."

"By the frozen hells of Laxxar! Show me the royal cabin."

"Yes, Sardar." The monitor showed Malo slumped on the couch, fast asleep. Good. She would deal with him later.

Now, Kefira must speak to her people on the freighter, to explain the situation. She didn't want them to panic.

* * *

Malo's head hurt as he attempted to rise from his couch. His brain fogged. He struggled to concentrate on his situation. Faint emergency lights pulsed toward the exit, but it was dark. He couldn't focus his eyes. Something was very wrong. He'd also lost time.

Using his sorcerer's gifts, he enhanced his senses and detected a foreign smell. Some kind of gas? He remembered the cabin was equipped with emergency breathing masks.

He rolled off the couch and crawled toward the compartment in the bulkhead. Could he reach it? Almost. He managed to get his feet under him and rise enough to grab and pull the handle. A clear mask fell off. He grabbed it, sank to the decking, and fitted the apparatus on his face, then pushed the button to activate the flow of oxygen.

He took a few breaths into the mask and his thoughts came into focus. He was sitting on the decking of his royal cabin, and his strength was slowly returning. He could also see better as his eyes acclimated to the dim light. "Computer, clean the air."

The computer remained silent. Incapacitated? Or ignoring his voice?

Malo rose to his feet and stumbled toward the exit hatch, but it didn't open. Not a good sign. "Open the door."

The hatch remained closed.

What happened while he was out? How long had he been asleep?

He had other ways to access information. Closing his eyes, Malo let his consciousness roam beyond the confines of his royal cabin. He wanted to call his men to open the door, but he couldn't sense the minds of his soldiers in the *Zantar*'s main hold. His wandering shadow found the hold empty. As for his soldiers, they were dead, floating in empty space.

"By the frozen hells of Laxxar!" Malo swore under his breath.

How did the little hellcat escape and regain control from under his nose? She was more capable than he realized. He felt like a prisoner on his own ship. And maybe he was... but not for long.

He let his disembodied shadow float through the bulkhead to the brig to rally the guard. But he found no guard on duty. When he scanned for the guards, he found them inside the cells, prisoners. Damn the Sardar princess!

And he felt the engines revving as the freighter was changing course. No!

Malo focused on the old captain's mind. "Resume course to the planetoid immediately... or else."

He felt the captain's mind open and recognize his presence. *"Padshad? Where are you?"*

"I am on the Zantar... anchored to the freighter... where else?"

"The Sardar queen said you were gone and left her in charge."

"All lies. The traitorous bitch put me to sleep. Obey me. She doesn't have to know I'm awake. Do not fear. You won't have to suffer a woman in charge for long. When we reach our destination, you will be handsomely rewarded for your loyal service."

"Aye, aye, Padshad. Correcting course in a wide curve, so the engines will not change their rhythm."

"Good man." Malo shuddered at the captain's fickle loyalty.

Now, he must order the Anvad generals to take care of Kefira for him, discreetly and efficiently... and free him from his golden cage.

Chapter Eleven

With Karak at her side, Kefira stood at the end of the oval table, in the freighter's conference hold, where she'd gathered her officers. Only six remained after the Marauders' attack. How things had changed in such a short time. Ten days ago, they had bowed and treated her with high honors. Now, they gave her sideways glances and grudgingly sat around the table.

Kefira's confidence plummeted when she realized these men valued appearances above all and only respected her Sardar nobility when she looked like a princess. Right now, without the rich silk uniform symbolizing her rank, she didn't look like a queen or a military leader. The officers glanced with disdain at her disheveled, ragged appearance, without makeup or jewelry, wearing maintenance overalls from the supply closet. And the drab lighting didn't help any.

The bruise at her temple ached and pounded her head. But she must soldier on.

"Where is our Padshad?" The young officer in impeccable blue uniform frowned at her overalls. "We only answer to Padshad Malo."

"Malo is no longer in charge. I am." Kefira straightened her back.

Karak huffed then calmly licked his front paw while displaying his long fangs. Great show of support. Good boy.

The officers fidgeted in their seats. At least, they did not leave the table. Small victory.

"Where is the Padshad?"

"Malo is safe." Kefira took a deep breath. "But I have distressing news... The dreaded Stygian Order, who nearly caused the destruction of all life in the galaxy three cycles ago, has returned... and Malo is an important member of that evil sect."

A general frowned, another's eyes widened. The other men at the table mumbled to each other. Did they doubt her words? The words of a Sardar?

Kefira shuddered at the thought but wouldn't be intimidated. "Helsara sent me a vision a while back, and now the threat has been confirmed."

"Confirmed? What threat?" An older man rose from his seat. "Sardar, with all due respect, we've seen no evidence of what you say..."

Since when did her word require evidence? She pointed to the bruise on her temple. "This is your proof. And a Sardar never lies!" They should believe that. "Malo wears the seal of the Stygian Order branded on his chest!"

The officers mumbled, some in shock, others in protest. They still didn't believe her. How could this be? Did Malo's grip on them still linger?

Kefira cleared her throat. "Padshad Malo lied to us. He is fulfilling the Stygian Order's agenda. He was taking us to an isolated planetoid, where he planned to deliver our people to be sacrificed to an army of bloodthirsty Cyborg."

The officers stared with wide eyes... surprise or incredulity?

"Cyborg? Ridiculous!" a strong voice shouted, but she didn't see who it was.

"It's the truth!" Kefira steeled her resolve. "Helsara showed them to me. They come from another galaxy, wear black armor, have weapons coming out of their metal arms, and they feed on blood."

An older general slammed his fist on the table. "This is blasphemy against our Padshad!"

"Watch your words in the presence of a Sardar, General. And think." Kefira wouldn't be intimidated. Her people needed her. Unlike these officers, only interested in maintaining their ranks and privileges, her people were innocent and deserved to live.

"Did Malo ever tell you where he was leading us, or why?"

"Not exactly. A Padshad has his reasons." The old general mumbled the words. "But I have no doubt he was doing what's best for our people."

"Malo only does what's best for Malo." She stared at the officers in turn. "I bet he promised you all kinds of rewards if you helped him."

The men at the table glanced at each other sideways. She didn't have to read their minds to realize they were guilty of taking bribes. All of them. Her blood heated at the thought.

"Sardar!" A seasoned officer called from the far end of the table. "For what possible reason would Padshad Malo ever betray his own people?"

"The usual reasons, greed and power. Or, maybe he's a victim of the Stygian Order and fell under their evil influence." Kefira kept her head high, aware any of these men could shoot her at any moment.

The officers remained silent, deep in thought. Did they believe her now?

"Malo was the one who hired the Marauders who attacked us two weeks ago."

A low murmur circulated around the table.

Kefira's hope returned slowly as she explained. "When the Marauders failed, he came in person. He had a small army on the

Zantar. If his ploy to be crowned Padshad hadn't worked, he would have raided our freighter and taken it by force."

"Sardar, these are grave accusations… and speaking against the Padshad is a capital offense." The warning in the male voice didn't escape her.

"With all due respect, Sardar, it looks as if you've suffered some trauma that may have caused the loss of your senses." That officer used a compassionate tone, but his threat was unmistakable.

Karak emitted a low growl that agitated his whiskers and bared his fangs.

"I am as sane as a person can be." Kefira wished she had a blaster, given that all these men were armed. Thank Helsara for Karak's loyalty.

An old general shook his head in disapproval. Not a good sign.

"I already spoke to the captain. We are sailing toward the Land of Many Waters again. After all, it was our initial plan. That's what Helsara wants us to do, and the safest place for our people."

"But, Sardar, it's highly irregular for the queen to give orders, even in the absence of our Padshad."

"Not at all." She stared down the young officer. "I am still your Sardar. A descendant of Helsara to guide our people. I used to give you orders all the time. And in the absence of the Padshad, I rule."

"But Sardar, what you say is outrageous!"

"Is it? When I confronted Malo, he admitted everything I just told you." Kefira didn't realize it would be so difficult to convince stubborn men, once they were free of Malo's influence.

When she attempted to read their minds, she hit a mental wall. How could they shield their thoughts since they didn't have Helsara's gifts? Was Malo still shielding their minds... did he still control them?

"Sardar, you have been through a lot. You should rest... and change into more suitable clothes for a woman of your rank." The old man's compassionate tone reeked of disdain.

Kefira glanced down at her gray maintenance overalls from the supply closet. "Who cares about clothes in a moment like this? Malo set us up for genocide, and all you can say is change into proper clothes?"

Picking up on her angry tone of voice, Karak growled menacingly.

The officer cast the big cat a circumspect glance and cleared his throat. "Trusting a woman is difficult enough, Sardar. But how can we believe the words of a queen who ignores proper decorum?"

"I see..." Something didn't add up. Before Malo showed up, these officers used to follow her orders without protest. By now, they should be free of his evil influence. And if they weren't, if Malo still controlled them in his sleep, Kefira must make sure the captain followed Helsara's route.

"Computer? Where are we headed?"

"We recently resumed course to the planetoid, Sardar." The synthetic voice emanated from the bulkhead.

Kefira raged inside at the captain's betrayal, but she managed to keep her voice calm. "Computer, make corrections to head for the Land of Many Waters immediately."

"Sorry, Sardar. Only the highest authority can order a change of course." The synthetic voice rasped. Was the computer mocking her?

"And I am the highest authority on this freighter." Kefira couldn't help the frustration in her voice.

Karak pivoted his ears, then huffed and snorted for good measure.

"I understand, Sardar." No nuance in the computer voice, only logic. "Still, I need the captain to confirm and approve, in order to alter course."

Kefira sighed. The computer wouldn't budge. "We are flying to our doom."

The officers around the table seemed strangely indifferent, almost bored. Did they not care? Or did Malo dictate their reactions?

Tightening her jaw, Kefira made eye contact with each officer. "Follow me to the bridge, and we shall discuss this matter with the captain in person."

Grudgingly, the officers rose from their chairs and slowly followed her along the corridors, dragging their feet, or waiting for something to happen.

As she marched toward the bridge beside Karak, Kefira wished she had her blasters and blades, but there had been no time, not for clothes, not even for weapons. She must regain control of the situation, and fast.

* * *

Kefira resolutely stepped on the command bridge. "Captain? Why did you disobey my orders?"

"I obey all legal orders, Sardar." The captain shuffled his feet. "Presently, I am following the Padshad's orders."

"The Padshad is not here. I am the queen, and I give the orders." Kefira projected her voice so all on the command deck could hear.

"But you are only a woman, Sardar. Why should I obey a woman while there is a legitimate Padshad?" He scoffed. "Especially a woman wearing a drab jumpsuit."

Karak growled and bared his fangs at the captain.

Kefira wished she had her blaster. "I will have you removed from your post for blunt disobedience, Captain."

"This is not your pretty little ship, Sardar. I am the captain on this freighter, and I decide whose commands to obey. I take my orders directly from our Padshad."

"Me, too." A general drew his blaster and aimed it at Kefira's head.

Karak leapt and pounced. The general fell back with a scream. The blaster fired in the rafters then fell to the decking. Then Karak crunched the man's neck, and the scream ended. Good boy.

Another officer drew and aimed at the big cat.

But Karak leapt high and swiftly disappeared in the overhead shadows. Good.

Kefira picked up the dead general's blaster and shot the officer who'd aimed at Karak. The man froze, a black laser hole in the middle of his forehead, and a surprised look on his still face. Then he fell like timber.

"Attacking a Sardar or her bodyguard is punishable by death." Kefira narrowed her eyes in warning. "Anyone else wants to challenge my command?" She spotted the big cat high up on the bracing beams, glad he was unharmed.

The remaining officers averted their gaze, looking down and sideways at each other.

Then she aimed her blaster at the captain's head. "Change course immediately, or I'll relieve you of your command with my next shot."

The old captain lowered his head in a reluctant nod of agreement, exposing the wrinkled skin of his bald head. "Aye, aye, Sardar."

Proud of herself, Kefira smiled inwardly. Finally, some respect.

Then a shot resounded behind her. Paralyzing pain exploded in her lower back. The blaster slipped from her grip as if in slow motion, then clattered to the decking. Someone she couldn't see had stunned her. She was paralyzed. How dare they shoot a Sardar?

Her vision narrowed. The bridge bulkhead closed upon her. She spasmed on the decking, unable to control her movements. She tasted metal and wanted to scream but could not. She wanted to kick the men who picked her up and dragged her by the shoulders out of the bridge, but she was powerless.

As they half carried half dragged her along the drab corridors of the old freighter, Kefira fell in and out of consciousness, unable to focus. Along the way, curious civilians gawked at seeing her manhandled. She must keep fighting, for them.

Then she recognized a sign indicating the direction to the freighter's holding cells. By the frozen hells of Laxxar! This was not her personal ship. This time, she couldn't use hidden emergency routines to get out of her jail.

Her attempt to regain control of the situation had backfired. Who would save her people now? May Helsara protect them all.

* * *

Malo rejoiced at Kefira's arrest, but he couldn't believe the incompetence of the *Zantar's* crew. Once freed from their cells by the Anvad officers, they should have been able to reverse Kefira's reprogramming of his ship...and gotten him out of his luxurious prison. What was taking so long?

"Can someone open the farking doors?" His voice came muted by his breathing mask. And with the com system down in his royal suite, no one could hear him.

Couldn't they at least restore communications in his quarters? As a result of his silent confinement, Malo could only express his orders in their thick minds, and roam the ship in a shadow state, invisible to them.

He swore under his breath as he watched his men fumble. He needed to get out with his physical body, look them in the eyes, intimidate them, and threaten them in person with his own voice. A mute, shadow presence did not have sufficient impact to maintain control for long.

As hard as he could focus on Kefira's mind, he couldn't read or penetrate it to figure out what she did to his ship. Damn her Sardar gifts! And how did she manage to jettison his small army into space? All Malo had now was the *Zantar's* civilian crew and the few Anvad officers managing the freighter.

The little lioness would pay dearly for this aggressive move. No one humiliated the Padshad in front of his officers. He needed them to control the populace.

Finally, the air cleared from the sleeping gas and Malo could remove his mask. Then the cabin hatch opened.

Malo stepped out, barely containing his impatience, and glared at the crewman in red uniform. "It took you long enough!"

"Sorry, Padshad." The man bowed deeply. "The encrypted programming was difficult to bypass."

"Tell it to someone who cares!" Malo marched angrily along the corridors. He hoped his father wouldn't learn he'd been bested by a pesky woman. "Computer, reinforce the red shield to battle frequency."

"Aye, Padshad. Shields at maximum."

"Good." Malo would make sure Kefira couldn't contact anyone. She was his to do as he pleased, and no one would come to her rescue.

He smiled inside. Her indomitable nature would contribute greatly to the offspring he planned on having with her.

*　*　*

Blake moaned as he turned in his sleep. This wasn't his usual dream about Kefira, where they talked and laughed, and enjoyed each-other's company. Nor was it a vague premonition of things to come.

In this nightmare, Kefira was dragged to a dingy cell. At least, it wasn't an airlock. But he saw it from above, through layers of metal bars, with the eyes of someone perched in the high cross-beams of the Anvad freighter.

The shock of seeing Kefira in such dire condition woke him. He sat up on his bunk, but the nightmare still went on in his mind. It wasn't a dream. Someone was transmitting these images directly into his brain, someone who cared, someone in anguish. *"Who is this? Identify yourself!"*

"Karak protect. Angel Blake protect. Mom need help!" The cat's panicked mind voice explained many things, yet, how could they communicate through the red shield?

Blake closed his eyes and visualized the Anvad freighter, on a parallel path to the planetoid. He probed the red shield with his mind, without success. It still held. Could this be a Stygian illusion? A trap?

Unlikely. These twisted cultists would never degrade themselves by using lowly animals. Besides, Blake recognized the big cat's mind voice, and his desperation felt genuine.

"Good boy, Karak. Show me what happened."

Images of Kefira's attempt at neutralizing Malo unfolded in his mind. Although simplistic and not fully understood by the big cat, they showed her initial victory, then the betrayal by her officers. And now, she was rotting in a dark, disgusting cell aboard the Anvad freighter.

"Well, Karak, my friend, don't despair. Since we can talk to each other, we must help Kefira together."

"Karak help. Karak protect. Karak like Angel Blake."

"Good boy, Karak. This is what we are going to do…"

Chapter Twelve

Slowly emerging from her lethargy, Kefira groaned. Her fingers cramped. As she attempted to stretch on the metal decking, all the muscles in her body screamed in protest to the paralyzing strike. The chill of the air scrubbers penetrated her overalls as she lay on cold metal. By Helsara! She'd failed... again. How could she save her people now?

A dim bulb flickered some distance to the left, barely dissipating the darkness. Over the purr of the engines and air-scrubbers, a faint regular drip ticked the seconds, like a leaky faucet. The smell of rust and decay made her want to retch.

By the unsteady light, she detected no surveillance cameras in the dingy cell or directly outside. Thick metal bars and solid locks lined rows upon rows of stacked metal cages. Why so many? She wondered what the freighter had carried in these cages in the past. Illegal prisoners? Slaves? Large wild animals? All illicit trades. The very thought made her sick to her stomach.

No wonder she never liked the shifty-eyed captain. What kind of Anvad would deal in such contraband? The kind with no honor… like the officer who shot her in the back. How humiliating. At least, he'd used the stun setting… killing a Sardar was still taboo, but for how long?

Malo had won… again. She had no doubt he now had full control of the *Zantar* and the freighter. He must be laughing at her.

Too bad her plan didn't work. She should have killed Malo at the coronation, but how? She shuddered at the memory of the blade unable to penetrate his chest, with not even a drop of blood… and he'd laughed at her. Could he be immortal as he claimed? If he were, how could she ever win?

She grabbed the thick bars and pulled herself up, struggling to get to her feet. She needed to learn more about her situation. "Hey, it's cold in here. Anyone listening?"

Only silence, except for the faint drip.

No other inmates, no guards, no one around. How long had it been since she'd lost consciousness? Hours? Days? Her stomach growled. How long since she last ate? She'd been abandoned without food or water, left to rot, and apparently forgotten.

At least, Karak had escaped. She found solace in that fact. *"Where are you, big boy, are you okay?"*

No response… she quickly erased from her mind the image of Karak being thrown out of an airlock. The big cat was agile and resourceful. By Helsara, she hoped he was alive. And if anyone hurt him, Kefira would make them pay.

A chill seized her as a cold presence invaded her brain. She closed her mind against being read but couldn't resist the intrusion.

"So, you are awake, little lioness." The familiar voice iced her spine.

"Malo? Get out of my head!" She shouted to hide her weakened state.

Then she saw him, stepping out of the shadows, the dim illumination barely revealing his face. Malo stood there, immobile, staring at her. His dark eyes shone despite the darkness.

"You really thought you could outsmart me?" His lips didn't move, but she could hear him in her head. *"Look at you, now. Your own people betrayed you, abandoned you, and no one is coming to save you. You will die alone, and no one will care."*

"How did you get inside my mind?" Her throat tightened.

"You thought you could resist me?" His self-satisfied smile reeked of pure evil. "Your Sardar gifts are no match for my talents, little lioness. You can't hide your thoughts from me anymore. And soon, I will control you like a puppet, and you'll do anything I ask."

"No." A slight tremor coursed down her spine. Could he really do that? By Helsara, she hoped not. "I would rather die than help you exterminate our people."

"I was afraid you wouldn't cooperate willingly." His raspy tone attested to repressed rage. "I could start killing children one by one in front of you."

"You are a monster." Would he dare? It didn't matter. "Since you intend to kill them all anyway, it won't change my mind. I will not help you."

An invisible dagger stabbed Kefira's heart. She screamed and collapsed on the metal decking of the cell. She moaned, clutching her chest, in excruciating pain, but no hilt protruded from her heart. Yet, she felt blood running down her body, and her life force slowly ebbing. Was she dying?

Sonorous laughter exploded around her. Malo's evil laughter. "No, Kef, you are still alive, but you will die a million little deaths like this one if you don't do what I ask."

The pain eased. Kefira caught her breath.

"And what do you ask?" Not that Kefira would give him anything but keeping him talking might give her time to recover.

"I have many plans for you, my little hellcat. But I won't tell you yet, since you are not ready to comply." His laughter echoed through the empty cages and off the metal bulkhead like a malevolent breeze. "In the meantime, I'm enjoying this new relationship of ours. This is the natural order of things, with the man dictating, and the woman submitting."

"I will never submit!" Damn the evil man. Kefira couldn't even plot against him since he'd found a way to read her mind.

Excruciating pain speared her mid-section... she cried and folded in two under the agony. How long could she tolerate this kind of torture? Not long enough.

Malo just stood there, waiting for her to give up. "If you joined me, you could become a great queen."

"I will never join you!" But his words gave her hope. He didn't want her dead, at least not yet. She must remain strong.

An invisible arrow shot her heart. She heard her own scream, as if it came from someone else. As if her body was foreign to her. Then she felt herself rising, leaving her body behind, hovering above it, seeing it lying, unresponsive, in the filthy holding cell.

She recognized the phenomenon. It had happened before, when she meditated, and her astral form traveled to higher planes, to consult with Helsara. She was tempted to remain in this disembodied state, where there was no pain. Maybe she could fly away and contact Blake...

As her astral form rose through the layers of metal, she hit the red shields and she slammed back into her physical body with a cry of anguish.

Malo sneered. "You can't escape so easily. I have important plans for you."

Kefira steeled her resolve. "I will not cooperate. I will never cooperate."

"Oh, but you will, little lioness." His silky voice caressed her. "You will carry my seed and raise my children."

"Never." Another invisible stab, in the shoulder this time, made her wish she'd remained in her astral state.

"It's not for you to decide. This is all your fault." Regret flickered in his dark eyes. "Our relationship could have been a glorious one, but you had to make things difficult."

"Me? You are the one leading our people to the slaughter." Kefira couldn't believe the self-righteous cur.

"Just an unfortunate detail." He smirked. "Once, we had it all. We were happy. Why couldn't you remain the sunny young girl I fell in love with?"

Past images of their happy life together flashed upon Kefira's mind. Not her memories, but his. Their love flourished then, in sunny details and bright colors. Then all turned gray.

"You spoiled everything with your stubborn attitude and twisted ideas!"

"You are the twisted one."

"No woman should ever rule. It's an insult to tradition." He frowned. "Your greed for power led us here. Because of your actions, I have no choice but to keep you where you can't interfere."

Kefira wanted to protest but realized it would be wasted energy. She must recover to continue the fight.

Malo sneered. "You only have yourself to blame for your pitiful condition."

He dismissed her with a wave then vanished into the shadows. Had he ever been there in person? Did she imagine his presence? No, she could still feel remnants of pain from the injuries. Would she die from them? Or was it all illusion and sorcery?

What if she died in that cell? Who would protect the Anvad? She must face the torture and keep fighting. Maybe, if she remained strong, she could get through to Malo and stop the genocide.

Kefira struggled to grasp filaments of her thoughts in order to remain awake, but her consciousness faded, ever so slowly. Darkness lurked at the edges of her shrinking field of vision. Was she dying?

As the black cold enveloped her, Kefira realized she'd lost. Her people were doomed because of her failure. Their deaths would be on her conscience. May Helsara protect them all.

But even Helsara would never forgive Kefira for this horrible fiasco.

* * *

On the freighter's command bridge, the old captain attempted to land the freighter.

Malo, hands clasped behind his back, rocked from foot to foot, like a man on a boat, to compensated for the unusual pull making the ship lurch and roll like a drunken sailor in low altitude. "Why is it taking so long?"

"Padshad, this is a big ship, and the bizarre gravity on this planetoid isn't helping."

Malo wondered what caused it. He didn't remember this from his last landing, when he'd come to be anointed. "Just do your job."

"Aye, Padshad. The instruments are going berserk. I'll have to land in manual." The old captain's face tensed as he leaned on the levers to compensate for the roll.

On the forward screen showing the approaching ground, Malo watched as his personal crew landed his royal raptor, the *Zantar,* on a pad near the main entrance, just in case... One should always be prepared for a quick exit. Old habits died hard.

He expected to be received with high honors. His first mission as First Lieutenant had been a smashing success. His father would be proud. But where was the welcoming committee?

Malo noticed a black ship of foreign design on one of the many landing pads, a Barracuda, with fins, gills, and a battery of weapons on the hull. He shivered as he sensed an alien vibe about it. Was it the

218

cause of the strange gravity and instruments disruption?

But Baalmordo, the Prince of Darkness, wasn't anywhere near the planetoid. So, who was that?

Malo let his mind explore the alien Barracuda. He recognized the energy signature of Baalmordo. He winced and withdrew his mind from the ship. Cyborg! The ship had brought an advanced party of black-clad Cyborg.

Since the Cyborg came from a different galaxy, their presence might explain the strange gravity field. But this was only a small contingent, probably an advanced delegation to insure a smooth arrival for their alien master, Baalmordo.

Why didn't his father tell him about this?

The captain finally landed the freighter, to the applause of the few officers.

A disembodied voice came over the com system. "Welcome everyone to our humble home. Now, please exit the freighter, and follow the marked path into the complex."

Malo and the officers went down to the lower level to make certain the debarking went well.

The ship had landed close enough to the rocky cliff, so that everyone could easily walk the distance. The quickest way to move five thousand offerings.

When the belly ramp unfolded, Malo felt the rush of fresh air on his face. He disembarked first, surprised at the lack of welcoming committee. He hid his disappointment. Why wasn't he officially greeted as the First Lieutenant? After all, he'd completed his important mission with flying colors.

He scanned the paved road leading to the cliff. Not to the main entrance, but to a narrow side tunnel with its own arched door. A row of stiff guards in black armor and blind helmets flanked the path on both sides to guide the passengers into the cave complex.

The black soldiers didn't wear the Stygian colors. They had human shape, but Malo suspected they were something else. A quick mind scan confirmed it. He flinched at the contact. These were Cyborg... more machines than living tissue, with a rudimentary brain, using blood as a main energy source... a design intended to motivate them to kill.

Malo couldn't help but shudder at the sight of these killing machines, but he also felt proud. Soon, according to plan, they would become his personal army. He would lead these Cyborg in the conquest of the galaxy in the name of the Stygian Order... Then he would get rid of his father and take his place as Sorcerer Supreme.

Hands clutched behind his back, Malo watched the Anvad people slowly walking down the freighter's belly ramp. They blinked in the pale sunlight, and a slight breeze ruffled their hair.

One woman attempted to go back inside, slowing the flow. An Anvad officer grabbed her arm and forced her to move forward. She panicked, refusing to disembark. Then the officer shoved her, and she fell. Several Anvad helped her back to her feet, glaring at the officer who had the gall to mistreat another Anvad.

A mistake on his part. Malo took note of the officer's clumsiness. He needed the Anvad to trust their superiors. Sheep behaved better when they trusted their shepherd.

The woman stood up, brushing a bloody knee, averting her gaze, like a good little sheep. A Cyborg standing next to Malo sniffed the air at the sight of blood and made a strange sound deep in his throat, like an animal smelling prey.

Malo shook his head in disgust. Unfortunately, the superior species often needed to use special warriors like these Cyborg, to impose their will on others. At least, these looked somewhat human… although Malo hadn't peeked behind the smooth helmet, he suspected they had a face.

The Anvad officers now smiled as they encouraged their people to walk faster. "All questions will be answered inside. Please keep moving."

The flow of Anvad people kept walking past Malo. He nodded and smiled like a benevolent sovereign. His presence would reassure his people. In their naivety, they trusted their Padshad. How pathetic.

After the crowd had filed through the arched door, the Cyborg followed them inside.

Then Malo's crew in red uniforms brought Kefira, in chains, half carrying and half dragging her by the shoulders. Her head was down, her short dark hair unkept. She looked unconscious, or she had no energy to resist. He may have gone too far with the torture... but she asked for it with her stubborn streak.

The Anvad officers still standing atop the ramp observed their Sardar being taken away in silence. One averted his gaze.

"Take her to her special cell, in solitary confinement." Malo kept his voice strong but seeing her like that was painful. He still missed their young love. He wished she had accepted his offer to reign at his side.

His red clad crew, familiar with the facility, nodded and half carried, half dragged Kefira toward a different entrance, a small metallic door at the base of the cliff.

Then the captain of the freighter emerged from his ship and walked down the ramp toward Malo, followed by the general and the four other Anvad officers.

The captain bowed. "What about us, Padshad? Where are our accommodations?"

"Ah, yes." Malo savored his power over lesser men. "I suggest you follow the same path as our people. It will become clear as you get inside."

The old man smiled, greed in his small eyes. "You also promised us a substantial reward for bringing our people here, Padshad."

"Your reward?" Malo bit his lips not to explode in laughter. These greedy traitors dared ask for payment. "Oh, you'll get your reward all right. Just follow the path to the arched entrance."

* * *

Safe in the *Blue Phantom*, cloaked and invisible to all, Blake approached the planetoid and scanned the area. A few small Cyborg ships of Barracuda design floated in orbit, although the full Cyborg force with the Leviathans was still several planetary systems away.

Since the Anvad freighter had landed, Karak should be contacting him soon. But would the big cat be able to do so? The red shield around the asteroid looked even stronger than the one generated by the *Zantar*.

223

Blake focused on the red shield surrounding the planetoid. Just as he feared, it reeked of evil magic. No way to bring the *Blue Phantom* to the surface, but he and his angels might be able to rematerialize on the other side.

"Karak, can you hear me?"

No response. He would have to wait for the big cat to initiate the link. For some strange reason, Karak could reach him through the shield, but Blake could not reach the big cat.

Maybe it was due to the difference in mind wave frequencies. The Stygian Order did not deal with lowly animals and never bothered to study them. They didn't consider them a threat, so their shields didn't stop their slightly different mind waves.

Then Blake recognized the big cat's particular mind vibration.

"Karak protect."

"Good boy, Karak. So glad you are safe. Tell me everything."

* * *

Kefira came to with the rattle of chains on the concrete floor. So, she was still alive… she hadn't died from her imaginary wounds… but she could hardly feel her body anymore. Two strong men in red uniforms dragged her along dark corridors that reeked of mildew. Were they taking her to another cell? No. This was stone and concrete, not metal. She suddenly realized this wasn't the freighter.

Had they landed already? Helsara help them all!

Barely opening her eyes, she raised her head and spotted a familiar shadow, moving up above on a ledge. She spoke to him in her mind. *"Karak?"*

The shadow froze then resumed its high parallel path. *"Karak protect."*

"Good boy, Karak, but stay hidden. Stay safe."

"Angel Blake here. Angel Blake protect." The feline's mind voice held much confidence and hope.

Blake was here? Kefira and her people could certainly use his help now. But it couldn't be. Blake was far away and out of reach. Yet, it must be true. The big cat would never lie. She forced her mind to focus on Blake, but her reaching thoughts only met the sinister vibration of evil shields.

She blinked when her guards dragged her into a brightly lit underground room. The place smelled like a hospital or a medical lab. She heard the beep of sophisticated instruments. This was no cell. They lifted her and dropped her on a cold metal table, where she collapsed. Bright flood lights blinded her. She was being restrained on a surgical table.

Then someone stabbed her in the arm, and all went black.

Chapter Thirteen

In the tunnel carved inside the rock, Malo stopped in front of an imposing door and nodded to the black sentry. A Cyborg! The guard grunted then opened the door, letting out the fragrant smoke of burning spices and sacrificial bones.

As he walked into the luxurious accommodations, Malo noticed the warmth of the open fire. Candles and torches cast dancing lights and shadows, giving the impression of live power. Red and black velvet curtains, as well as tapestries of serpent and dagger in a circle hung on the walls, warming the cold stone.

Against the back wall, his father, Matchitehew, sat on a red velvet throne, in white ceremonial robes and red cape. The black crystal stone on his chest flared. So many theatrical elements in the setting and the mannerism... could they be hiding a lack of true power? In any case, self-importance was a weakness Malo could exploit.

"Father!" Malo stepped with confidence. He felt his father probing his mental shield, but the shield held. Good.

"Son!" Matchitehew rose majestically at Malo's approach. The sorcerer's honeyed smile made it impossible to guess his true feelings. "Welcome home. Today, you make me very proud."

"It doesn't feel like it." Malo bit back a harsher comment, glad he could hide his thoughts from his father. "I was expecting a more public welcome, especially since I fulfilled my mission so brilliantly."

"You did, and I understand your need for recognition... but more pressing matters required my attention." The haughty turn of the head forbade any question or comment on the subject.

Malo held his frustration in check. "What's happening here? Why do we have Cyborg soldiers working security?"

"The Exalted Lord Baalmordo is closer than I first believed. We must show him we can provide for his Cyborg." Matchitehew caressed the black gem on his chest. It flared again and emitted a strange purple light that pulsed like a living thing.

"Why is the crystal active now?" Malo could feel the pulse in his very bones. He'd only seen the gem do this inside the temple, during ritual sacrifices.

Matchitehew's smile widened. "Since the Dark Prince entered our galaxy, the black crystal comes alive of its own."

"Baalmordo is feeding the crystal?" Malo realized the jewel could channel great amounts of dark energy. "Does the black stone enhance your powers as a sorcerer?"

"At least a hundredfold. It's exhilarating... and it also gives me new abilities." Matchitehew held up the black crystal and gazed at it with wonder in his shiny black eyes.

Malo would definitely have to get hold of that stone. He could use its power.

His father released the pendant and his face turned serious. "But the Exalted Lord's demands keep increasing... especially in blood."

Malo scoffed. "I brought you plenty of blood."

"Yes." Matchitehew nodded. "But we may need more to seal the pact."

"More blood?" Malo wondered whose blood and how much, but he didn't dare ask. And who would be left to rule over, after the Cyborg had killed the masses?

Matchitehew nodded. "We should feed the Cyborg delegation, and soon."

Malo smiled. "May I suggest we sacrifice the Anvad officers first? I isolated them, but when they finally realize they struck a bad bargain, they might stir up trouble and become a nuisance."

"Now, you are thinking like a leader." Matchitehew flipped back the sides of his red cape, as if for dramatic effect. "I should also tell you that you need not worry about the Sardar princess."

"Kefira?" Malo didn't trust his father. "I wasn't worried." Until now…

"I gave the order to extract her genetic material." His father sounded proud. "After that is done, she will no longer be needed, and can be sacrificed."

"Sacrificed?" Heat crept up Malo's neck. Kef was his, and only he should decide her fate. No one else.

He wanted to vent his outrage but something inside him strangled his words. As hard as he tried, he could not express his feelings or speak against his father. When he reached for his blaster, he realized he couldn't raise a hand or a weapon on him either.

Fark! His father never had so much power. Did the black crystal protect him?

This didn't bode well for Malo's future plans. He would have to use deceit and finesse rather than confrontation and brute force. Maybe he could help his father hang himself by triggering his weaknesses and insecurities.

Matchitehew seemed oblivious to his son's struggle. "The blood of the Sardar princess will constitute a special treat for the Exalted Lord Baalmordo himself, later, when he arrives in the flesh."

"Of course, Father." Malo bit his lips, hating the submissive words pronounced against his will.

He never agreed to sacrifice Kefira. And he hated being used. But a superior power prevented him from expressing even the slightest objection. At least, he could still keep his thoughts from his father, and he had a little time to maneuver before this Baalmordo arrived. Malo wouldn't give up the dream of Kefira ruling at his side.

"In the meantime, we are having a ceremony to feed the Cyborg advanced party. Upon your suggestion, we shall sacrifice the Anvad officers." His father stepped aside to leave then glanced back. "I'm counting on your attendance at my side."

Malo felt himself kneel and bow against his will. How humiliating. He seethed inside but couldn't help the words flowing out. "Of course, Father."

After his father left the room, Malo was free to stand up and move again. So, the protective power of the crystal only worked in close proximity. Maybe Malo could keep his distance as he orchestrated an unfortunate accident for his father…

Then Malo would inherit the title and take possession of the precious black gem.

* * *

Kefira regained consciousness on the cold surgical table but kept her eyes mostly closed, peeking between her thick lashes.

She was naked under the white sheet and surrounded by medical staff.

"We now have plenty of DNA," a medic said. "We were lucky she was ovulating. We have more than we need."

They'd harvested her genetic material? That's what Malo meant when he said he had plans for her and she would carry his children. Kefira wanted to protest, but she couldn't move or speak. And she had difficulty focusing her thoughts.

"Get her into a ritual robe and take her to her special cell." The man's order came from beyond her field of vision.

Two sturdy medics dressed her in a long white dress of simple linen. Strange choice of garment for a prisoner. Then they lifted her from the table, and dragged her limp body along brightly lit concrete corridors. She peeked between her eyelashes and saw wall markings and banners... Stygian symbols of serpent and dagger in a circle.

Helsara help her! This must be the order's secret base. She was in the maw of the evil sect. Her stomach churned. She would have retched if she'd had anything in her stomach.

"Karak protect. Angel Blake protect." The big cat's voice roamed inside her head.

Was she imagining it? Maybe not. Paralyzed and helpless, Kefira focused on Karak's reassuring presence. *"I'm glad you are free, big boy. Did you say earlier you spoke to Blake? Is he close by?"*

"Angel Blake watch."

"From his ship in space?" Kefira assumed the planetoid and the Stygian complex were shielded... with more than technology. Even deep underground, she could feel the disturbing vibrations of evil energy.

"Yes." The big cat sounded certain. *"Angel Blake watch."*

"Where are the Anvad people. Are they alive? Are they okay?"

"Okay, yes." Karak sounded grave and solemn. *"In big cave."*

Kefira released a long breath. There was still hope. *"How do you communicate with Blake?"*

"Karak speak... Karak show Angel Blake." The big cat sounded proud.

So, Karak could transmit words and images through the Stygian shield. Good to know.

"Show Blake where our people are held. Show him the inside of the cave complex. Tell him to free the Anvad first. The bad people need me, so I am in no immediate danger." If these mad sorcerers wanted her to carry Malo's children to term, they wouldn't kill her anytime soon.

"Karak tell. Karak show."

"Good boy." Of course, since they had her DNA, Kefira may no longer be needed...

and they called the white dress a ritual robe. For what kind of ritual? but Malo specifically said she would carry his children, not just provide DNA.

Her handlers stopped in front of a heavy metal door. One medic applied his hand to a pad on the side. The door slid open with a puff of compressed air. The medics threw Kefira inside the brightly lit cell. She fell limp on the white floor. It smelled of strong disinfectant. The door closed with a definite clang.

She was a helpless prisoner.

She called Karak in her mind, but no longer felt his presence. She let her mind roam but could not see, or sense anything outside her cell. These special walls prevented her from communicating mind to mind with the outside.

She shuddered at the thought of her people being led to the slaughter. How could she help them from inside a prison?

Kefira's last strand of optimism broke. Her fate, and that of her people were out of her hands. She felt so helpless… and paralyzed by drugs, she couldn't even wipe the tears rolling down the side of her face.

"Blake, I'm counting on you. May Helsara protect us all." But although he might be listening, she suspected the angel couldn't hear her plea.

* * *

Blake hurried toward the control bridge of the *Blue Phantom.* Karak's most recent images, and the rapid advance of the Cyborg army pounded in his head like a dark omen. In the cat's simple mind, the dire condition of the prisoners, and what was done to Kefira seemed ominous. Blake must find a way to rescue them before it was too late.

As he stepped in, five angel officers sat in a circle in midair, eyes closed, guiding the ship through space.

"Graziella?" Blake still hoped they could save Kefira and her people. "Can we manifest through the red shields or not?"

Graziella opened her eyes. Her levitating body lowered itself to the blue crystal bench, then she unfolded her legs and stood. "The readings indicate traces of a chemical compound surrounding the planetoid."

An image of the shields and list of their chemical composition manifested in front of them.

Graziella indicated a specific element. "This deadly compound is generated by the red shields and will destroy any living tissue attempting to cross without the proper codes."

"What if we cross in ethereal form?" Blake's patience was evaporating.

"We may or may not survive the trip through the shield... but it would definitely kill the human prisoners we plan to transport through." Her last words echoed like a final verdict.

"By the frozen hells of Laxxar!" Blake struggled to control his frustration. "Can we materialize on the planetoid, then disable the shields once we are on the surface?"

"Maybe… assuming we survive the one-way trip, but there is no guarantee of that."

An unbidden glimpse of Kefira, crying, paralyzed, helpless in a bare white cell flashed on Blake's mind. He blinked and the image vanished. Was it a message from Karak? No. The flash had a different feel. It came in real time, not through someone's mind. Were the shields glitchy? Or did his feelings for her play tricks on his mind?

No. He didn't imagine this. He could feel her, so close… yet, he couldn't reach her or speak to her. She and her people might die because he couldn't cross the Stygian shields.

He sighed his frustration. "Keep probing these shields. Find me some way to circumvent or disable them. We must rescue the Anvad before they become Cyborg fodder."

"Aye, aye, Captain." Graziella returned to the meditation bench, sat, crossed her legs, and closed her eyes. Then her body rose straight up, to join the circle of officers levitating in midair.

"May the Formless One help us!" Blake mumbled as he stepped out of the command bridge.

But the Formless One only cared about the balance of good and evil in the universe. To such an entity, Blake's personal feelings and preferences didn't matter at all.

* * *

Malo smiled inwardly as he waved his hand over the pad controlling the door of the luxurious holding cell.

His smile widened as he nodded to the Anvad officers sitting on the velvet couches, sipping a stiff drink. "Gentlemen, I hope you are enjoying your special accommodations. They are reserved for visitors of the highest rank."

The six men set down their glasses and rose to meet him.

The general saluted. "Much obliged, Padshad. But the snake and dagger symbols are a bit overwhelming. What kind of place is this?"

"You have the great privilege of being valued guests of the Stygian Order." Malo enjoyed their fear. They were traitors, all of them... and they shot the Sardar queen without his permission, then manhandled her. They deserved what was coming to them.

"I see…" The general raised his brow. "Also, it seems the door locks from the outside, Padshad."

Malo's smile came naturally. "It's for your own safety, of course. There are some unsavory characters wandering about. You wouldn't want to meet a bloodthirsty Cyborg in a dark corridor, would you?"

The officers glanced at each other with wide eyes.

This particular part of the job amused Malo immensely. "Now is the time to get your reward. There is a special ceremony planned for you. If you follow me, I shall lead you there."

Relief washed over their faces.

The old captain raised his hand. "Padshad, since there are less of us now, shall we also receive the share of the two officers who died?"

The captain was referring to the officers Kefira and her hellish cat killed on the command bridge of the freighter before her arrest. How precious! Malo nodded. "You will get all the riches you were promised and more."

As Malo led the small group through the torchlit corridors carved into the cliff, the old captain, the general, and the four lesser officers seemed to relax. Eagerness animated their eyes. Nothing was more entertaining to Malo than a sinister character getting his just reward.

"Padshad," the old captain bowed as he walked. "Where is the ceremony taking place?"

"In the temple, of course." The irony was priceless.

"What kind of temple? A Stygian temple? But we worship Helsara." The general straightened his posture and his walk turned stiff. He obviously didn't approve of the Stygian Order.

"Do not fret, General. The temple is just a gathering place where we bestow the highest honors." Malo's smile took no effort.

"Padshad, you wouldn't be a member of the Stygian Order, would you?" The general stopped himself from saying more. Was he starting to understand?

"What if I were?" Malo smiled inside.

The general gasped then marched in silence.

They walked past the wide arch of an artificial cave carved in the rock and closed by an iron gate with thick bars. Malo indicated the people visible beyond the gate. "This is where we housed the rest of the Anvad people... close to the temple. As you can see, your accommodations are much better than theirs."

"Indeed..." The general glanced right and left suspiciously. "If you don't mind my asking, Padshad, what's in store for the Anvad we brought here?"

So, be it. Malo took a deep breath. "I wish you hadn't asked, General, but since you did, they are going to be sacrificed."

"Sacrificed? You mean killed?" The look of horror on the general's face was priceless. "This is barbaric."

"I know." Malo relished their unease. "I am sad to say it's by necessity."

The captain of the freighter cleared his throat. His face turned pale. "All of them?"

"All of them." Malo managed a jovial smile. "Aren't you the lucky ones?"

The officers exchanged worried looks but as Malo read their minds, he realized they still believed they would be spared. How precious.

The old captain's eyes shifted toward his colleagues. "After we get our gold, we'll need a shuttle to leave this planetoid."

"Of course." Malo jubilated. "And what are you going to do with your loot?"

The old captain chuckled. "I'll go somewhere warm, with sand beaches, and pretty young women."

The general seemed to take heart. "I shall buy some estate on a newly settled planet and enjoy my retirement as a gentleman farmer."

"I wish you all good luck in your future endeavors." Malo found it so easy to feed their hopes. "Here we are."

The old captain pointed to the small arched door. "Is this the door to the temple? It seems small."

"It's a side door, Captain. For special guests only." Malo pushed the door open and stepped through the arched opening. "Please, come in."

The six men entered the empty temple then halted and gawked at the sight. Fires burned at both ends of the long altar. A few monks in red robes and capes busied themselves with last minute preparations, whispering in a quiet hurry.

"All that grandiose setting just for us?" the general asked in an awed whisper.

Malo relished this part of the job. "Your invaluable service deserves the greatest honor."

The door closed and locked behind them, startling the officers.

Malo smiled and pointed toward the central altar. "This way for our most honored guests, you are getting the best view of the festivities."

"Front row?" As he walked, the old captain glanced all around and up at the hanging banners, uncertainty in his steps. "That's a lot of serpents and daggers."

A lower rank officer nodded. "There is also a very unusual vibration in here. I wish I had my instruments. This must be a phenomenon specific to the planetoid."

"It's a very special place." Malo rejoiced. They could feel the vibrating power of dark energy. Good.

He led the officers around the altar, toward a group of burly hooded monks. He nodded to the monks. The strong men approached the Anvad officers from behind, seized their nape, and kicked the back of their knees, forcing them to kneel.

Cries of protest surged from the officers at this mistreatment, but the monks quickly tied their hands behind their backs.

"What is this?" The general struggled to stand up, but the big monk behind him pushed him back down.

"Glad you asked." Malo couldn't help a grin as he watched each monk swiftly tie the feet of his assigned officer then hook them to a long chain.

"How dare you?" The old captain's face turned red then purple.

"As I said…" Malo took his sweet time, enjoying every second. "You are the guests of honor. The highest honor of all. You are going to be the first of the Anvad sacrificed on this altar." Well… after his mother… but they didn't need to know that.

"This is an outrage! You gave us your word. What kind of Padshad doesn't keep his word?" The general was so naïve… but all the Anvad were.

A lower rank officer sniffled. "Please, Padshad. I'm so young. I cannot die yet."

"You should have thought about that before you betrayed your people." Malo felt no pity for the sniveling traitor.

The general growled. "Queen Kefira warned us you were evil!"

"Did she? You should have trusted her." Malo laughed. "She could have saved you all. Now, it's too late."

As insults started to fly, Malo nodded to the hooded monks.

They deftly taped the officers' mouths, ending the protests. Then they pulled the chains attached to pulleys above the altar. As the monks slowly turned the gears, the chains rattled, and the struggling officers couldn't prevent the rise of their feet. Then the monks hoisted them upside down, in a line. Soon, the officers hung by their feet, heads dangling a foot above the long altar.

Then attendants set up the sacrificial daggers and the golden bowls below each of them in preparation to collect their blood.

The six hanging men struggled for a while, but quickly realized they were doomed. Only fear remained in their widened eyes.

Malo exulted. This ceremony would mark the beginning of his ascent to power.

Chapter Fourteen

Malo stood next to Matchitehew on the central platform of the temple, enveloped by the rhythmic chant of the monks. Reminding himself to show a cool exterior and reserved demeanor. He slowly inhaled then released a calming breath.

Hundreds of followers in red masks and hooded capes filled the floor of the sanctuary. They stood in concentric rows, surrounding the altar... and in total anonymity. Not so for Malo and his father, whose faces remained fully exposed. Although Matchitehew wore a stripe of black makeup across his eyes... another superfluous dramatic effect.

The soft light of the torches, bouncing off the gold daggers and bowls on the altar, added a solemn air to the ceremony. The heat and the fragrant smoke of the sacred fires at both ends of the altar twirled toward the high vaults. Hanging banners with snake and dagger symbols floated gently down the length of the stone columns.

As the new First Lieutenant, Malo wanted to be perceived as the solid rock of power behind the Sorcerer Supreme... in stark contrast to his father's melodramatic tricks and performances.

Cheap illusions wouldn't gather much respect from the military elite. A sober image would serve Malo better when the time came for him to lead. Let the Stygian leaders and members at large see Malo as the true pillar of the organization. Soon, his father would reveal his deranged nature and discredit himself in the eyes of the military leaders.

The vibration from the black crystal gem on his father's chest increased in intensity and pulsed with purple light. Malo wondered about its power but hid his concern. The voices of the chanting monks reverberated louder throughout the entire cave complex. Muted drums beat a slow tempo.

Malo remained in shadow when Matchitehew stepped up to the long altar, above which the six Anvad officers hung upside down, bound and gagged, like cattle on a hook, waiting to be butchered.

Matchitehew opened his arms wide under the cape, in a solemn gesture. "Today we reclaim the might of the Stygian Order. Today we welcome the first elite soldiers of our new army. This gift from the Exalted Baalmordo, will revitalize our ranks and give us unrivaled power."

"Baalmordo, Baalmordo, Baalmordo," the acolytes repeated in unison.

"And as an offering to our mighty benefactor, we shall feed the Cyborg he sent ahead with the blood of these Anvad officers." Matchitehew signaled a red guard at the side door.

The arched door opened, and two dozen Cyborg in black armor and blind helmets entered the temple. The drums marked the tempo of their quick steps as they jogged in perfect sync along the aisle toward the altar.

Many heads in the crowd turned to watch them with open curiosity.

Then the Cyborg lined up in four straight rows in front of the long altar and lifted the front of their blind helmets.

The attendees gasped at the monstrous sight of their half-furry, half-machine faces.

In the waving light of the fires, the non-human faces looked ominous. The Cyborg grunted, snorted, and raised their lips, baring sharp fangs. Saliva dripped from their pointy teeth, as they sniffed around for fresh blood. How disturbing.

Malo remained impassible but quietly willed his heart to slow down. What ugly, scary creatures. Of course, they had been engineered to incite fear in their enemy... or rather their prey. Yet, they seemed disciplined. Blunt warriors... Malo hope he could control them.

The six officers, upside down at the end of their ropes, twitched and struggled... uttering insults muffled by the tape. Their eyes widened in horror as they finally understood the gory details of their grim fate. Malo felt no sympathy for them. These traitors had mistreated Kefira. They deserved a gruesome death.

Malo had learned long ago not to concern himself with the suffering of others, and he wouldn't be intimidated by the scary Cyborg faces.

His father did not show any reaction to the way they looked either. He calmly handed his red cape to a monk, then he picked up a gold dagger and held it high in the air, reciting litanies in a long-lost dialect. Although some rituals held power, this entire performance didn't. The dramatic effect only served to influence the weak minded.

The drums beat faster. The air in the temple electrified. The red clad followers held their breath.

Hands clenched behind his back; Malo remained still as the stone columns while he observed the Cyborg kneeling in front of the altar. He mentally explored their minds but could only read bloodthirst and impatience.

Then the drums stopped. Matchitehew aligned himself with the first upside-down officer... the Anvad general. The man twisted violently, making the chains rattle, and muttered under his gag. What a futile and cowardly move.

Matchitehew raised the gold blade then struck downward in a savage blow, piercing the soft tissue of the general's belly. Blood spurted then flowed down and poured into the gold vessel below. Matchitehew smiled like a demented man as he reached down with his hand into the chest cavity and ripped out the man's heart.

Then he held it up for everyone to see, uttering the name like a mantra. "Baalmordo, Baalmordo, Baalmordo."

The acolytes repeated the chant, and the Cyborg swayed from foot to foot, salivating profusely.

"Baalmordo, accept this offering!" Matchitehew threw the heart into the closest fire.

A few followers gasped, others remained frozen, eyes wide with fear, or entranced by the barbaric spectacle.

The Cyborg nodded and huffed, and turned to each other, waiting impatiently for a signal giving them permission to feed... like trained animals. Malo read their agitated minds. Images of carnage floated through their thoughts. Despite their forced obedience, these ruthless soldiers had such a strong bloodlust, they may not be entirely reliable.

Then Matchitehew, his white robes spattered with blood, moved to the next offering, and the next, and the next, stabbing down, ripping hearts, all the time smiling and relishing each kill. He seemed to enjoy being drenched in blood, a sickening sight.

Keeping his face unreadable, Malo observed the barely restrained Cyborg, and analyzed their potential danger. These creatures had no sense of loyalty, only a switch. What if they turned against the Order, or against Malo himself? What then?

As Matchitehew threw the last heart in the fire, he laughed out loud and motioned to the Cyborg to come up to the altar and feed. Then he handed the first Cyborg the sacred vessel to drink from it.

The creature grunted, pushed the vessel back down to the altar, then buried his face into the sacrificial bowl, slurping fresh blood like an animal. When another Cyborg shoved him off to take his place, the monstrous tusks dripped crimson.

Malo shuddered at the disturbing scene. The followers in red capes, although used to witnessing human sacrifices, seemed aghast, and remained immobile and silent. Were they holding their breath? Malo could sense their fear... a powerful motivator. Something he could use.

And so, the Cyborg fed, six at a time, taking turns, coming for seconds, until all the blood was gone. A few snarled and growled and gouged each other with their tusks as they fought over the last drops. Then they leapt onto the altar and buried their faces inside the victims' bodies, devouring their bloody guts.

Malo focused his mind on restoring order. He willed the monks to strike the gong. A loud metallic boom resonated above in the high vaults, then echoed throughout the temple. The Cyborg looked disoriented. Malo willed them to reform their ranks. He felt relieved when they did.

His father glanced at Malo with a look of reprimand. The disgusting man had enjoyed the ghastly spectacle. Too bad. This wasn't a gore feast. Baalmordo was watching from afar, and Malo wanted his respect.

Several monks scurried to the altar and took down the corpses. Then they pushed the corpses into the sacrificial fires at both ends. The bodies sizzled in the hot fire, and the smell of burning flesh filled the entire temple. Malo wanted to retch.

He also realized he would have to figure out some kind of protection against his Cyborg army. He would use their savagery and military skills for his purpose, but he would never trust them. Although the Cyborg obeyed his command, he could sense the resentment emanating from them.

Matchitehew cast Malo a resentful side glance. Obviously, he didn't like his gore feast cut short. Then the Sorcerer Supreme raised both arms to the high vaults and chanted an incantation. "O Exalted

Baalmordo, accept our blood sacrifices and guide us to victory. Help us enslave the many planets of this galaxy and gain absolute power over them."

"Baalmordo, Baalmordo," the acolytes chanted in a trance.

A strange wind whistled in the high vaults. The cold draft swept through the sanctuary, sending the flames of fires and torches aflutter.

A black cloud manifested above the altar where the sacrifices had hung earlier. The Cyborg fell to their knees, head down, as if in prayer. Then the inky cloud crackled.

A strong, low-pitched voice surged from the cloud and resonated throughout the complex. "I am Baalmordo, and I take you under my protection, as we embrace the same dreams of domination over this galaxy."

Malo squinted to see through the inky cloud floating above the altar. He thought he saw an undulating shape. Like an enormous black snake, hovering vertically, and twisting its coils. Then the cloud faded, and the reptilian creature became clear as it took substance. The giant black serpent with a white belly had the pale chest and arms of a man, and a scaly but human-looking head.

The followers gasped at the unholy sight, holding their breath.

Matchitehew fell to one knee and bowed his head. Everyone in the temple followed his example... except Malo.

Malo remained standing, partly in shadow. He didn't buy into all that drama. He suspected this wasn't Baalmordo himself, just an apparition, a shape meant to spread fear among his followers. But something clicked in his mind. Legends talked about the Naga, nasty serpent beings with human heads and torsos. But there was nothing human about this Dark Lord.

Then Matchitehew, in his bloody white robe, stood up and opened his arms in welcome. "We are grateful for your presence among us, O, Exalted One."

"You did well, Sorcerer Supreme," the voice hissed. "I am pleased. You took good care of my soldiers."

"We welcome them, O Exalted One." Pride shone in Matchitehew's peacock stance.

"Good. Now, I have some news for you, Sorcerer." The floating reptile observed the crowd with cold black eyes and flicked his forked tongue. "There is an angel ship in your vicinity. The *Blue Phantom*. And the traitor you seek is aboard that vessel."

"We suspected that much, O Exalted One, but the *Blue Phantom* remains invisible to us."

"Not for long. When I arrive in the flesh, I will reveal it to you, and you can have your

revenge... I want you to destroy that ship."
The words cracked like a whip.

"Yes, O Exalted One." Matchitehew bowed. "With your help, the *Blue Phantom,* its captain, and its crew will be annihilated. I swear it."

"Good. I am counting on you. Your reward will be great, but... do not fail me." The last words sounded ominous.

Malo wondered why such a powerful being as Baalmordo, with a large army of Cyborg, relied on his father to neutralize the *Blue Phantom.* Did the Dark Lord have limited powers against the glowing ship and its so-called angels?

Matchitehew bowed low. "It will be done, O Exalted One."

The giant serpent turned its human head and stared directly into Malo's eyes. An icy cold seized Malo's heart. Then the evil snake simply vanished.

Matchitehew rose, brushing his bloody white robes.

The Cyborg raised their heads.

The monks intoned a new chant.

Something in this deal with the evil lord bothered Malo. Yes, his father needed the armies of the Dark Lord to conquer the galaxy. But Baalmordo wasn't all powerful, and needed the Stygian Order as well. To what purpose? Malo would find out.

In any event, Malo realized that no amount of blood would ever satisfy the

Cyborg. And no living being would ever be safe as long as the Dark Lord and his Cyborg army resided in the galaxy.

* * *

May Helsara protect her! Kefira was losing her mind. What substance did the medics inject into her body? One minute she was lying paralyzed on the sanitized floor of her white cell, the next, she was running barefoot through tall green grasses, and frolicking with Blake under the golden sun, on a lush planet, where the breeze carried the fragrance of sweet blossoms and heady spices.

Blake's usually pale skin had a swarthy glow that enhanced his striking blue eyes. He looked so handsome out of uniform, with strong muscles bulging through his sleeveless shirt... and he smiled.

She didn't remember seeing him with a big smile... ever. He was always serious and sometimes moody in their real-life encounters. But in her waking dream, he had a winning smile and dimples that softened his entire face.

Kefira wanted to remain in that green paradise with Blake forever. She knew it was only a dream, but it was tempting to float away from the harsh reality and enjoy the attentions of the man she loved. Loved? How was this possible? They hardly knew each other, yet deep inside, she knew he was the only one for her.

May Helsara help her remain grounded. Kefira must escape and free her people. But as hard as she tried to remain conscious and rooted in reality, she kept sliding off into that insanely attractive dream with Blake.

* * *

Blake smiled at the recurring dream. Kefira kept popping into his mind, smiling, happy, laughing at the touch of a butterfly, smelling blossoms, and inviting him to lie down on a bed of fresh grass... speaking of love. But this was a life he could never have. He didn't deserve paradise, and he must honor his mission to roam the confines of black space, to save the lives of the worthy.

As much as Blake enjoyed the daydream, love could never happen for him. Besides, he couldn't afford distractions right now, and the dream was a figment of his imagination. Kefira didn't even like him. Since true communication was impossible through the red shield, it couldn't come from her.

Yet, something about the dream felt familiar... like a déjà-vu, or maybe a glimpse of things to come. Blake shook his head to force his mind back to reality.

Standing in the observation dome of the *Blue Phantom*, he watched the familiar military ships gathering around the planetoid. Battleships and destroyers from the former GTA fleet, equipped with a deadly arsenal. Human ships come to support the Stygian Order…

Not all the GTA ships were destroyed in the final battle, as a few were scattered at the far ends of the galaxy at the time. These were the battleships who'd survived. And somehow, their captains had rejoined the more-secret-than-ever Stygian Order.

They reminded Blake of his previous command, and allegiance to the Stygian Order and the GTA. The *Blue Phantom* had once been such a ship, but no longer. The blue crystal at its core had changed its very nature, and most of all, it transformed its crew.

"Graziella, any luck on the shields?"

"Not yet, Captain."

"Any response from the Azuran Council?"

"No, but we have unusual visitors."

A flash of light illuminated the dome.

Blake did a double-take. Some tall and imposing beings, nine of them in white robes, with long white hair held back, sat in a circle above his head on floating stone thrones.

"Who are you?" Blake could feel them invading and reading his mind. He was helpless to stop them and didn't like the feeling.

The most imposing one gathered his robes around his knees. "We are the Archons governing this galaxy. We usually contact the Azuran leaders on their home planet, but it seems you and your crew are involved in an unusual situation."

By the frozen hells of Laxxar, Blake never suspected the Azurans themselves answered to superior beings. Yet, he remembered a strange group of ancient sages showing up in the final battle. They'd help vanquish evil on that fateful day.

Blake bowed with respect. "It seems the Stygian Order is back and has acquired a new Cyborg army."

"Yes." The chief Archon paused, as if wondering how much to tell him. "They are in contact with a dark entity from another part of the universe. A Naga, a nasty reptilian lord who calls himself Baalmordo."

So, Blake had guessed right. "These Cyborg have done much damage already. They move from planet to planet, killing and drinking the blood of their prey. They are a threat to all life in this galaxy."

The Archons glanced at each other. Blake could tell they were having a serious conversation mind to mind, but he couldn't hear them.

Finally, the chief Archon straightened on his high seat and exhaled slowly. "I know you attempted to contact the Azuran Council."

Blake stopped curses from passing his lips. These Archons had violated his mind. "I made several calls, without success. The Azurans have gone off the grid. They isolated themselves from the rest of the galaxy. All our efforts to contact them have failed."

The Archons glanced at each other and nodded.

The chief Archon stared at Blake with luminous blue eyes. "Maybe we can contact them for you..."

Chapter Fifteen

Malo hated when his father summoned him... like a child, or a servant. The disturbing Cyborg guarding the entrance grunted, then opened the door for him.

Malo shielded his mind as he entered the luxurious chambers, deep inside the cave complex, noticing a different mood. No fancy lights or incense this time. The smell of cold candles stagnated in the cold air.

Strange. His father may not be entirely stable. His need for impressing others seemed to come and go, and falter at times. Malo would find a way to exploit his father's inflated ego and expose his weaknesses. The Stygian Order deserved better leadership... Malo's leadership.

Matchitehew barely raised his head at Malo's approach. Hunched in his red velvet throne, without his gruesome face paint, he looked old and beaten... such a contrast from the bloodthirsty Sorcerer performing human sacrifices earlier. His father didn't even force him to bow or show respect.

What happened to him? He showed high and lows, and mood swings, like a drug addict. Was he taking mood enhancers? It wouldn't be surprising. Another weakness to exploit.

Malo resolutely stepped on the plush rug, toward his father. "I walked through half a mile of cave tunnels to see you. I hope this is worth my time."

His father straightened and regained some of his natural pride. "You could have ridden one of our many antigrav vehicles. They are fully automated."

Malo repressed a tart retort. His lazy father never walked anywhere. "Well, I'm here now."

"It's time to act, my son. We must destroy the *Blue Phantom* before the Exalted Baalmordo arrives." Was it fear widening his father's eyes and making his hands shake?

Malo savored his father's apprehension. "What's the hurry? Didn't the Dark Lord say he would reveal the *Blue Phantom*'s location when he arrived?"

"That's what he said, but it's a test." His father's gaze darted right and left, as if he sensed someone watching. "The Dark Lord is challenging us."

"Why would he do that?" Malo frowned. He sensed no one watching them. "Or maybe, you are desperate to earn his respect... you want to impress him, don't you?"

Matchitehew straightened. "The Dark Lord believes he can command us and use us for his own purpose." New pride inflated his father's chest. "We must show him we are equal partners, and perfectly capable of solving our own problems... without his help."

"I doubt we can demonstrate we are as strong as he is. The Dark Lord has a Cyborg army." But Malo started to understand his father's concerns. The old man was losing his confidence. "You do not trust the Exalted Baalmordo, do you?"

"Evil can never be trusted, my son." Matchitehew sighed. "It will turn on you at the first sign of weakness."

"How true..." Malo nodded. He was thinking of dethroning his own father.

Matchitehew shook his head. "We need to look strong and powerful, or Baalmordo will use us, then crush us like bugs."

"How insightful." Malo couldn't help but pity his father. He really was a sorry excuse for a sorcerer. The man should have realized long ago that Baalmordo was too powerful to be controlled. "What do you propose, Father? Or more precisely, what do you want me to do?"

Matchitehew nodded several times, as if in deep thought. "Seize the *Blue Phantom* and arrest its crew before the Dark Lord arrives."

Easier said than done. "And by crew, you mean Captain Blake Volkov... the traitor who caused the fall of the Order in the final battle."

"Yes. The traitor cannot be allowed to escape." So much hatred and determination in his father's eyes. "He caused your sister's death."

Malo hated to be reminded of his sister. Besides, all her impressive abilities had failed to protect her. She was dead now, and Malo was alive and bristling with new powers... not to mention almost impossible to kill. "How do you expect me to locate the angel ship?"

"Simple. The traitor is waiting for an opportunity to land. He wants to save the Anvad. If we open the shields, he won't be able to resist the bait." Matchitehew offered a crooked smile. "All we have to do is lower the shields and wait for him to fall into our trap."

"That sounds risky." Given the strength the Azurans demonstrated in the past, Malo wondered at his father's sanity. "You let him in... then what? Close the shields again?" Malo still didn't see how he could win. "We do not have a military force on the planetoid."

"We'll use the Cyborg contingent already here." His father relaxed against the back of his throne and linked his fingers in his lap.

"What if the angels overpower the small Cyborg force? What if they free the Anvad?" That would really piss off the Dark Lord.

His father had a slow, diabolical smile. "But the angels won't succeed. We know exactly where they are going, and you'll have an ambush waiting for them."

"Easy for you to say." Malo didn't trust his father.

"I have faith in your abilities, my son. You are my blood, my First Lieutenant... and a fine strategist to boot." The older man knew how to flatter.

"This won't be easy." Malo could see many ways it could fail.

Matchitehew relaxed in his high seat. "Ideally, we'll capture the captain and his angels, then sacrifice them for the Dark Lord when he arrives... as a treat. Angel blood has to be especially sweet... maybe even sweeter than Anvad blood."

"No doubt." Blast his father! The flattery was working, and Malo couldn't possibly refuse without looking like a coward. "The crew of the *Blue Phantom* has proven deadly against the Marauders. They demonstrated powers we do not understand. What if we don't catch them before Baalmordo arrives?"

"You will, my son. I have full confidence in your training and your superior abilities... Unless you are not up to the challenge." The gem on his father's chest flared and pulsed purple.

Damn his father to the frozen hells of Laxxar! The man was washing his hands and passing the buck. If Malo succeeded, his father would take full credit, and if he failed, Malo would be the only one blamed in front of the Dark Lord. There would be reprisals.

Did his father suspect Malo's intention to take over the Order? Did he purposely set his son up for failure?

Malo felt a pull in his stomach. His knees buckled and he hit the deck. Then his head bent against his will, and words came unbidden. "Your will be done, Father."

As he managed to raise his head, hating the forced submission, Malo realized he may have underestimated his father's abilities. Matchitehew was smiling, but Malo shivered at the malevolent streak in his shiny eyes.

* * *

Kefira felt the moment the red shields dropped. As if a weight had been lifted from her shoulders. The paralyzing drug was finally wearing off, and she sat up, legs crossed, on the pristine white floor. What was she wearing? White robes. The medics called them ritual robes... for what ritual? Unease weakened her gut.

There was no time to waste. With the shields down, she might be able to send a message. She focused her thoughts on Blake. *"Blake, if you can hear me, the red shields are down. Please save my people from a gruesome death."*

"Kefira! Are you all right?" The concern in the familiar mind voice warmed her insides.

She could sense Blake, almost smell his scent. *"I am okay right now, in a special isolated cell, wearing strange white robes... I'm not sure why."*

"The shields were deliberately turned off. I think it's a trap."

"A trap?" Kefira wanted to save her people, but she couldn't let Blake die with them. His angel longevity didn't protect him from being killed. *"If it's an ambush, you shouldn't come. I don't want your death on my conscience."*

She heard Blake chuckle in her head. *"It seems you care a lot about what happens to me."*

"Of course, I care." Kefira felt a hot flush creeping up her cheeks. Good thing he couldn't see her. At least, she hoped he couldn't.

Blake sighed. *"I care about you, too... and about your people. My mission is to save you all, and I intend to do just that."*

"Thank you, but be careful." She wanted to say more, but doubted Blake felt the same way about her. He said he cared... not that he loved her.

Her fancy dreams were hers alone. He was an immortal angel, sworn to roam the galaxy and protect worthy travelers for millennia to come. And he was sterile to boot. She was a short-lived Sardar queen, expected to breed many heirs to insure the future of the Anvad people.

They couldn't possibly be destined for each other.

* * *

Blake broke the mental link and opened his eyes, then he let his body float down to the crystal bench and uncrossed his legs. There was so much he wanted to tell Kefira, but his love for her must remain his secret. He refused to place such a burden on her. She had her own obligations to fulfill.

Something else scratched at the edge of his thoughts. Something she said… strange white robes? Like those of a virgin offering. That couldn't be good. He hoped she wasn't among the first to be sacrificed.

"Graziella?"

"Aye Captain." His second in command manifested in front of him. "The red shields are down."

"I know. It's an ambush." Blake paced the crystal deck to gather his thoughts.

"So, what do we do, Captain?" She stared at him, too respectful to invade his thoughts. "Do we still land the *Blue Phantom*?"

"No. Too risky." Blake shook his head. "If they close the shields, the ship would be trapped there."

266

Graziella's eyebrows rose. "So, we keep the *Blue Phantom* in space, in invisibility mode?"

"No." Blake scratched his chin. "So close to the planetoid, the Stygian Order might be able to detect it with their extra-sensory abilities."

"So... what do we do?" She planted herself in front of him, at attention, hands behind her back.

"We hide in plain view." Blake had done it before. Nothing more invisible than a single ship among many other similar ships.

Graziella blinked. "I'm listening."

"We camouflage our ship in the middle of the enemy fleet... alongside the Stygian destroyers." A risky move, but Blake must find a way. He had to rescue Kefira and her people.

Graziella took a deep breath, as if to give herself time to consider the proposal. "The ships are identical in size and shape. I guess, we can hide the glow..."

"Or, we alter the ship's shields to generate an illusion, make the *Blue Phantom* look like an ordinary Stygian destroyer, with the black hull and the red snake and dagger symbols." Blake shuddered at the desecration, but he would do anything to get results.

"It could work." Graziella nodded. "Our ship used to look exactly like theirs, so it shouldn't be too difficult. But what if they still detect our different vibrations?"

"It's unlikely." Blake remembered his time as Fleet Captain in the GTA. "The military leaders are not sensitive enough. But even if they suspect something, in such close proximity, they won't be able to attack us without damaging their own destroyers."

"Okay." Graziella straightened her frame. "So, we materialize on the surface... in invisibility mode."

"Yes. Thanks to Karak, we know where the prisoners are. We'll set up a diversion at the gate while other angels manifest inside the large prison cave." Although Blake planned to rescue Kefira personally.

Graziella's eyebrows rose. "What about the guards?"

"According to Karak, the guards are posted outside the holding cave, guarding the door." Blake chuckled. "They don't know we don't need doors to get in."

"But we can only transport the Anvad two or three at a time through the rock." Graziella bit her lips. "It will take a long time to evacuate them all to the freighter then take off."

Blake realized that was the real trap. "That's the only problem. We must keep the shields open long enough to evacuate them all."

"I think I know where the shield controls are." Graziella gestured in the air and a map of the enemy facility popped in midair. "See this structure with a transmission tower, on a cliff near the Stygian base? It spiked when they turned off the red shield." She pointed to the tower on the map. "I'll take care of it. Either I'll disable the shield from the control room, or I'll destroy the tower. Piece of cake."

Blake noticed the structure was a klick away from the main complex. "Be careful, that tower compound will be heavily guarded."

Graziella smiled. "That's when being invisible comes handy."

"Don't forget we are dealing with sorcerers, many of which have extra-sensory abilities." Blake remembered the demonstrations of power he witnessed years ago, in the Stygian temples. "These are not regular people, or even soldiers. They might sense our presence."

Graziella bit her lips and nodded. "Duly noted, Captain."

"I also sense a small Cyborg presence on the surface. And the Cyborg army itself is getting closer." Blake could see in his mind a sizeable contingent detaching itself from the main horde, a few planetary systems away, and speeding toward the planetoid. "We don't have much time."

"We can handle the small Cyborg contingent. And we'll work fast." Graziella closed her eyes briefly, then she opened them. "The crew is ready, Captain, waiting for your order to execute."

"Make it happen. May the Formless One protect us." With so many unknowns, Blake hoped he wasn't sending his angels to the slaughter.

After Graziella vanished, Blake focused on his main ally on the planetoid. *"Karak, get ready. We are coming down very soon."*

The big cat purred in his mind. *"Karak ready. Karak protect."*

* * *

Kefira stood up at the sound of a metallic groan. She faced the opening hatch, expecting Blake. No such luck. Two imposing red guards, masked and armed with blasters and blades, stepped into her white cell.

She poised herself, ready to fight. A red mist came over her eyes and she couldn't move. She was paralyzed. As if time slowed for her but not for the guards. Chemical agent, or dark magic?

The two guards grabbed her, turned her around, and forcibly tied her hands behind her back. Kefira struggled against her bonds... with sluggish movements, as if she'd fallen in a vat of thick sludge.

The towering men flanked her, lifted her by the upper arms and marched her out the door. No amount of resisting made any difference.

"Where are you taking me?" Kefira's words came out as a garbled moan.

No reaction from the guards. They hurried their steps along the stone tunnel, carrying her vertically, her feet never touching the ground.

Kefira calmed herself enough to explore their minds. Their open thoughts told her they were taking her to the temple… to be sacrificed? A blood ritual! So, that explained the white robes. Her heart beat like a demented drum. She panicked and struggled but could barely move. The burly men tightened their grip on her upper arms and walked faster.

Helsara, protect your humble daughter!

She could sense the frightened minds of her people nearby. The Anvad were scared but not hurt. She could also tell the shields were still down. Maybe Blake had landed.

Daring to hope, Kefira closed her eyes to send a desperate call. *"Blake! They are taking me to the temple right now… to be sacrificed!"*

Karak's mind voice answered. *"Angel Blake busy. Karak come. Karak protect."*

"Good boy." Taking comfort in the big cat's response, Kefira couldn't glimpse him or his swift shadow anywhere. Where was he?

She hoped a rescue would come quickly, because she remained semi-paralyzed, unable to speak, or struggle, or defend herself in any way... like in a nightmare.

Bountiful Helsara, please protect us, please keep your children safe!

* * *

Standing at the gate of the holding cave, Malo fumed as he cast rays of red energy through the air at invisible angels... in vain. They couldn't pierce his personal shield, but they were destroying his Cyborg force. He'd already lost half of them, decapitated by sharp blades, while the rest just shot lasers in the air and batted at invisible ghosts. They had no clue how to fight this sophisticated enemy.

The angels could also fly. Malo couldn't read their thoughts or influence them. He could vaguely sense their presence, but he couldn't see them, or locate them any other way. His Cyborg army seemed useless against such fighters.

The gate to the holding cave would soon fall. Malo would be blamed for the loss of five thousand choice offerings. He hated his father for manipulating him into taking this assignment. The twisted man had succeeded in making him look inadequate.

His father's voice sounded in his head. "Lord Baalmordo will be here any second to attend the immolation ritual. Join me in the temple immediately."

"But I don't have any angel blood for your sacrificial blade, Father! I need more soldiers."

"Don't worry about it, Son. The entire Cyborg army is assembling in orbit." His father chuckled. "Lord Baalmordo can defeat the angels himself."

Malo didn't share his father's confidence. He could sense the Dark Lord's cold presence approaching the planetoid and shuddered. Lord Baalmordo would not react kindly to his failure to squash the angels.

"Meet me in the temple immediately to greet our new master in person." His father's voice had a steel edge.

"Your will be done." Malo couldn't believe his father could make him say the words through the tons of rock separating him from the temple. "I'm on my way."

Chapter Sixteen

Blake lunged and severed the Cyborg's head. Although they couldn't see the attacking angels, the black armored warriors seemed to have a sixth sense as they managed to face the angels raiding the gate. Fortunately, the Cyborg couldn't fly, and their radars weren't very accurate.

As he stabbed and sliced through armor, Blake couldn't help but think about Kefira. He must rescue her, but first he must clear the gate.

Focusing on Graziella, Blake called. *"How is it going at the shield tower?"*

"It seems they are on to me, Captain." The melodious voice in his head sounded surprised. *"They can sense me, although their weapon strikes keep missing, so I assume they can't quite locate my position."*

"Same here. How close are you to succeed? Show me." Blake flew away from the fight, behind the protection of a stone wall, then closed his eyes.

He watched through Graziella's vision as she flew up the rocky needle toward the lofty tower complex. Black Cyborg and red

274

Stygian soldiers scrambled down the slope to meet her but seemed confused as Graziella hovered above them and they couldn't see her.

She flew down and decapitated one red soldier with her glowing sword. "Five more to go, on the way to the tower."

"Be careful. Good luck." Blake sighed and blinked away the visual connection.

He glanced around the stone corner. At the gate of the holding cave, the remaining Cyborg, although clumsy, kept hacking and firing in the air, fighting tirelessly, like demons with unlimited energy.

Dodging a laser strike, Blake returned to the protection of the stone wall and focused on the angel leader of the evacuation group. *"How is the rescue going?"*

"Slow and steady, Captain." The angel chuckled. *"The Cyborg haven't realized the battle at the gate is also a diversion and we are transporting their prisoners through stone."*

"Good." At least, that part of the plan was working. *"We still have a dozen Cyborg to neutralize here. When we clear the gate, be ready to guide the flow of refugees to the waiting freighter."*

"Aye, Captain," the male voice said resolutely.

Blake then focused on the crew left in space on the *Blue Phantom*. *"Time to release our three Cyborg prisoners."* He hoped when the virus in their brain was released, it would spread to the rest of their military force, since all their brains were linked. *"Make sure they think they escaped on their own."*

"Aye, aye, Captain."

Blake focused on the three Cyborg prisoners and connected with their secret angelic programming. He winced at the brutal nature of the Cyborg psyche. The three quickly realized the clear wall of their cell was down. They stepped out and, glancing left and right, followed the only route left open for them, encountering no angel on the way to the landing bay.

Blake sensed their resolve and their excitement as they stole and boarded a small craft then flew out into space, away from the *Blue Phantom*, toward the Cyborg fleet. Cyborg fighters came to meet the small angel craft. Blake felt their unease as the escapees connected with other Cyborg minds. When their brothers recognized them, they cleared them to land on one of the Leviathans. Good.

Blake almost retched at the oppressive vibes inside the black monster ships. A few Cyborg came to greet the returning soldiers. No warm emotional effusions among their brothers at their escape and return, but no hostility either. The escaped prisoners were accepted back into the fold, communicating freely with their counterparts. They were reconnecting with the hive. Good. When released, the virus would spread.

So far, the plan was working, and Blake hoped it would work all the way... he also hoped the false memories and false coordinates implanted in the escapees' brains would keep the location of the *Blue Phantom* a secret.

Blake returned to the fight at the gate. Only three soldiers left. He decapitated one. Then he sensed a change in the vibrations throughout the cave complex. Something was happening in the temple. Kefira!

He sent a mental message to Karak. *"Where are you, big boy? Do you have eyes on Kefira?"*

"Kefira in temple. Bad people. Karak ready."

"Good boy. I'll be with you very soon."

* * *

Malo still fumed as he stood by his father's side at the center of the temple. Torches and sacrificial fires burned, and their smoke mixed with incense and a few psychedelic drugs meant to soften the resolve and influence the minds of the acolytes.

In front of them, on a low altar, a human form lashed to the stone lay under a white sheet, emitting muffled sounds. The special offering... a woman judging by the shape of her hips. Probably an Anvad virgin. Malo was reminded of his mother, sacrificed on that same altar, just a few weeks ago.

The ceremonial drums beat a slow rhythm while the acolytes hummed a chant, repeating the Dark Lord's name like a mantra. "Baalmordo, Baalmordo, Baalmordo…"

A flash of lightning, a roll of thunder, and a black cloud manifested above the altar. Soon, it morphed into the solid shape of a being, with the torso, head, and arms of a man… standing in midair. The upper body, although relatively human in shape, showed gleaming white scales instead of skin. But the lower body was that of a huge black snake with a white belly.

Definitely a Naga! The previous apparition was just an image, but this was a heavy being of flesh, behaving like a snake. Malo shuddered as he remembered the legends of Nagas throughout the universe.

Most of them had a nasty reputation. Hard to believe such entities did exist… and this one looked terrifying. A forked tongue flashed out of the human mouth. Then the Naga hissed… like a snake.

Malo stood, transfixed.

His father bowed. "Exalted Lord Baalmordo, welcome to our humble temple."

The creature's cold smile resembled a rictus... with fangs. "Do not thank me yet,

Sorcerer. I sense angels on this planetoid. And their ship is hiding among your fleet."

Matchitehew bowed. "With your help, we shall exterminate them all, My Lord."

"Yesssss." The forked tongue flicked, and the thick serpent body undulated in eager anticipation. "But first, you promised me a special sacrifice."

"Yes, My Lord." Matchitehew bowed again. "A real treat. The purest and noblest Anvad blood."

Malo noticed the veiled offering moving slightly under the sheet. Something in his brain clicked. He stepped up to the altar and uncovered the woman's head. His blood turned cold. "Kefira!"

Malo trembled with barely contained rage as he marched up to his father. "What is this? I never agreed to this."

Matchitehew's painted face hardened. "I do not need your approval, Son. As Sorcerer Supreme, I rule this temple."

"You can't kill her. She is mine!" Malo drew his Kirpan blade and raised it above his father.

A sudden cold paralyzed Malo's body. He couldn't move... or speak, stiff as an ice statue, dagger poised.

The Naga abomination lowered itself and slithered along the altar. He sniffed Kefira with gusto, flicking his forked tongue, then he rose in front of Malo and faced him with open curiosity... The strange eyes turned red with bloodlust… reminding him of a vulgar Cyborg.

Paralyzed, Malo couldn't vent his revulsion and struggled against the force holding him, but he couldn't fight it.

"How dare you question my authority in front of our honored guest!" Matchitehew growled to his son. "Now, you must pay the price of disobedience."

Pay the price? What price?

When Malo saw his father brandish the golden dagger, he realized not only he couldn't save Kefira, but he was about to become a snack for the monstrous Naga.

The drums rolled faster, and the acolytes raised their voices as they chanted the Naga's name. Matchitehew closed his eyes and seized the sacrificial dagger with both hands. The evil snake at his side undulated in a happy dance.

By the frozen hells of Laxxar!

Heart beating a frantic tempo, Malo remembered blades couldn't penetrate his skin. Besides, he couldn't be killed unless his head was severed from his body. Helpless, he watched the golden blade coming down in slow motion.

To his horror, the sacrificial dagger, imbued with strong magic, planted itself in his chest. Malo felt the stabbing pain but couldn't scream. His heart beat even faster as blood pooled and bubbled and flowed over his yellow silk shirt.

He didn't fall but remained standing, watching helpless, as his father ripped his heart out of his chest and held it up for him to see. Terror spread through Malo's mind.

Then the Naga rose, facing Malo's frozen form. The monster bared his fangs and buried his scaly face into Malo's chest, slurping and eating his insides. The loud tearing of flesh overwhelmed Malo's hearing through the impossible pain.

He wished he could die. As he glanced at his father, he understood the old man planned to sacrifice him all along. He'd used Malo to gather the Anvad, but never intended for his son to rule.

When the Naga slithered back up and hovered in midair, Matchitehew glared at Malo and drew his long blade. "All traitors must die!"

Matchitehew aimed for Malo's neck and sliced it in one smooth stroke. Then all went black, as if someone flipped a switch. There was no more pain, no sound, nothing but cold silence.

* * *

Watching a few feet away from the altar, in invisibility mode, Blake couldn't believe what he'd just witnessed. The Naga monster was now writhing in Malo's blood like a drunken worm, all over the floor of the central platform.

Blake approached the altar where Kefira, wide-eyed, seemed paralyzed, mouth open as if in a silent scream.

"It's me, Blake," he whispered as he untied Kefira.

Then he lifted her and dematerialized with her. But some inexplicable force pulled him back to the stone floor, where he fell, dropping his precious cargo, fully visible to all. He attempted to restore his invisibility but failed. What now?

The acolytes beat the drums and chanted faster, like they did before the previous killing. The infernal Naga, now fat and engorged, with blood rivulets dripping from his fangs, straightened up and hovered vertically to face Blake.

Kefira, slowly rose to her feet, apparently shocked out of her stupor.

Blake glimpsed the big cat slinking toward Kefira. Good boy.

"Karak protect."

Matchitehew marched toward Kefira brandishing his blade. Blake wanted to interpose himself, but the Naga stood in his way.

Karak stepped up to face the sorcerer and roared, holding his ground. Then the big cat bared his powerful jaw and pounced on the hand holding the blade. The knife clattered to the stone floor. The old man paled and stepped back. Dark magic didn't work on lowly animals like Karak. Their minds were immune.

But it seemed to work on Blake. His vanishing and flying abilities failed him as he now faced the Naga. Still, he briefly focused on the evacuation and could see in his mind the Anvad still running out of the cave toward the freighter. He must distract the Naga and the sorcerer. Give the Anvad people time to escape.

The serpent's human half crossed his arms on his torso and sneered at Blake, hissing between his fangs, and flashing a forked tongue. "Your kind is a calamity for my entire race!"

Blake drew his glowing sword and faced the Naga. "And your kind is a black mark on this entire universe."

Somewhere on the periphery, Blake glimpsed Matchitehew cradling his bloody hand and retreating behind his acolytes for protection. Karak was guarding Kefira, who stood, ready to fight, holding the sacrificial knife like a dagger.

The Naga rose straight up and undulated in midair. "Light and darkness are both necessary for life to thrive, Angel, but your kind only respects light."

"And your kind worships the darkness." Blake stabbed, but the Naga easily dodged his sword.

Then the Naga snapped with his fangs and reached toward Blake with fists and coils. Blake struggled to fend off the attacks, slashing, punching, stabbing. His opponent kept sliding off and slinking away like a snake.

Then the acolytes seemed to realize their deity faced a real challenge and might be in danger. They broke their ranks and rushed toward the central altar with blades drawn.

Blake found himself at the center of a melee, back-to-back with Karak and Kefira. While he faced the Naga, they faced the acolytes. The Naga was losing strength. His acolytes also wavered.

Somehow the drums still beat a savage tempo, matching the strokes of swords and knifes, punctuating the dying screams of the acolytes when a blade impaled their hearts, or Karak's fangs pierced their skulls or ripped their throats. The smell of blood grew overwhelming.

The sorcerer was nowhere in sight. The acolytes were losing ground under Karak and Kefira's strikes.

The Naga's eyes flashed red. "You can match me strike for strike, Angel of Light, but you cannot win against my army."

The Naga vanished into thin air. The few acolytes still standing ran away.

Blake could feel his angelic abilities returning. He deployed his wings then focused on the evacuation team. "Are all the Anvad on the freighter?"

"Aye, aye, Captain. All accounted for."

"Graziella? How are you doing with the shields?" He gasped, out of breath from the fight.

"The shields are disabled for good, Captain."

"Then take off with the freighter and connect it to the *Blue Phantom*. That way, it will be hidden and protected by our shields."

"Aye, aye, Captain."

Blake sheathed his angel blade and smiled at Kefira and Karak, relieved they'd survived this ordeal. "Good job, you, two. Let's get back to the ship."

He seized Kefira's hand, enjoying the soft contact of her skin, then he grasped Karak's scruff and dematerialized with them both.

Chapter Seventeen

Kefira rematerialized with Blake and Karak under the clear dome of the *Blue Phantom*. By now, she had gotten the hang of this strange dematerialization. As he let go of her, she laid her hand on his strong arm, but not for balance.

Her people had been saved. She owed it all to Blake, and she was elated. "Thank you for liberating my people. I am eternally grateful."

Blake gazed into her eyes and gave her a rare smile that dimpled his cheeks. "You should thank the crew of the *Blue Phantom*. They evacuated your people to safety."

"While you were saving my life in the temple with Karak." Kefira's legs wobbled at such charm and modesty. "Where are my people now?"

"In their freighter, just below the *Blue Phantom*, hidden and protected by our shields." He folded his wings in a ruffle of white feathers. "But do not thank us yet, Sardar. We are far from safe."

"Even with your ship's protection?" Kefira imagined an angel ship must somehow be all powerful, and immune to ordinary means of destruction.

"We are sworn to fight evil and surrounded by many enemies." Blake gestured to the space beyond the clear dome.

The planetoid's orbit swarmed with military destroyers, black leviathans, and barracudas. And in their midst, floated a red vessel of strange design, like a coiled serpent raising its three heads. Kefira shuddered as she guessed whose ship that was.

The big cat hissed and growled at the red monstrosity. *"Karak not like snake."*

Kefira petted the cat's furry head.

The enemy vessels seemed to be regrouping in some kind of alignment. Small black ships flew in and out of the maw of the Leviathans. Kefira sensed the contingents of Cyborg inside, restless, and hungry for blood.

She shivered. "Can they see us?"

"Not with their eyes." Blake stared at the red vessel, rigid, his face unreadable. "Unfortunately, that infernal Naga has detected us by other means."

"But your shields and weapons are more powerful than theirs, aren't they?" Otherwise, what good would it do to be an angel ship? "My people are safe, aren't they?"

"Not really." Blake pinched his lips together and shook his head. "Our enemies haven't blasted us to smithereens yet, but only for fear of damaging their own vessels." He shrugged. "Or, maybe, they don't consider us a real threat."

"But what if their fleet moves away from us and targets us?" It just didn't feel safe.

"If they do that, our odds are not good." Blake didn't seem overly concerned.

Kefira couldn't imagine he had planned so poorly and gambled her people's lives. "So, what's the plan?"

"We wait." Blake sighed, staring far into black space, beyond the evil armada.

"Wait for the fatal blow? For the Cyborg to drill holes in the hull and infiltrate your ship and the freighter?" Kefira's patience eroded quickly. "We should do something. Fight, run, disappear like you did before… anything but sit here waiting to be blown to smithereens."

"Captain, I discern movement around us." Graziella's voice echoed inside the dome.

A chill of foreboding coursed down Kefira's spine. The enemy destroyers floated away to form a wide circle around the *Blue Phantom*, and their turrets pivoted so their cannons could target the angel ship… and the freighter below it.

"Captain?" The lovely voice of Graziella interrupted. "Enemy firing."

Blake closed his eyes. "Brace for impact!"

Kefira looked around for something to hang on to, but the deck was clear. Karak moved closer to her and anchored his claws into the decking. She went down on one knee for better balance and hung on to the cat. Several projectiles hit the angel shields in a firework of red and blue streaks.

The *Blue Phantom* wavered and bobbed like a cork on tempestuous waters. Kefira knelt on the deck, still holding on to Karak. She hoped her people in the freighter below the angel ship didn't get hurt. May Helsara protect them!

Blake had deployed his large wings and hovered a foot above the deck. His eyes stared into nothingness, as if he were looking within. "Counter-strike!"

A bright blue wave flashed from the *Blue Phantom* all around, its ripples propagating in a wide circle. The enemy destroyers rode the wave, but several of them were shoved and knocked against each-other like small rafts on a turbulent sea. Three vessels exploded on contact with others. One floated, belly up, dead in space.

Kefira rejoiced. "Yes!"

The big cat sneezed his enthusiasm. *"Karak like angel."*

Small Stygian fighters, like a flock of tiny black triangles, surged from their destroyers, headed for the *Blue Phantom.* Another strike wave from the *Blue Phantom* knocked them out in a perfect circle, exploding them and throwing them against the destroyers. But more barracudas now emerged from the maws of the Leviathans.

Kefira's heart hammered her chest as she relived her nightmarish vision. "The Cyborg are coming!"

Blake still hovered in midair, staring faraway. "Graziella, trigger the virus. Now!"

"Aye, Captain." Graziella sounded eager. "Virus deployed. It might take a few moments to spread, though."

"A virus? What virus?" Kefira felt left out of the loop.

"Well," Graziella's disembodied voice volunteered. "Earlier, we implanted three Cyborg prisoners with a computer virus. Then we let them escape, unaware that they carry special commands in their brains. Since the Cyborg are all linked, the virus should spread to the others."

"Thanks for telling me." Kefira felt a little better. Still...

Blake came out of his trance and nodded. "If it works, most of the Cyborg will ignore orders and feed on each other, and on the Stygian personnel aboard the military destroyers."

Silence took over the dome. Kefira could hardly breathe as time stood still. The Barracudas slowed their approach. Kefira scanned the enemy fleet with her mind and detected fear and chaos. Closing her eyes, she could see the Cyborg feasting on the Stygian crew. It made her want to retch. How barbaric!

Blake's clear blue eyes stared at the enemy ships, as if he were seeing what happened inside through their hulls. The shadow of a smile washed over his face. "Our plan is working."

"Diabolical." Kefira straightened her back and narrowed her eyes on Blake. "Are you sure you are a good angel?"

"Absolutely not. I told you I never was." Blake chuckled.

Graziella gasped, the sound of it filling the dome. "Captain, we have company."

"Finally." Blake gestured in the air. An enhanced view of far space manifested in front of them in 3D. What kind of technology was that?

Some strange blue light seemed to pierce the black and grow larger as it came toward them, so fast, it was already here. Kefira marveled at the spectacle. Glowing blue ships flying in formation. "Are these angel ships?"

Blake smiled. "The Azurans answered the call."

Kefira remembered Azurans were angels, too. "So, we are saved?"

"Not necessarily, but our odds just went way up."

"Good." Kefira breathed easier. She noticed many little blue dots in space all around the angel ships. "And what are those?"

"Ah!" Blake sounded satisfied. "They brought the AI Legion of Avenging Angels."

As the image enhanced itself, Kefira squinted and saw each little dot grow into a luminous humanoid, seemingly made of glowing blue crystal and silver, flying in formation around the Azuran fleet.

As the 3D image dissolved, Kefira could now see the angel fleet directly with her naked eye, through the clear dome. It quickly surrounded the evil armada.

"Captain, the enemy destroyers are turning their weapons to target the Azuran fleet." Graziella paused. "Should we move out to join the other angels?"

"Not yet." Blake closed his eyes, as if he were waiting for something, but what?

Kefira could tell he was communicating with some other entity, mind to mind but she couldn't tell whom, or what they were saying. Blake obviously had a plan but wasn't sharing with her. How frustrating!

The big cat came to her, as if feeling her unease and rubbed his head against her hip. *"Angel Blake protect. Karak protect."*

Kefira scratched the furry head. "Thank you, Kitten."

Outside the dome, the Stygian destroyers shot at the angel fleet, but their missiles exploded halfway, or splashed harmlessly against the blue shields. The Cyborg leviathans also shot red hot projectiles at the angel ships, but none seemed to make contact. They all burst or dissolved on impact with the blue shields.

Then the angel fleet retaliated with luminous blue strikes spreading wide like speeding waves.

"Brace for impact!" Graziella's steady voice.

"Karak, come." Kefira knelt next to the big cat, holding on to him. She hoped her people on the Anvad freighter below were also bracing.

The *Blue Phantom* rode the blue wave unharmed.

Kefira rose and noticed that the angel strike did not breach the red shields of the Cyborg and Stygian vessels. "This kind of battle could go on forever."

"Not if I can help it." Blake opened his eyes. "Graziella? Are we ready for EMP?"

"Ready on your command, Captain."

"An electromagnetic pulse? In space?" Kefira tried to analyze the implications. "It could disable the entire fleet... including yourself, the Cyborg, and the luminous AIs."

Blake chuckled. "Angel technology is immune to EMPs. No electronics onboard. We run on mind power and crystal power."

Kefira wasn't sure what that meant, although she hadn't seen any computers or electronic gadgets of any kind on the angel ship. She also remembered the battery on her blasters died the first time she boarded the *Blue Phantom*. "What will the EMP do to the freighter below us?"

"Nothing. It's currently protected by our shields."

"Captain, movement in the enemy ranks." Graziella's voice remained even.

Kefira stared through the clear dome as the scaly red ship of the Naga Lord uncoiled then swam resolutely to the front to face the angel fleet. A red glow surrounded the Naga ship, like an ominous cloud. The very sight of it made Kefira sick to her stomach.

"What now?" Kefira was trembling.

Blake straightened. "All angel ships, EMP, now!"

Kefira braced herself with Karak again. She didn't know what to expect. A sudden flash blinded her. She sensed something happening among the Cyborg. As if all their minds went blank.

When she opened her eyes and rose from the deck, Kefira could tell the destroyers, as well as the leviathans and barracudas seemed disoriented, floating in space willy-nilly, some of them belly up, others spinning around. None seemed able to bring their stabilizers online, and even less their weapons.

Kefira exulted. "Yes! You did it!"

Blake shook his head. "Not quite." He pointed to the Naga ship. "Look."

Kefira could see the Naga ship remained stable, unaffected by the EMP. "They, too, must run on another kind of energy."

The army of angelic AIs rushed toward the Naga ship.

"Are they attacking it?" It seemed incredibly dangerous, even reckless.

Blake nodded. "Their weapons can pierce the hull. They can breach the ship and take it over."

"Wow!" Kefira stared, transfixed, unable to look away.

A red bubble extended around the Naga ship, enveloping it on all sides and growing. The AIs stopped their advance, but she watched in horror as the first wave came in contact with the bubble. The unfortunate AIs seemed stuck on that energy shield, unable to move... like so many insects caught on a sticky web.

Then a red cloud manifested atop the ship, and the Naga lord materialized from it, hovering in space, like a giant hologram, facing the angel fleet. His scaly face snarled, and his forked tongue flicked. Then he hissed.

"Well played, puny angels." The strong voice of the serpent resonated inside the *Blue Phantom*, and probably inside every other ship as well.

The Stygian and Cyborg fleet seemed dead in space. The Angel fleet stood at attention, in perfect order, ready to strike.

Kefira couldn't believe what she was seeing and hearing. Before she met Blake, she had no idea such powerful creatures as angels, sorcerers, and Nagas roamed the universe.

The Naga's chuckle oozed with malice. "I now call upon the poor little AIs paralyzed by my shields. I give you a choice. You can serve me and thrive with me forever, or refuse to serve me and be destroyed like puny insects."

Kefira shivered. "What will happen if these AIs switch allegiance?"

Blake laid a gentle hand on her shoulder. "Let's hope he doesn't turn them. It happened once before, during the final battle. These AIs are a formidable force."

The big cat butted his head against Kefira's hip.

She petted his strong neck. "Don't worry, Kitten. It will be all right."

"Karak protect." The big cat meant it.

The AIs who weren't caught in the red bubble hovered together and started to hum. The sound vibrated so loudly, Kefira could not only hear it, but she could feel it and see the red bubble vibrating with thousands of sonic waves, like a choppy sea in a storm.

Soon, the AIs caught on the bubble shook themselves loose. They seemed disoriented, affected by the experience, but free of the sticky web.

"Never underestimate an AI." Blake smiled. "These new AIs are incorruptible... and very resourceful."

As the red bubble reinflated, its surface smoothed around the Naga ship, and the AIs now kept their distance.

The giant image of the Naga lord wavered. He hissed and red smoke surrounded him. "This galaxy is not worthy of my attention. The Stygian Order is undeserving of my gifts. Like its useless leader, a lowly sorcerer with dreams of grandeur. The objects I once imbued with my powers throughout this galaxy will become poison to those who covet them."

"What happened to that horrible sorcerer?" Kefira didn't remember seeing him after the fight in the temple.

"He vanished." Blake narrowed his eyes. "But I still can sense him, hiding in that cave complex on the planetoid."

Another voice, soft and melodious, rose amidst the chaos. "Baalmordo, Naga lords are not welcome here. You have lost, and we give you a choice. Stay and be destroyed, or leave this galaxy never to return."

"How dare you threaten me, puny angels?" The Naga's voice wavered.

"We dare, in the name of the light."

A powerful beam of blue light flashed, emanating from the angel fleet to strike the Naga ship.

Kefira held on to Blake and Karak, transfixed.

Under the angel strike, the red bubble around the Naga ship burst, propagating a red wave.

The *Blue Phantom* rode the red wave safely. But all the enemy vessels disabled by the EMP, unable to control their movements, collided from this new wave and many caught on fire. As they exploded, Cyborg and people poured out of their broken shells.

Kefira noticed that even as they gasped for air, the Cyborg still grasped their prey, attempting to drink their blood. Her stomach heaved.

The Naga lord screamed, loud enough for Kefira to cover her ears. Karak growled his discomfort. Blake's face blanked as he communicated with other angel minds.

Then the Naga vessel flared and vanished with the few Leviathans still in one piece, leaving the planetoid's lower orbit littered with floating debris and dead bodies.

Kefira released the breath she'd been holding. Relief flooded her and she slumped. "I hope he never comes back!"

Blake shook his head. "Hard to tell. Evil is not easily dissuaded."

* * *

298

Kefira held onto Blake as they rematerialized with Karak on the planetoid, near the main entrance of the cave complex. Her gentle touch on his arm tingled. She looked up at him and met his gaze. Did he feel the tingle, too?

She removed her hand and brushed imaginary dust from the blue silk of her uniform, then she straightened the blades at her belt. "It was nice of your angels to retrieve my clothes and Kirpan blades, but I miss my blasters."

Blake chuckled. "Sorry. Angels do not like to handle blasters... or any electronic devices."

"I know." She remembered they were incompatible.

Other angels manifested on the vast landing pad, some familiar from the *Blue Phantom* crew, others strangely alien, bald, with blue skin, others with webbed fingers and tentacles as hair. Among them a few luminous AIs with wings. Strange... angels weren't a uniform race.

Blake walked up to them. "I can sense a few acolytes still wandering around, so be careful. They are armed and could still be hostile."

Several angels saluted then vanished.

Blake closed his eyes, like he did when he communicated with his crew. "Graziella, make sure Kefira's people are all right after the battle. Help them with whatever they need to settle down comfortably."

Graziella manifested in front of Blake and Kefira. "Of course, Captain."

Kefira lifted a resolute chin to the tall woman angel. "Now, the Anvad need to think about nominating a new captain for the freighter, and new officers among the most capable of them. I'll make the final decision from their selections."

Blake smiled, as if impressed by her decisive attitude. "Graziella? Did you get that? Any questions?"

"No, Captain. All is clear to me." Graziella saluted then walked away toward another group of angels.

Kefira stared at Graziella's retreating figure, then she turned to Blake, unable to hide a hint of jealousy. "You seem very chummy with your very attractive second in command."

"That again?" Blake shook his head. "I told you we are linked. Our minds work together on the *Blue Phantom.*"

"Still..." Kefira wasn't convinced. How could a lovely woman working so close to Blake not be attracted to him, or him to her? "You said you could locate that despicable sorcerer. He can't get away with kidnapping my people and murdering my officers. He must be brought to justice."

Blake nodded. "I sense his bio-signature, deep in the lower levels of the complex, but it's very weak. He is alone, and his energy is low."

"Then, let's get the bastard." The harsh words sounded odd as Kefira uttered them. She scrunched up her face to look fierce.

The big cat huffed his agreement. *"Karak go. Karak protect."*

"I can take us directly into that deep recess, but it could be dangerous." Blake's protective attitude was touching. He cared about her safety. "Although the Naga took away his powers, that sorcerer still is a very dangerous man. He may be armed and could have many tricks left in his arsenal. Be prepared to fight if need be."

"I am prepared." Kefira nodded and pressed her lips in what she hoped to be a resolute expression. "Let's do this."

Blake seized her arm and grabbed Karak's gruff. Kefira felt the tingle of vanishing.

* * *

Blake rematerialized with Kefira and her big cat inside a recess in a deep natural cave, lit by the hesitant glow of a single torch in a sconce. He found the spectacle of this beaten man, sitting on a small boulder with his eyes downcast, shocking. But that was no innocent. The disgraced sorcerer didn't deserve his pity.

Blake cleared his throat. "The time has come for you to face justice, Sorcerer."

"My name is Matchitehew," he sobbed. "I was the most powerful sorcerer in this galaxy." The broken man raised his head and tears rolled down his cheeks, melting the gory black and red paint on his face, and dripping onto his blood-spattered robes.

"It seems you caused your own downfall." Blake steeled himself not to feel pity for the man… it could be a trick.

"Look at me now. I am alone and I lost my powers, my children are dead." The voice barely whispered. "My acolytes are dead, the few survivors have fled, no one cares about me."

Kefira stepped up. "You should have thought about that before you sacrificed your own son to that horrible Naga. What kind of father does that? Malo was a good man once. You turned him to do evil deeds, then you killed him yourself."

The big cat growled for good measure. *"Karak not like Malo. Not like sorcerer."*

The shadow of the man Matchitehew used to be crumpled and sobbed. "Since I lost my daughter three cycles ago, things have never been the same."

Blake remembered that battle. Ciara had died horribly that day, when he'd turned his destroyers against the love child of the evil Kalishtar with this abject man. "She was a

302

threat to the galaxy. She had to be stopped, and I'm glad we did."

"No! She was our best hope!" The man shouted, raising his head, then he crumpled again. "Now, I have no future. How can I face my failure?" He sounded like a spoiled child deprived of his toy.

"You should have known our actions have consequences." Kefira's voice remained harsh. It seemed she wouldn't fall for this dramatic display. Good.

"Even the black crystal that once gave me power has turned against me. Look." The broken man extended mangled fingers toward the black medallion sitting next to him. The bloody hand was Karak's work.

"Stop. Don't touch that thing!" Kefira brandished her Kirpan blade, ready to strike.

The big cat stared at the sorcerer and bared his fangs, ready to pounce. *Karak not like sorcerer. Karak protect.*

The old man scoffed. "You are in no danger from me."

As he touched the gem, it flared and sizzled. The man quickly pulled back his blackened finger, with smoke coming from the tip. "See? It has become deadly to me."

"You have to come with us and face your sentence, Sorcerer." Kefira's words sounded reasonable, but his only sentence from her people would be death. He had committed too many atrocities. "Maybe confessing your sins to the Anvad will make you feel better."

Blake felt pity despite his resolution. "As a former Stygian member, I understand the need for redemption. Maybe you could do something good to redeem yourself before you die."

The broken sorcerer slowly raised his dripping face and resolve firmed the line of his trembling mouth. "I do not want your pity. I do not want to redeem myself. I am Matchitehew, Supreme Sorcerer of the Stygian Order!"

Blake shook his head. "Not anymore."

"I curse your kind. I curse the Anvad. I curse all who oppose the darkness." His eyes shone with a maleficent gleam. "I choose my own destiny, and no lowly human or angel will dictate whether I live or die."

Kefira turned to Blake. "This human garbage doesn't deserve a trial. We should kill him now. Let him join his son and daughter."

Blake shook his head. "It's against the Angel code to strike a defenseless man."

"Good." The sorcerer flashed a demonic smile. He reached behind his back then stood up holding two Stygian blasters, one in each hand. He aimed at Kefira and Blake. "Whatever hell I'm bound for, you will share it with me."

Karak pounced. The old man fell backward on the flat boulder, smack on top of the black crystal. The two blasters clattered to the flagstone. A strange light flared.

The big cat stepped back, realizing something was happening.

Matchitehew grimaced as he clutched his heart. "I will return from the dead and punish you all for the calamities you have caused."

Then he uttered a long scream as he burst into flames, and his face melted. The smell of sizzling meat filled the cave recess. In the midst of the inferno, Blake stared in shock as the black jewel disintegrated itself along with the sorcerer's body.

Soon, only a smoldering mound of ashes remained.

Blake sighed. "That is a fitting end for such a despicable soul. Pure evil should be allowed to die."

"Wow!" Kefira's voice trembled as she stared at the incandescent ash. "Did he just curse us?"

Blake emitted a nervous laugh. "I wouldn't worry about it too much... although I suspect evil never truly dies. But it often returns in another form."

When Kefira took his arm, Blake felt the pull of her soul calling his... but it could never be.

She smiled. "At least, now we can resume our voyage to the Land of Many Waters."

Blake smiled back. "I sense you are going to need an escort on that voyage."

"Yes. And I'm hoping it will be you." Despite the inviting tone, a shadow crossed her face. "And, I guess, Graziella."

"About Graziella..." Blake struggled not to laugh. "You may not know it, but before she became an angel, she was an Amazon from the planet Skeera."

"An Amazon?" A crimson glow crept up Kefira's neck and face.

"Yes. You know... a warrior woman... who prefers the company of other women." Blake chuckled.

"And you let me be jealous of her?" Kefira punched his arm.

Blake rubbed his arm and emitted a soft laugh. "I thought a Sardar would be above common jealousy."

She laughed with him. Then Kefira's grip on his arm tightened. "Also, I wanted you to know that I am over my anger at your past mistakes. I guess, some people are redeemable, and others are not."

"Glad to hear I have your approval." Blake covered her hand with his. "Does this mean I am forgiven?"

"Yes." Her beautiful brown eyes gazed into his. "Now, if only you could forgive yourself and stop being so sad."

Blake sighed. "I promise to try."

The big cat harrumphed for good measure. *"Karak like Blake."*

Blake petted the cat then dematerialized the three of them, leaving the ashes of the dead sorcerer in his cold, deep, dark grave.

Chapter Eighteen

The Land of Many Waters, a month later...

"Sardar?"

Kefira turned at the call and blinked in the late afternoon sun. She smiled at the young woman, noticing she wore the traditional pink skirts of a maiden. Other young people came running toward the trestle tables set in the middle of the temporary camp, surrounded by large dormitory tents... for now.

The young people bowed to her. Kefira smiled and motioned for them to straighten. Here, on Helsara's land, after only a few days, Kefira's power had grown stronger, and her people could sense it.

"Several young people wish to take a mate, Sardar." The girl's eagerness indicated she must be one of them. "Where should we build Helsara's temple?"

"Let's see..." Kefira closed her eyes and communed with the energy of the planet. She could sense Helsara everywhere, whispering in the ocean breeze, bathing in the rivers, fertilizing the land, and inviting the sun. Then an image popped into her mind.

Kefira opened her eyes and nodded. "Helsara has spoken."

"Yes? Where will the temple be, Sardar?"

Kefira pointed to a rocky prominence. "Up there. The perfect spot, overlooking the fields, and the river's estuary, where it meets the deep blue ocean, with soft winds, and plenty of sunlight."

The Master Builder in overalls stepped forward. "What should this temple look like, Sardar?"

Kefira took the offered sheet of paper and pen and set it on the trestle table. She drew a sketch of her vision. "The temple should be circular, and made of white stones, with a cupola roof, many high windows, and plenty of space inside to welcome all our people."

The Master Builder stared at her drawing. "I see… What about the inside?"

Kefira kept adding cross-sections to show the inner layout. "It should also include flower gardens, a large water fountain and tall trees to provide shade from the summer sun."

"What about a statue? Our sculptors are eager to start." The Master Builder sounded excited.

"We'll hold a contest." Kefira smiled. It was so easy to channel Helsara in this idyllic place. "The winning representation of Helsara will stand in the temple. The other statues will grace the gardens."

Karak pawed her back and pulled on her sash. *"Karak like sand."*

Laughing, Kefira handed the rough drawing to the Master builder. "Let me know how it goes, or if you have questions."

The man rolled the paper and bowed. "Yes, Sardar."

Then Kefira followed the big cat toward the beach, glad for a moment of peace and quiet, enjoying the feel of this virgin world, the Anvad's very own planet. It harbored no dangerous predators, only the small animal species who survived the destruction ten millennia ago.

As her foot sank into dry sand, the ground shook, and flocks of birds took flight. Kefira recognized the feel of falling trees. She scanned the neighboring hill, were men and women called to each other as they roped and cut down tall trees. On the lower slopes, carpenters sawed and hammered planks to build the first houses.

The civil engineers surveyed the land, planning the future bridges and dams, as well as the irrigation canals for the fields, and waterworks and clay pipes to bring clean water from the mountain springs to the future town.

Already, the farmers cleared and plowed the fields where they would plant the seeds they brought with them. Others would start orchards with the fruit trees the *Blue Phantom* provided. Women and children scoured the countryside for native fruit and vegetables. The few domestic animals they brought along would multiply and provide dairy, meat, and eggs.

The Shamaness, headed toward the camp with a basket full of herbs, nodded at Kefira. "I already collected many medicinal plants, Sardar. It seems Helsara is blessing us with her bounty."

"Excellent." Kefira resumed her walk, wondering if those plants included the secret poison of Sardar queens and princesses, but she didn't ask. There would be time enough later to plan for the worst. Right now, she only wanted to nurture constructive thoughts.

As Kefira walked along the sandy shore, Karak loping at her side, her booted feet slushed into wet sand. Some small fish jumped in the wavelets that ebbed and flowed, and the big cat ran and pounced around them like a kitten on catnip.

The rays of the setting sun turned the water ripples to liquid gold as well as the waves breaking offshore. The tall reeds at the top of the sand dunes also turned golden. Kefira breathed the salty air full of aromatic scents and sweet tropical fragrances. Seabirds flew overhead, calling and diving for the last meal of the day.

She'd finally reached the very planet she had seen in her dreams, the Land of Many Waters, the planet of her ancestors, Helsara's promised land. Her people settled nicely, safe and happy. They had every reason to envision a bright future.

So, why did her heart feel so heavy?

Over the trills of colorful birds, and the song of the cicadas, Kefira heard children laughing and playing, their happy shouts carried by the breeze. A reminder of her sacred duty to continue the Sardar line.

Although Kefira had fulfilled her promise to Helsara and to her people, she felt no satisfaction. In her dreams, Blake remained at her side... but she couldn't ask him to sacrifice his mission. Captaining the *Blue Phantom* and saving deserving souls in distress was his calling, the means to his personal redemption. And even if he did want to stay with her, his sterility would disqualify him as a consort.

Karak head-butted her hip, and Kefira scratched the furry head. "Are you happy on our new planet, Kitten?"

The big cat harrumphed. *"Karak protect."*

"I may no longer need protection since we are safe and at peace. Maybe it's time for you to roam free, enjoy frolicking and hunting in the wild."

The big cat shook his head with vehemence. *"Karak protect."*

"I understand. I would miss you, too." Kefira plopped on the dry sand to watch the sunset. "But eventually, you might warm up to the idea of freedom."

"Karak free. Karak protect." The big cat sat next to her, purring, rubbing his big head against hers.

"Guarding me is a labor of love, isn't it?" She hugged the big cat. "I love you, too, big boy."

* * *

Blake manifested at the top of the dune and folded his wings. As he watched Kefira from a distance, the idea of leaving her forever made him miserable. Blinking into the setting sun, he stepped down toward Kefira and Karak, his boots sinking in the shifting sand.

The big cat pivoted his tufted ears then turned his head. *"Karak like Angel Blake."*

"Good boy." Blake couldn't help but smile. "I like you, too."

Kefira turned around. Her face lit up as their eyes met. She patted the sand beside her. "Is the *Blue Phantom* ready to depart?"

"Almost." Blake sat down at her side, facing the sunset. "I've been thinking about us."

"So have I." She stared at the sunset, her hand absently caressing his fingers.

Why were goodbyes so difficult? Blake swallowed the lump in his throat. He didn't want to abandon her. "So, what is your take on us?"

"I love you and I will always love you, but we can never be together." She kissed his fingers, unaware of the profound effect she had on him. "You have your duties, and I have mine. I understand that."

Blake wiped the tear rolling down her cheek. "Is that some antiquated rule set by an overbearing king in the faraway past?"

"No. Helsara's line must go on. As the only Sardar alive, it is my highest responsibility. Even if you choose me over your mission, I can't be yours... you can't have children."

"Not on the *Blue Phantom*, no." Now faced with separation, Blake realized his self-imposed punishment had lasted long enough. Kefira deserved happiness, and maybe so did he.

"What do you mean?" A glimmer of hope flashed in her brown eyes.

Blake seized both her hands. "I mean, if I lived away from the ship, let's say on this planet, after a few weeks or a few months at the most, I would lose my angelic abilities, my wings... I would return to the simple human I used to be... and I could procreate again."

Her brown eyes softened at the revelation. "Such a big sacrifice, losing all

314

your abilities… I can't ask you to renounce everything you are."

"You are not asking." He gazed deep into her eyes, feeling the strong pull of her soul. "I'm offering… if you will have me… not as an angel, but as a common man."

"But didn't you take a solemn vow?" Her voice cracked.

"It wasn't a vow as much as a self-imposed punishment." Blake realized that, now. "I would rather spend a short lifetime with you than contemplate an eternity of loneliness as an angel."

"What about your mission?" Hope filled her voice.

"The *Blue Phantom* can go on without me. It can continue its mission with the same crew, and a new captain." Blake realized he'd made his decision. His heart beat like a demented drum.

"Really?" Hope and joy battled on her face as the reality of his decision dawned on her.

Blake closed his eyes and made mind contact with the *Blue Phantom.* Then he opened his eyes on his new reality. "I just asked Graziella to be the new captain and she accepted."

"Good choice. She will perform beautifully." Kefira's gaze turned golden as it caught the sunset glow. She laid her hand on his knee. "What made you change your mind?"

"I recognized you from my dreams, but Angels don't have dreams, only visions of things to come. So, I suspected we may have a future together." He pressed his hand over hers. "It took me a while to realize you wanted me to stay, and even longer to understand that the *Blue Phantom* could go on without me."

She picked up his hand and gently kissed his fingers. "There will always be evil in the galaxy, but it's good to know there are also righteous angels to fight that evil when the darkness threatens to smother the light."

Blake felt as if a weight had been lifted from his shoulders. Finally, the world around him made sense. Only he and Kefira existed at this moment. Now, his gaze slid down to her lips. How he wanted to kiss her!

She leaned toward him and her lips opened slightly.

He enveloped her into his arms, brought her closer, and tasted the sweetness of her kiss.

Birdsongs filled the cool evening breeze. String music and drums rose from the nearby campfires. Blake could get used to planet living... especially with Kefira in his arms, looking at him like she did now.

She curled up against his chest. "The Anvad people are rejoicing. Soon they will be dancing, and the young people will choose their mates."

Blake softly kissed her hair. She smelled like a summer field in bloom. "Don't you think it's time for their queen to think of her own happiness? Isn't it time for you to dance and take a consort?"

"You once told me that dancing wasn't on your list of special abilities."

"Well, it's never too late to learn something new... especially since my list of abilities is about to shrink significantly."

"Are you sure that's what you really want?" She caressed his cheek. "Life on a planet is nothing like life on a ship."

"I know. But I want a family with you." He kissed her forehead.

"Really?" Kefira flashed a happy smile. "Then, as soon as Helsara's temple is erected, we shall be the first couple to wed."

The big cat rubbed his head on Blake's shoulder. *"Karak like Angel Blake."*

"I like you too, big boy. But soon, I won't be an angel anymore. I won't be able to read your mind." To many it might seem like a sacrifice, but to Blake, the prize was worth it.

Kefira scratched the cat's furry head. "But when we have a baby, he or she will have Sardar abilities like me, and will become your friend."

"Karak protect baby." The big cat emitted a contented purr.

Kefira turned to Blake and kissed his neck. "Are you sure you'll never regret this decision?"

Blake enjoyed the light shiver of her kiss and smiled. "Maybe after we have many children, if we feel that one lifetime together isn't enough, we can always return to angel life among the stars... together."

"You thought of everything, didn't you?" She pointed at a blue streak in the darkening sky. "Look!"

"It's the *Blue Phantom* leaving orbit." Blake closed his eyes and wished them well. He didn't feel sad anymore. He gazed at the first rising stars in the foreign sky of his new home planet and squeezed Kefira's shoulder. "I feel like the luckiest man in the universe."

The End

Also published by BWL Publishing Inc.

from author Vijaya Schartz

Byzantium series:
Book 1 - Black Dragon
Book 2 – Akira's Choice
Book 3 – Malaika's Secret

Azura Chronicles series:
Book 1 - Angel Mine
Book 2 - Angel Fierce
Book 3 - Angel Brave

Chronicles of Kassouk series:
Prequel: Noah's Ark
Book One: White Tiger
Book Two: Red Leopard
Book Three: Black Jaguar
Book Four: Blue Lioness
Book Five: Snow Cheetah

Ancient Enemy series:
Book 1 - Anaz-Voohri
Book 2 - Relics
Book 3 - Kicking Bots

Single title sci-fi romance:
Alien Lockdown
Snatched

Archangel twin books:
Archangel Book 1 – Crusader
Archangel Book 2 – Checkmate

Also check out Vijaya Schartz's
medieval fantasy series
based on Celtic legends: CURSE OF THE
LOST ISLE

Book One – Princess of Bretagne
Book Two – Pagan Queen
Book Three – Seducing Sigefroi
Book Four – Lady of Luxembourg
Book Five – Chatelaine of Forez
Book Six – Beloved Crusader
Book Seven – Damsel of the Hawk
Book Eight – Angel of Lusignan

Vijaya Schartz also published
contemporary romance

Ashes for the Elephant God
Asleep in Scottsdale

2020 Bestselling Author
Vijaya Schartz

Award-winning author Vijaya Schartz never conformed to anything and could never refuse a challenge. She likes action and exotic settings, in life and on the page. She traveled the world and claims she comes from the future. Her books collected many five-star reviews and literary awards. She makes you believe you lived these extraordinary adventures among her characters. Reviewers compared her stories to Indiana Jones with sizzling romance. So, go ahead, dare to experience the magic, and she will keep you entranced, turning the pages until the last line. Find more about Vijaya and her books at http://www.vijayaschartz.com

BWL Publishing

bwlpublishing.ca